Maverick Squadron

By
Don Falgrim

Maverick Squadron
First Edition
Published by DreamStar Books, November 2008
ISBN: 978-1-904166-31-3
EAN: 9781904166313

Drovers House
Craven Arms
Shropshire
SY7 9BZ
Tel: 0870 777 3339
e-mail: dreamstar@jakarna.co.uk

Set in 'Garamond'

Printed and bound in Great Britain by Biddles Ltd

About the Author

Born in Norfolk and educated at King Edward VII Grammar School, Don has settled in a small Hampshire village after a varied career as a soldier, salesman, musician and writer. He has written extensively for radio and TV in Australia, having had two, 3-act stage plays produced in Perth, Australia. He also has experience as a copywriter. He has written over 100 novels, principally thrillers and has also written several novels about aerial combat over French skies during the Great War. His latest book, titles 'The Witch of Wootton Marsh' was published in December 2007 by DreamStar Books.

Dedication

To my wife – Margaret,
who had to endure many lost hours of companionship

And to Gordon Rushmer – artist extraordinaire,
for his fantastic book cover illustration

Chapter 1

"Who the hell are you?"

Bob jumped a foot into the air at the sound of the voice in his ear. He dropped his suitcase and kitbag to the still-moist grass and jumped to attention.

"Lieutenant Spiers, sir, reporting for duty." He gave what he thought was a smart salute.

The man in the Sidcot flying suit regarded him sourly, walked around him as if inspecting a prize bull, looking him up and down.

"How old are you Lieutenant?" he rasped. Bob noticed he had a limp.

"Seventeen sir… going on eighteen," said Bob, staring out over the converted cowshed, rigidly to attention.

"Relax Lieutenant, nobody's going to bite you," said the man standing before him. Bob eased his cramped muscles. "Where are you from?"

"Alton, Hampshire, sir," said Bob, gazing at the man with awe.

He was a big man, over six feet, broad at the shoulder, bull-necked, a mop of black hair and beetling black eyebrows. His nose was a massive lump of flesh with wide nostrils that jutted out parallel to the high cheekbones. A moustache covered the hare-lip, giving his mouth a perpetual impression of a snarl. Under the Sidcot jacket he wore jodhpurs encased in cavalry boots, the clips for spurs encompassed the heels.

"I mean what was your last post, for Chrissake?"

"2nd Basic Training Flying School, sir, Sidcup, Kent," stammered Bob.

"How long Lieutenant?"

"Three weeks," said Bob, "…Sir."

"Jesus H. Christ!" said the man, "Sending me babes in arms now."

Bob felt an angry flush spread over his face. The insulting sonofabitch… no wonder we weren't winning the war with nasty bastards like this one around.

"Feel insulted do you Lieutenant… all hurt are you? Think you know it all do you?" jeered the man.

"No sir!" said Bob, wanting to hit him.

There were some giggles from a group of young men in flying kit standing at the entrance to a Nissen hut to his left.

The big man swung around. "What the hell are you lot laughing at?" he roared. "Get down to that bloody hangar and look your aircraft over!" He turned back to Bob.

"Leave your kit there, Johnson will see it into your billet" he said in a more kindly voice. "Go into the mess and get your flying gear on."

"Now sir? This minute?" asked Bob, unable to believe his ears.

"You wanna learn to fly, don't you Lieutenant?" rasped the man, in his hectoring voice.

"Oh yessir!" Bob looked eagerly out over the flat field at the three Farman bi-planes, looking like birds nests with wings, parked on the tarmac before the huge ungainly canvas hangar. The windsock was limp against the pole at the far side of the field.

"Well, the sooner we get started, the sooner you'll have the opportunity of maiming me for life, won't you Spiers?" said the big man. "My name's Jessop, and believe it or not, I'm a flying instructor. That means I risk my life every single day teaching you infants to fly those bloody death-traps over there in the service of His Majesty King George and for England… God help me."

Without another word Jessop turned and began marching over to the hangar his lame leg dragging slightly behind him. "Come on you high-born ponces!" he screamed, "have you checked every one of those flying wires, ailerons, rudders, oil leaks, canvas, struts? Think you're fucking immortal do you? Think that these modern miracles are going to fly themselves?"

His voice faded as he reached the group of young men in flying kit.

"I'll get your kit into your billet, sir" said another voice, quietly behind him. The man was like a little garden gnome, misshapen, a slight hump on his back. He was about five feet two and his RFC uniform looked as if it had been made for a man twice his size. His face was wizened, half his teeth missing. "Captain Jessop isn't all that bad sir," said the little corporal, picking up Bob's suitcase and kitbag as if they were feathers. "He gets a bit irritable at times… suffers from that leg of his."

"War wound is it, corporal?" asked Bob, following the gnome-like figure across the damp grass to the nearest Nissen hut.

"God no sir… crashed a few months ago, young officer couldn't manage the Farman, wouldn't let go of the stick. Piled up along that road sir." The corporal pointed to a line of telegraph poles that lined the field. "May have to have is leg amputated if it doesn't knit."

They reached the squadron hut.

"The mess is over there sir, if you want to change into your kit. Major Brent is in the office there."

Bob walked into the tiny office and looked aghast at the pile of yellowing paper on the desk; at the cobwebs festooned from the windows and shelves; the ink stains on the blotter atop the ply board suspended on several beer crates that did duty as a desk. A vision of utter chaos.

"Come in Lieutenant… Spiers, isn't it? I'm Brent." The smallish man with the sandy eyebrows, thin lips and aquiline nose sat behind the desk and was smiling at Bob.

"Looks a bloody mess doesn't it? Dead right – it is! Welcome to Denham old man. No need to tell you to abandon hope, is there?" Brent offered him his hand in greeting, "Already met Martin have you, I see?"

"Yessir." Said Bob, saluting after shaking the man's hand. The grip made him wince.

"An unforgettable experience, I'm sure, Spiers. Good instructor though, the best… lives for the job . . . pity about his leg." Brent picked up a paper from the untidy heap and read it. "2nd FTS at Sidcup, eh, Spiers. Know Major Rigby?

"The Commanding Officer sir? Yes, he was there directing training sir," said Bob.

"Good man, keen as mustard, eh? Six months at the Front before he got that wound. Four victories over the Hun," said Brent, "Glad to have you Spiers. Go and get your flying gear on and get down to the hangar." Brent sat down again and began reading a stained paper from the ply desk.

Bob swung another salute that Brent ignored, turned about and walked down to the hut Corporal Johnson had said was the mess.

A narrow board with paint flaking from it held the legend 'Officer's Mess' fixed over the entrance.

The interior stank of stale beer, cigarettes and perspiration. There were other odours, oil, leather, polish and sawdust, all mixed. The place was deserted.

The leather flying suit felt stiff and awkward to Bob as he struggled to get into it. The lamb's wool tickled his skin and the helmet looked perfectly ridiculous. The boots felt two sizes too small and were hard to lace up. He waddled out of the mess into the June sunshine feeling like a brown penguin.

An ear-splitting roar sounded out as he was halfway across the springy turf to the hangar, which died away to an asthmatic spluttering. A Farman bi-plane seemed to waddle out of the hangar into the sunshine, the sun's rays glinting on the doped fabric of the wings and sparkling on the maze of crossed wires that held the wings in place. The skid under the nacelle was splintered and had been bound with wire.

Another engine roared into life, and then another until three Farman FE 2b's were lined up on the tarmac outside the canvas hangar. The young men who had giggled at him a short time before were all swarming over the planes looking at ailerons, rudders, wires, engines and wheels. There were two men in two of the Farmans. Captain Jessop was in the third beckoning to him angrily, gesturing at the front cockpit impatiently.

A fitter held the ladder for him as he climbed stiffly into the cockpit which resembled a child's bath. The joystick had also been bound with wire at some time in the past and the wires leading from the rudder bar had been joined by knots of wire. The noise was deafening.

A thump on the shoulder and a voice in his ear bellowed, "Safety belt idiot, you wanna fall out?"

He fixed the belt tightly across his waist and adjusted his goggles.

"Put your hands on the stick, but don't do anything.. just feel it...OK?" roared the voice from behind him. "Your feet on the rudder bar... and for fuck sake don't panic!"

Before he could reply the Farman's 70hp Renault engine broke into a thunderous cacophony of sound and the aircraft was lurching and bumping over the turf, the summer air already beginning to whip at his cheeks.

When he thought the mass of wood and wire would break up under the battering it was receiving from the earth, all was suddenly smooth and the ground was falling away beneath him. He grabbed the side of the cockpit wildly in panic; the aircraft seemed to be slipping sideways.

"Get your foot off the fucking bar, you twat!" screamed a voice and a fist clouted him on the ear.

He let go of the sides of the cockpit, grabbed the stick, which seemed to be moving with a life of its own, easing his feet from the rudder bar. The earth seemed a long way below now, a chequerboard of green and brown, doll's houses and animals in fields.

Another thump on his ear and the same hysterical voice bellowed, "Let go of the stick!"

He realised that he'd gripped the wirebound stick in panic and was holding it rigid. The plane was wobbling from side to side and the horizon seemed to have disappeared. The engine was screaming behind them in protest.

The bottom of the cockpit seemed to fall out and his stomach went with it. He grabbed the side of the cockpit again. The horizon was above his head now and some trees were floating lazily up towards them.

When it seemed that the Farman would take the topmost branches off, it swerved and the wing-tips were pointed at an angle of forty-five degrees to the ground. Bob was convinced they were going to pile into the trees.

The horizon levelled off and assumed an almost stable state for a few seconds before the other wing-tip leaned downwards, throwing him to the side of the cockpit. But for the safety belt he was sure he would have gone over the side.

"OK . . . take it . . . it's all yours" screamed the voice in his ear.

Bob grabbed the joystick again, placed his boots on the rudder bar. The Farman lurched upwards in a stomach turning curve.

"Keep your nose on the horizon!" yelled the voice, thumping him again.

The Farman seemed determined to frustrate his efforts at keeping it on a level flight. First one wing, and then the other would droop earthwards. Each time he received another thump on the head, and he would correct madly.

After he had been flying for about a century, it seemed, the aerodrome and the canvas hangar showed below him.

"Turn it to the left . . . not too much rudder, a touch on the bar," roared Jessop.

The Farman seemed to be skidding out of control, the ground coming upwards.

"Nose up, idiot!" yelled Jessop. "Not too much""

The yawing had ceased and the Farman seemed to be behaving itself now, the hiss of the wind in the wires was music and the satisfying roar of power behind him from the 70hp Renault engine was fulfilling.

A fist banged him on the shoulder. "Down!" yelled the voice.

The Renault seemed to miss a beat, and then the aerodrome was lurching up towards them as the roar of the engine died away to spluttering and coughing.

"Stick back, man!" bellowed Jessop. "Keep your wings level . . . aim at the sock!"

The earth seemed to be approaching at a horrible speed. Bob was convinced that the Farman was about to plough into the ground. The windsock seemed to be dancing around like a drunken man. He tried to keep the Farman in a direct line with the advancing pole, but the wings seemed to be swaying up and down beyond his ability to control them.

"Let me have her!" roared Jessop.

Bob released the stick, removed his feet from the rudder bar, and grabbed the side of the cockpit.

Suddenly, the Farman seemed to behave itself, the wheels bounced gently on the turf once, twice, then there was a continuous grinding, bouncing and bumping, and the Renault was coughing into silence. The windsock seemed to be over their heads and all motion had ceased.

Jessop throttled up again, the Farman turned sluggishly and taxied towards the distant hangars and the waiting ground crews.

Bob nearly jumped out of his skin as another Farman crossed the field in front of them, bouncing and thumping over the turf in a decidedly addled manner.

"You fucking clown!" screamed Jessop at the unknown pilot of the other Farman.

The other Farman suddenly stopped as if held by something, the nose went over, hung poised for a moment, then crashed back to its tailskid. Bob could have sworn he saw the two miniature figures in the cockpit jump into the air.

He felt his legs trembling and shaking uncontrollably as he climbed stiffly out of the cockpit to the ground.

Jessop was already out, grinning, and clapping him on the shoulder. "Not bad, Spiers," he yelled, "You'll probably last a week!"

****

Chapter 2

"Hey, look, you chaps, here's Jessop's pet monkey!" said the sneering voice.

Bob stared at Lieutenant Martine with distaste.

The tall young man was standing, back to the mess bar, his blond hair long and combed back in a thick wing either side of his head. His blue eyes were pale deep-set, high cheek-bones, and a wide downwards curving mouth.

"Something bothering you, Lieutenant Martine?" asked Bob, witheringly.

"As a matter of fact there is, old boy." Martine looked at his bunch of sycophants for approval. A motley collection of public school types all with the same asinine expressions on their faces, the same accents and the same scarves round their necks. There were perhaps a dozen of them, all watching Bob with various expressions of disapproval.

"You'd better get it off your chest then, Martine . . . old boy, hadn't you?" said Bob quietly. "I'd hate for you to become all frustrated."

"How is it, Spiers, that you get on alright with that monster Jessop, but we find him an obnoxious type . . . boorish, caddish and certainly not a gentleman," said Martine. "It evidently has something to do with your backgrounds." Martine looked down at Bob from his six-foot two height to Spiers' five-nine, an expression of disgust on his face.

"That's right, Martine, we both had to work for our living . . . working-class I believe you'd call us," said Bob, still softly "Something you'll probably never know anything about!"

"The little squirt . . . punch his nose for him, Charles," said one of the other young men, a Lieutenant de Vinguind, tall, lean, round chin and sleepy eyes. "These socialist types are getting more uppety every day."

"Whenever you feel like having a go, de Vinegar," said Bob "I'd be delighted to have it out behind the hangar . . . any time."

"You jumped up little man . . . crawl back into your woodwork," sneered another, taking a step forward. "Go back to your wooden hut and your lice!"

Nobody saw Spiers' fist until it had connected with the man's unprotected abdomen. The man, Lieutenant Launcey-Moore, doubled up, breath whistling between his teeth.

"No, hold it, you chaps, I'm going to teach this bounder a lesson," said Martine, restraining his companions from jumping on Spiers, ". . . a lesson he won't forget!"

Martine carefully removed his uniform jacket, folded it, laid it on the mess table, rolled his shirt sleeves up, after unfastening the gold cuff-links.

He then stood with his fits poised in the classic Jack Johnson pose, right fist extended beyond his left, feet apart.

"Come on, you working class little cad, let's see how you tackle a real gentleman," he said, his voice thin and waspish.

Spiers ignored him, grinned at the Sergeant in charge of the bar, who was watching the proceedings with a look of contempt on his features.

"You unutterable little oaf!" snarled Martine, and lashed out at Spiers, in a straight, orthodox right punch.

Somehow, Spiers wasn't there, but out to his left, still grinning. The infuriated Martine jumped at him, lashing out, both fists. Spiers easily avoided the blows until he fell over a table. The others began cheering Martine on, offering advice how to finish off Spiers.

Spiers saw Martine standing over him waiting for him to rise. The fall had hurt Spiers' elbow. He sat there amidst the wreckage of the table, rubbing his elbow gently, regarding Martine from his sitting position, the grin still on his face. Launcey-Moore was still gasping and wheezing, being held upright by his fellow officers.

"Wipe it off his face, Charles, the oaf!" yelled one of his companions. "You've got him now!"

"Get up!" commanded Martine, his face flushed with triumph. "Come and get your medicine."

"Sure you wanna go through with this, Martine?" asked Spiers, gently, from the floor.

"I'm going to thrash you within an inch of your life, Spiers," said Martine.

"Oh, dear," said Spiers, uncoiling like a snake. His head went into Martine's chin, a fist like a pound of lead, connected with Martine's chest, just under his heart, another landed like a steam piston on the side of the tall man's face, and a veritable rain of blows fell on the man from every angle.

He fell into a heap.

"What in hells' going on here, gentlemen?" rasped a voice from behind them.

Major Brent stood in the doorway, a hard look on his face, his swagger stick lashing his boot in anger. His thin lips and sharp nose seemingly vibrant with irritation.

Martine struggled to rise, blood from his cut face and nose streaming onto his shirt. He dabbed at it, trying to staunch the flow.

Brent walked into the mess, glaring at the young men, stick still lashing the side of his boot. "Brawling, are we? Got enough energy left to scrap amongst yourselves, have we, eh?" Brent looked taller somehow in his peaked cap, shiny boots and Sam Browne belt, his face suffused with displeasure. "I want to see you, Spiers, and you Martine, in my office in the morning . . . eight a.m. sharp. Is that clear? And the rest of you are confined to quarters until further notice. Is that clear? Pity you weren't all in the infantry, you could have worked your spleen off against the Hun on the Western Front, instead of carrying on in this disgraceful fashion." Brent swung on his heel and left the bar.

Spiers appeared unruffled, save for his elbow when he fell over the table. He walked over to Martine "Let me fix your face for you, Martine," he offered, quietly.

Martine shook off his hand, violently. "Don't touch me, you little cad!"

Spiers watched the Martine brigade file out of the mess, a slight smile on his face.

"You'll have trouble with that one, sir," said Sergeant Miller, offering Spiers a glass of beer. The Sergeant's craggy face was neutral.

"I'll have to take my chances, won't I, Sergeant?" said Spiers, licking his knuckles.

"Fancy piece of fisticuffs, sir," said Miller. "Where'd you learn that style?"

Spiers grinned. "They breed 'em like that in Hampshire, Sergeant!"

****

"I will not tolerate this kind of cretinous behaviour on my patch. Do I make myself clear, gentlemen?" rasped Brent. "You'll have ample opportunity to fight when you get to France. Now, what was it all about?"

Martine's face was a mess. His nose was swollen, the side of his face was puffy and inflamed, and he looked sick.

"Personal matter, sir," he said, thickly, through his puffed out lip.

"Spiers?" Brent glared at the younger, slighter man.

"My fault, sir. I suppose I was a little upset . . . still a personal matter though," said Spiers.

Brent glared at both young men, his blue eyes hard. He sighed with irritation.

"Very well, since you both seem to have difficulty in sorting yourselves out, I'm going to sort it out for you." Brent pushed a heap of old paper aside, leaned his elbows on the desk, stared at the two officers. "If either of you create any further disturbance on this base, I personally will see to it that you are transferred to the infantry. Do I make myself clear? I don't know what has caused this hostility between you. I don't care. But I won't have any more of it. Is that clear?" He waited until both officers had nodded. "Very well. You are both confined to quarters for seven days, outside normal duty."

"There's no need to punish Lieutenant Martine, sir. It was my fault, sir," said Spiers.

Brent stared at Spiers coldly. "I appreciate your chivalry, Spiers, but it takes two to make a quarrel," he said, crisply. "Now get out of my sight!"

****

At the end of two weeks at Denham, Spiers had flown a total of two hours' dual with Captain Jessop, in the Farman Longhorn bi-plane, with its pusher engine, located behind the wings, and to the rear of the bath-like cockpit. Jessop still roared and snarled at his young pupils in a boorish manner, Spiers being not exempt to the tongue-lashing. But his rough and ready methods began to pay off. Spiers began to get the feel of the ungainly craft, and was soon able to make turns without the threat of a spin. Take-offs and landings were practised until Bob felt convinced that he was able to make the solo flight without further instruction. Jessop held off making the concession until one morning fifteen days after Spiers had arrived at Denham.

"Alright, Spiers," said Captain Jessop, after a successful trip round the aerodrome one morning. "Off you go!"

Spiers gaped at the officer's jutting black eyebrows, the grin that split the man's hard mouth. "Now?" he asked, uncertainly.

"I told you when you arrived, Spiers, that you might last a week. You lasted two. What's the matter? Want to live forever?" snapped Jessop over the spluttering of the Renault.

"No, sir, I mean, yessir!" said Spiers, shaking, now that the moment all novices dreaded had arrived.

"Well, go ahead . . . see if you can kill yourself, man . . . and Spiers, try hard not to smash that aeroplane, won't you? We can replace you any day, but the plane . . . ?" Jessop shook his head, regretfully.

Bob climbed into the rear seat, feeling naked and alone. The sunlight glinted off the doped fabric wings, the spluttering of the engine behind him, the smell of castor oil, the watching mechanics and ground crew just beyond his line of vision. He took a deep breath, as the mechanics lifted the tail and pointed the Farman into the wind.

He pushed the throttle forward, hearing the engine behind him howl and roar, then the Longhorn was bouncing and clattering over the soft turf, the joystick shaking in his hand. He felt the plane lighten as the rush of air came under the wings. Easing the stick back, he saw the ground slip away beneath him. He was airborne! He eased the Farman up in a gentle climb, a feeling of exultation supplanting the initial panic. No clouts on the ear for making wrong moves, no bellowed insults, he was in command of an aeroplane. The ground looked a long way down, but the altimeter registered a mere fifteen hundred feet. Jessop had always insisted the height could save your life, gave one time to think. Close to the ground, the options open to a pilot with an engine failure were few.

He put the plane into a gentle bank to the left, seeing a herd of Jersey cows in the field below him. There were buttercups massed amongst the greenery, he saw. A farmhouse slid beneath the wings. White faces were staring up at him from the buildings. Over to his right he could see Uxbridge, and to his left the villages of the Chalfonts, St Peter and St Giles. On the horizon he could see Rickmansworth, nestling below the escarpment. Batchworth Lake glinted in the morning sunshine.

At two thousand feet he levelled off. The Renault was roaring smoothly behind him, the minute drops of moisture on the wings were bubbling in long strings backwards towards the trailing edges.

He came to with a start. He had been daydreaming. Panicking, he stared out over the cockpit coaming at the ground. Where the hell was the airfield? He was completely disoriented, and had no idea where he was.

A church steeple passed under his wings, a long ribbon of road stretched into some woodlands, and a group of farmhouses showed red roofs, but of the aerodrome there was no sign. He looked at the fuel gauge. No worries there . . . plenty, showing over half full.

He made another turn to the left. What looked like a canal was below him. He could see locks and several barges being drawn by horses on the towpath. In the distance, he could see a factory chimney.

Shit! The sun was behind him; therefore, since the time was nearly noon, he must be heading north. The compass said he was travelling south, and was acting in a wild manner, the needle flickering all over the place. He saw with a start that he had lost height and was now down to less than a thousand feet.

Jerking the stick back, he felt the Farman buck slightly.

Without warning, the engine cut out, ending with a few asthmatic snorts . . . !

****

Chapter 3

Don't panic, he told himself, feeling an icy dread begin to paralyse his power of reason. First solo and the engine has to cut out on me! Looking below, he tried to select a field that would be suitable for a landing with a dead prop. There were cornfields and others with suspicious-looking lush greenery. He recalled Jessop telling him that deep green invariably indicated crops of some sort, turnips or mangolds.

There was a field to his right with some cows at the far end of it. Pasture. It would have to do, the altimeter showed six hundred feet. The wind was soughing in the wires and the fabric was drumming somewhere. The wooden struts were creaking. All normally concealed under the roar of the engine.

He remembered to switch off the ignition. "More men die from leaving the ignition on than do any other way, in the normal course of events," warned Jessop a few days after his arrival at Denham.

The trees swam up towards him. Christ! He was going to overshoot! The cows were looking up at him, startled. The altimeter said two hundred feet, but he knew there was something crazy about that information . . . the bloody trees were just under his wheels. He put the nose down sharply. There was no time to make a turn to get over the next line of trees. The grass was rushing past him now, the trees coming towards him with frightening rapidity. He pulled the stick back, gently. The Farman shuddered as it lost way and began to lose buoyancy. Less than two hundred yards, he told himself, his mouth dry with fear.

The wheels struck, bounced, the plane juddered sideways, wing-tips down to his right. Over-correcting, the Farman slewed into the opposite direction. He had barely time to jerk the stick to the right before the wheels hit the turf again, and dragged. The plane bounced, jarring his teeth, struck again, bounced, and then with a series of tiny hops came to rest ten yards from the line of oaks.

He began to tremble and shake, violently, as a cow ambled over and began to stare at him, curiously, chewing cud, a mournful expression in its eyes.

He jumped from the cockpit, his knees buckling under him, his hand went into a recent cow-pat.

Perspiration, cold and unpleasant was running down his back.

He had barely time to wipe his hand on a clump of grass before he heard the sound of a Renault coming closer. A few seconds later, a Farman swooped over the trees, two helmeted heads peering down at him from the cockpit nacelle. A hand waved. He waved back, and then a minute later the plan reappeared over the trees to effect a perfect three point landing, taxiing up to his stranded aircraft and switching off.

He recognised Captain Jessop as the big man jumped from the rear cockpit, and ran over to him. "You alright, Spiers?" he rumbled, glaring at Bob's Farman. His companion was no other than Charles Martine, smiling faintly.

"Yessir . . . engine cut out on me!" said Bob, trying to stop his hand shaking.

"Any damage to the plane?" rasped Jessop, walking round the aircraft, staring critically.

"Not that I'm aware of, sir," quaked Bob.

"Here, have a swig of this, Spiers," said Martine, holding out a gold brandy flask.

Bob took a swig gratefully. The liquid fire in his stomach eased the tension.

"Not bad . . . not bad at all, Spiers . . . you were dead lucky, mister," said Jessop, after a tour of inspection. His voice was grudging. "You're still alive and the plane is undamaged . . . remarkable!" He clapped Bob on the shoulder. "You'll make a pilot yet, Lieutenant!"

****

In the mess that night, Martine, his nose still swollen and sore-looking, lifted his glass to Bob. "Here's to the working class, you chaps!"

he called out to his colleagues around him. "Spiers isn't such a bad fellow after all!"

Bob found himself having to repeat the story of his escapade endlessly over dinner, to Brent for his report, to the NCOs in the mess bar, to Jessop, who wanted know exactly what had happened, to Martine, who then asked him to repeat it all again for the young men in the FTS.

He went to bed that night, slightly drunk, and believing that maybe he had misjudged Martine after all. For an upper-class nit, he wasn't too bad. That ass de Vinguind and Launcey-Moore were true-blue ass-holes . . . talking about the French defence of Verdun as if they, personally, were involved, and offering the French Commander Petain 'ADVICE ON HOW THE DEFENCE SHOULD BE ORGANISED'. de Vinguind's father had been present at the Battle of Loos in Flanders the previous year, and had been wounded. He felt, somehow, this gave him a prescience over the opinions of his comrades, on military matters.

The next day, Bob was advised that he was being posted to Gosport in Hampshire for his final training. Approval had been given by Major Brent on his solo performance and his air ticket would be allowed. The coveted 'Wings' on his uniform to denote his final approbation by the Air Ministry, would depend on how he performed on the Avros and BE2Cs at the FTS at Gosport.

"Well, Spiers, old man," said Martine, the night before his posting. "You seem to have landed on your feet . . . made your solo first time . . . and with a forced landing under your belt, as well. Good luck at Gosport." He held out his hand.

Bob shook it, unsure, still, whether Martine was being serious or just piss-taking. The man seemed genuine enough and seemed to hold no grudges over the battering Bob had given him in the mess.

"I was lucky, that's all," he said, smiling.

"Nonsense, old boy, you did marvellously. All of us here are envious of your skills. Quite frankly, I'd have been scared to death if it had happened to me."

"I'm sure your performance would have been equal to mine, Charles," said Bob, using the man's first name. It sounded even more formal than 'Martine' somehow.

"How about dinner in the Hare and Hounds tonight, old man?" asked Martine. "On us, of course. The jolly old pater's paying for the jaunt . . . bringing my sister along to keep us in order."

Bob was in two minds whether to accept or not, but finally agreed.

Martine and his two companions hired a car to take them from the aerodrome at Higher Denham to the village. The Rolls-Royce pulled up outside the mess at six-thirty and they all piled into it.

A table had been laid in a private room at the 'Hare', the cutlery gleaming and the table napkins crisply white.

"Meet my father, Robert," said Martine, pointing to where a fifty-year old man in a tweed suit stood next to a shining Hispano-Suiza, open tourer.

A girl stood next to the man, remarkable for her resemblance to Martine himself. Dark, broad face, high cheek-bones, almond eyes of blue, slim figure.

"Meet Robert Spiers, Father, the best budding pilot at Denham, and this is my sister Michelle."

Martine's father was as tall as his son, grey hair cropped short, waxed moustaches, angular, and looked very fit.

"Pleased to meet you, Robert," he smiled. His voice was softer than his son's, with a faint accent.

Michelle held Bob's hand for a fraction of a second, and then she was chattering away with easy familiarity to de Vinguind and Launcey-Moore.

He found that people calling him Robert instead of Bob made him ill-at-ease, as if they were according him a status he did not possess. The opulence of the dinner amazed him. Food like this, pheasant, jugged hare, trout and fresh salmon were not things the Spiers' household knew anything at all about.

He found himself sitting on Michelle Martine's left hand at the table, and was deeply conscious of her perfume and fine clothes.

"Well, Lieutenant, you seem to have gained a reputation already," she said, suddenly into his ear after the entrée had been cleared from the table.

"Unfounded, I assure you, Miss Martine," he said, blushing.

"Charles doesn't think so. He was quite enthusiastic about your accomplishments," she said.

"He'll make a better pilot," said Bob, subconsciously acceding to status.

"I hear you and he had a fight," she said, smiling, her eyes twinkling with merriment.

"Insulting you, was he?"

"Yes," said Bob, bluntly.

"Oh, dear, hit a nerve, have I?" she mocked. "You shouldn't be self-conscious, you know, this war will level out a lot of inconsistencies in social standing."

"I doubt it," said Bob. "My father works on the railway . . . the Southern . . . and he belongs to a Trades Union . . . hardly qualifications for nobility."

"All our aristocracy come from robber baron stock . . . Norman, Saxon, Danish, very few Celts are Lords or Ladies."

She was diverted by de Vinguind and said little else to him during the remainder of the meal. The tall de Vinguind seemed resentful of Michelle's slightest inattention.

The whole affair was depressing for Bob. Illustrating the wide social differences that existed between them. He was smitten with the girl, but her preference for the foppish de Vinguind made her appear unattainable. He tried to dismiss her from his mind. But the memory of those almond eyes and short, but thick black hair remained with him.

Martine and his colleagues were all in bed when the RRC tender arrived to take him to the station at Denham. Jessop was up, however, and came across to shake his hand. "You lasted more than a week, Spiers," he rumbled. "Which was longer than I expected. Keep your eyes open when you get to France, and never fly in a straight line."

The meaning of Jessop's enigmatic remark only came back to him months later.

"Thank you, Captain," he said gravely.

"One other thing, Spiers . . . don't get a chip on your shoulder over men like Martine. Just remind yourself that their crap smells just the same as yours," said Jessop.

Bob grinned, swung into the seat beside Corporal Johnson, the misshapen NCO who had taken his kit from him on his arrival at Denham. The Crossley Tender wound up until the engine fired smoothly, and he was on his way. His last view of Denham was of Captain Jessop standing in front of the mess-hut, waving to him as the Crossley turned a bend in the road.

He shook hands with Johnson on the platform, the little man standing back and saluting him, before he left.

Just before the train pulled out of the station, Bob saw a tall figure hastily prop a bicycle against a wall and rush onto the platform. It was Charles Martine. Breathlessly he ran to where Bob was leaning from the carriage window. He held out his hand. "Goodbye, old man, perhaps we'll meet again sometime," he said.

"Sorry about your nose, Charles," said Bob, grinning.

Martine fingered the still slightly swollen member tenderly. "Memento of Denham," he grinned. "Michelle sends her regards . . . you made an impression on her last night."

Bob felt himself blushing again.

Martine remained on the platform until the train turned a bend and the man's figure was hidden by a cloud of smoke from the locomotive.

****

The mess and quarters of the trainees at Gosport were housed in a disused fort of the coastal defence. The concrete blockhouse was star-shaped and damp during most of the year, save for sustained periods of hot weather in the summertime.

Upon his arrival, Bob was told that he would be flying BE2Cs, bi-planes with shallow exposed cockpits and a thin, pencil-shaped fuselage. Powered by a 120hp Beardmore engine, the machine was slow, but very stable.

The next day found him flying 'dual' over Southampton Water with a Sergeant Blake as his instructor. He found that his episode of landing a Farman Longhorn with a 'dead' propeller on his first solo flight had even reached the FTS at Gosport and the Sergeant was duly impressed by his apparent skills.

Bob found the BE an easy machine to fly and was soon making banks and turns without difficulty. The shallowness of the cockpit after the bath-tub impression of the Farman made him uneasy at first. The earth seemed, somehow, closer. He quickly adjusted and, two weeks later, Sergeant Blake, a taciturn man with an East Anglian accent, told him he could go 'solo' the next day.

With some trepidation, Bob went round his machine the next morning, ignoring the ironic smiles of the ground crews, inspecting wires, fabric and testing ailerons and rudder, inspecting control wires. The mechanics at Gosport were more skilled than those at Denham and, although this machine had several patches along the fuselage where rents had been repaired in the past, there were no botched up control wires or splintered struts lashed together with twine and doped over.

"Switches off!" called the fitter swinging the propeller.

"Switches off!" Bob repeated.

"Switches on!"

"Switches on!" yelled Bob.

The man swung the propeller lustily. The engine fired, spluttered and died. The process was repeated, with Bob conscious of the watching men. Three times he had to go through the proceedings before the Beardmore caught and settled down to a steady roar.

"Chocks away," he roared. The two fitters removed the wedge-shaped wooden blocks from the wheels by jerking the strings attached, and then the BE was lumbering over the ground in hollow bumping. He eased the stick back when the machine felt light, and then the ground fell away beneath him and he was out over Southampton Water. The bad start had upset him somewhat, but after a few minutes his natural ebullience returned and the BE was performing well. He made several turns, dives and climbs over the smooth water of the river blow, and then turned in for a landing.

The wheels bounced once, the BE sprang up into the air. Again the wheels touched and this time settled to a steady, ragged bouncing, until the tailskid dragged and he was down.

Switching off, he noticed that his hands did not tremble as much as they had done on landing the Farman Longhorn in the field outside Denham.

There was a mild cheer from the ground crews, as they came in at his wing-tips to guide the BE towards the hangars.

"Nice work, sir," approved Sergeant Blake, coming up to him as he got out of the exposed cockpit. "You'll be getting your wings in a day or so."

The silken emblem in the shape of a bird's wings was the envy and goal of every budding pilot and it indicated a landmark in ability. A man could actually fly one of those crazy wooden and canvas flying machines and held a certificate to say so.

****

Chapter 4

The train from Waterloo to Alton was late, but his father was waiting for him, dressed in his Sunday suit, a new trilby on his head, shoes polished until you could see your reflection.

"Hello, Dad," he greeted him.

There was a suspicion of moistness in the man's eyes, but his smile was all pride and respect. "See you've got it at last, son," was all he said, after shaking Bob's hand.

"Yes . . . look good?" he asked.

"Fine, my boy, just fine."

"How's Mum?"

They went on, talking about mundane things, the situation the French were facing at Verdun, the British on the Somme, price of food, scarcities and the allotment, then back again to the war and the news of another offensive being planned. This was the big one, to end it once and for all. The Somme was merely the opening stages of the offensive, which was going to drive the Hun from France for ever.

Bob was impressed by his father's evident knowledge through study of the positions of the British, French and German armies, and how they would ultimately fare in the battles now raging. There had been appalling casualties amongst Kitchener's men, up to sixty thousand in one day. Mr Spiers considered that this was just the heaviest part before the German line broke.

His mother greeted him with tearful joy, her wet cheek pressed against his in pure happiness. They chattered away about the usual things that had been of pressing interest a few months ago, the lads who had joined up, the news of those wounded and those killed, how Mrs Jones was faring with her husband and two sons, all in the Royal Artillery.

Then the conversation went flat. Somehow, Alton looked smaller. The house he had lived in all his life until joining the RFC, now seemed cramped and uncomfortable. He tried to tell himself that this was what he had been looking forward to for the three months he had been in the Flying Corps. But the flavour had gone. He found himself at the end of the first day smiling mechanically to the inevitable question "How long have you got?" as if leave was a blasphemy in view of the battles along the Somme in France, and his presence at home was a contradiction of the exhortations of the Government that everyone do their bit to defeat the Hun.

His brother, Melvin, younger by two years than himself was morose and indifferent to his brother, avoiding him whenever he could. He resented the fact that his own call-up was still a possible two years away and being a big lad, people were already asking him why he wasn't 'at the Front'.

At the Station Arms pub the beer was warm and weak. The locals stared at Bob with awe. the wings on the left breast of his uniform were known to be a coveted decoration. They concluded that Bob had joined the ranks of the toffs, and was no longer persona grata. His Second Lieutenant's single pip on his shoulder was evidence enough. They were polite because he was with his father, and then the conversation severed all contact with him.

At the end of the second day he was beginning to wish he was back at Gosport amongst people who had the same interests as himself. There was nobody that knew anything at all about flying aeroplanes or the war in the air. The odd soldier who was on leave were all infantry or Army in some capacity, and looked upon the RFC as a bunch of glamour boys without any credibility.

"Why don't you go and see Barbara?" asked his mother on the third day, when the hours began to drag and he had used up all his social contacts. All his friends were in the Army, and time hung limply on his hands.

"She's engaged to Bill Townley, isn't she?" he asked.

"Bill was killed a few days ago . . . at Fricourt," said Mrs Spiers.

"She'll hardly want to see me, will she, then?" said Bob, tersely.

"I'm trying to be helpful, Bobby," said Mrs Spiers.

"Yes, of course you are, Mum," he said, contritely.

"What's the matter with you, Bobby, you don't seem happy to be home?" His mother's lip trembled slightly.

"It's hard, Mum, coming home to peace and quiet, when all I've heard over the past three months are men's voices and orders, and aero-engines." He knew he was wasting his time. She didn't comprehend. "I'll go and see her," he said, to short-circuit any more tears.

Barbara Welland lived at Chawton with her widowed mother, not far from Jane Austen's birthplace.

"Hello, Bob," she greeted, delightedly, when they came face to face at the door.

If she was upset about Townley, she didn't show it. "How nice to see you . . . My! Aren't we smart in our uniform . . . RFC . . . an aeronaut . . . Mummy, come and see Bobby Spiers in his outfit!"

At least she didn't ask him how long he'd got, and a load of bloody stupid questions about how many Huns had he killed or what is it like in the trenches.

Mrs Welland, whose widowhood didn't seem to have impaired her capacity for enjoying herself, came in, and the two women made him blush with their praise.

Both Barbara and her mother were natural blondes, blue eyed, and with those willowy figures that seemed to go with their Nordic looks. He had heard that Welland had originally come from Norway to settle in England. Barbara was good-looking and her mother was not far behind her, despite being twenty years older.

"Come in, come in, Bobby, have some tea with us . . . we're man starved, aren't we, Babs?" said Mrs Welland.

Over tea and scones he had to answer a thousand questions about the RFC, and before he really knew it he was talking about his experiences with gusto. He didn't leave till well after nine o'clock. Barbara went with him to the gate.

"How about tomorrow, Babs?" he asked, breathlessly, as she was only six inches away from him over the gate.

"Where are we going?" she asked.

"How about Guildford for tea and then go to a cinema?" he asked, wondering whether he wasn't being too forward.

"That would be nice, Bobby," she murmured.

"Will your mother come too? . . . I mean . . . " He came to a stop, stammering.

"Chaperone?" chuckled Barbara. "Oh, my God, Bobby, this is the twentieth century, you know . . . I know all about conventions, but Mummy and I have had to manage without a man around the house for a long time now."

"What time then?" he stuttered, astonished at this liberal view of association with the opposite sex.

"You're the boss, Bobby," she whispered, the smell of honeysuckle in the air and her perfume gave his senses a delicious fillip.

"Two o'clock?"

"Marvellous . . . wear your uniform, won't you? I want everyone to see me with my flying ace boyfriend," said Barbara, mischievously.

She gave him a kiss that made his toes curl.

On the way home, he wished his leave would last forever, instead of another four days.

His father entreated him to go down to the Station Arms with him. He willingly agreed. The leave seemed somehow brighter and full of promise. What of, he had a hard task deciding. Even the cretinous remarks about the RFC passed over his head that night. He felt no resentment or belligerence.

He was at Chawton by half past one the next day, and they caught a train by a hair's breadth, just as it was about to steam out of the station. He helped Barbara into the compartment, his hands around that slim waist. It felt sensational. She sat close to him, fanning herself with her straw hat. He could feel her thigh alongside his own, exciting and deliciously forbidden.

"Don't you miss Bill Townley?" he asked suddenly, as the train was pulling into Alton station and a few farm people got in.

"I'm sorry for poor Bill, but it wouldn't have worked out, Bobby," she said, smiling.

He was baffled and delighted. Her novel approach to relationships cut across everything he'd been fed by his mother about women . . . dark whisperings about 'women's complaints', 'breach of promise cases', 'getting girls into trouble', all muttered when the neighbours thought he and Melvin weren't listening, warnings that girls were only out to get husbands to look after them.

He found that they could talk easily and she flattered him by her endless questions about his flying activities. She was not only shrewd but intelligent . . . something that women were not supposed to be, according to his mother.

They chattered all the way into Guildford, over tea, and then saw a film about a heroine being rescued by a tall handsome man from a villainous and cruel husband. She held his hand in the darkened cinema, all through the flickering films and only relinquished it during the pauses for changes in the reels.

They caught the nine p.m. train back to Chawton. The gas lamps were lit on the tiny wayside station at Chawton as the train pulled in.

"Won't your mother be worried about you?" he asked, as they began walking up the long dusty road to the village.

"She's not some Victorian old harridan, you know, Bobby," she murmured. "I don't know where you picked up all these weird ideas about us women. We're not frail and sickly, you know . . . at least I'm not, and I like doing things . . . I can't stand embroidery and knitting . . . I only wish to God I'd been born a man, then I'd be flying with you."

She squeezed his hand, gently. The scent of the summer night came to him, flowers, grass, hay, and the sickly sweet smell of cows. It was all mixed with the perfume that Barbara wore.

"You're very unusual, Babs," he said, softly.

"All women will be like me, some day, when they wake up to life," said Barbara, fiercely.

"Mrs Pankhurst has the right idea . . . votes for women and playing our part in life, not sitting at home, waiting for hubby to arrive, slippers warming by the hearth. God! I couldn't stand that . . . I want to do something . . . !"

Before he knew it they were outside the gate of the Welland cottage.

"Well, aren't you going to come in for a cup of cocoa, and show Mummy that you've brought me home safe and sound?" she demanded.

"Is it alright?" he whispered.

"Of course it is alright," she said, loudly, pulling him into the house.

Mrs Welland seemed genuinely pleased to see him, plying them with questions as to what they had seen at the cinema, where they'd had tea and then, like Barbara, she began asking him more questions about flying.

It was nearly midnight before he realised it.

They promised to meet the next day, for a picnic. Mrs Welland would hire a pony and trap and they would go into the countryside for a feast and a walk.

"Do you know what time it is, Bobby?" demanded his mother, upon his arrival home. She was all determination and anger.

"Gone midnight," he said, smiling, his memories still with Barbara Welland.

"It's disgusting!" exclaimed his mother. "That woman is leading you astray . . . she's well known in the town for her funny ideas."

Before he knew it or wanted it, they were rowing furiously, about loose women and staying out late, up to no good, etc.

He pointed out to her that it had been her idea in the first place that he go and see Barbara Welland, and now she was being unreasonable.

"She's after getting you for a husband!" snapped Mrs Spiers. "That mother of hers is putting her up to it."

"Oh, do give over, Mum, she couldn't care less about marriage and babies and homes."

A dissertation on the lack of virtue of such women followed.

He escaped to bed.

He arose early, shaved and washed carefully, putting on a pair of grey flannels and a roll-neck sweater, and a pair of old walking shoes, that somehow seemed tighter since he had last worn them.

His mother was all tight-faced and sullen at breakfast, packing his father's and brother's sandwiches for work on the railway. Melvin was a trainee fireman and his father a guard.

The Welland women were all ready for him when he arrived, the little pony looked mettlesome and the trap beautifully painted and varnished. They were both soon asking questions about the BE2B.

He gave them the facts . . . the 70hp Renault engine, 'V'-8 water-cooled, wingspan thirty-five feet and half an inch, length twenty-nine feet six and a half inches, height ten feet two inches, did seventy miles an hour and had a cruising altitude of nearly ten thousand feet.

"It must be marvellous to be able to look down on people and see them like midgets . . . must be a god-like feeling," said Mrs Welland, laying out a crisp new table-cloth on the grass and putting out plates, knives, forks, spoons and plates of ham sandwiches, tiny little home-made cakes and other goodies. She set up the Primus stove and soon had a kettle boiling with water from the stream. He then had to recount his experiences leading up to his first solo flight in the Farman MF7 Longhorn. They wanted to know why it was called a 'Longhorn' and he had to explain about the long skids, and the forward elevator which gave it its characteristic appearance and name.

By the time they had finished their lunch, Bob began to feel like a veteran and an ace. They went for a walk over the lush fields and returned to Chawton soon after six o'clock. Barbara kissed him again when he left. He walked home feeling ten feet tall.

He saw her again for the remaining two days of his leave, and then regretfully it was all over and he had to report back to Gosport.

"Write to me, Bobby," she begged him. "Promise?"

He was so full of remorse at leaving that he couldn't speak.

His mother was tearful and disapproving of the amount of time he had spent with the Wellands. His father saw him off, but his brother, Melvin, was indifferent and resentful of his brother's notoriety and refused to come to the station with him.

****

Chapter 5

The first FE2s he had seen arrived in Gosport at the beginning of September, creating a sensation amongst the trainees and instructors of the FTS. It was equipped with a Beardmore 160hp 6-cylinder engine, water cooled and was yet another 'pusher' type aircraft, more mounted inside the 'V'-frame of the aircraft, the propeller facing backwards. It was bigger by some ten feet in wingspan than the BE2B, longer by some three feet and its performance was impressive compared with the BE2. It had a maximum speed of 91mph and could, at a pinch, rise to eleven thousand feet and had a range of around 180 miles. These machines, destined for the Front, all had 303 Lewis machine-guns fitted on the front nacelle, covering a wide hemispherical field of fire forward.

Every single pilot on the FTS was anxious to have a chance to fly the machine but for many this dream remained just that. The planes were for a new RFC Squadron forming to go to France.

The CO of the FTS called Bob into his office one day, soon after his return from leave.

"Feel ready to go to France, Spiers?" he asked, leaning back on the rear legs of his chair.

"Oh, yessir!" Bob was astounded by this offer. There were pilots on the base who had been waiting for a draft order to be assigned to a squadron for weeks.

"Very well. You will report to Major Charlesworth, and tell him that you are to go along with his lads to No 1 Aircraft Depot at St Omer. I can't promise you you'll stay with the Major . . . it will be up to the state of the squadrons at the front at the time. I'll see that the necessary transfers are made."

Bob saluted the Major with speed and rushed from the office, just in case the man changed his mind.

He shared a batman with another officer who had been recently posted to Gosport.

"Corporal, I shall need my kit packing and despatching to St Omer as quickly as you can!" he ordered.

"Yessir!" said the little man. "See to it right away, sir."

Bob went in search of Major Charlesworth.

He found him in one of the hangars listening to a flight sergeant tell him about problems he was having with one of the Beardmores on an FE2. He was dressed in greasy overalls, and had oil over his face. His major's crown was on a sheath of serge under the epaulettes on the overall.

"Yes, what is it, Lieutenant?" he growled, pausing for a moment.

Bob saluted. "I was ordered to report to you at my earliest, sir, by Major Ransome, to go to St Omer with you!" He got it all out in a rush.

"My God!" muttered Charlesworth. "How old are you, Lieutenant?"

"Seventeen, sir, nearly eighteen," stammered Bob, his heart sinking.

"Jesus Christ," said Charlesworth, softly, "And you want to commit suicide like all the rest, do you, Lieutenant?"

"Not exactly, sir, but I certainly would appreciate flying with your squadron."

"How many hours have you done, Lieutenant?" Charlesworth was not tall, but stocky and powerfully built.

"Six on Bes, sir, and five on Longhorns, sir."

"Eleven hours," muttered Charlesworth, staring at Bob, up and down, plucking at his underlip.

"Reckon you could fly one of these?" he asked, tapping the nacelle of the FE above his head.

"Yessir!" said Bob, confidently.

Charlesworth stood for a moment, looking at Bob, whilst the ground crew tried to hide smirks of doubt at this cocky little bastard's ability.

Bob saw the grins, and flushed.

"OK . . . get your gear on, Lieutenant, we'll see what you're made of," said Charlesworth suddenly.

After his first experience of this sudden decision-making at Denham, Bob hid his surprise with aplomb, hurried out to fit on his Sidcot.

He arrived back to find an FE2B already ticking over on the tarmac, Major Charlesworth in the front cockpit.

"What's your name, Lieutenant?" he roared.

"Spiers, sir!"

"OK, in you get, and if you kill me or us both, God help you!"

The FE2 felt heavier than the BE or the Farman. The controls seemed tighter and harder to manipulate. He had spent a good ten minutes, whilst Charlesworth watched this performance, of going round the FE inspecting ailerons, wires and engine, testing the controls, trying out the throttle and working the rudder-bar and stick to see if all the elevators, rudder and ailerons were working properly. He nodded approvingly when Bob finally got into the cockpit. "It's all yours Spiers!" he yelled as Bob opened the throttle.

It seemed ages before the controls lightened and the aircraft came unstuck from the ground. The boundary fence seemed to be leaping towards him. He kept the nose level until the last moment before easing it back and they were airborne. Out over Southampton Water, the air was rich and stable, hardly any wind and the FE handled well.

"Go down near the water!" yelled Charlesworth, jabbing his thumbs downwards.

Bob took the FE down gently until they were travelling at about twenty feet above the tiny waves, heading towards the Isle of Wight. They passed the Victoria Hospital at Netley and then Charlesworth signalled for him to climb.

At five thousand feet he levelled off and looked down.

The water was under his wings, the hulk of the Isle of Wight out in front of them, the City of Southampton behind and the peninsular of Portsmouth out to his left.

"Dive!" ordered Charlesworth.

Bob obliged, until the wires were screaming and the wings juddering. The Major signalled him to pull out. He eased the FE out of the dive, carefully. The tales of wings stripping off under the wind pressure when coming out of steep dives were legion. The Major nodded approval, and then signalled turns until Bob was performing the most difficult of all turns, a ninety degree turn with the wing-tips directly pointing at the earth blow. With the rudder then becoming an aileron and vice versa, it needed nimble thinking and a cool head not to put the machine into a spin. The dreaded spin! In most machines it spelt death or at the least disablement. Few had ever come out of a spin.

Bob brought the FE back on even keel easily and with little trouble.

"Back home!" roared Charlesworth, pointing.

"Not bad, not bad at all, Spiers . . . you're a natural!" said Charlesworth on getting out of the front cockpit on landing. "You're on!"

Bob joyfully wrote to Barbara that night that he had now joined a squadron and was going to France. The memory of those days in August back in Chawton seemed remote now, but still as vivid.

Two days later, on the 12th September, the squadron was assembled on the tarmac ready to take off for St Omer. The nine FEs were lined up in diamond formation. The streamers of the flight leaders streaming back from rudders in the lash of power from the Beardmores. Bob was assigned to 'B' Flight, under Captain Jones. Jones had been in France for six months and had three 'victories' to his credit. The various flights took off in sequence, Charlesworth leading. Over Southampton Water they turned south-eastwards and were soon out over the Channel with the Isle of Wight on the right.

In just under two hours they were circling over the narrow airfield at St Omer, awaiting their turn to land.

The thought of landing in France, the scene of all the action, was an exciting, if slightly daunting, prospect. Not many miles away, the armies of Germany and France and Great Britain were locked in trench warfare, men being killed. At St Omer, a scene of great activity was enacted, men, machines, workshops, stores, lorries, cars, horse-drawn transport, were constantly being moved from one point to another, like some cosmic chess game.

Some individuality was lost on arrival at this seething metropolis of a clearing depot. Bob was pushed from pillar to post on apparently pointless errands, taking guard duty one night, mess officer the next, and even supervising the maintenance of the FEs of 49 Squadron the next.

All the pilots of the squadron were becoming thoroughly bored and irritated by this lack of direction and aimlessness. After a week of endless parades, and lectures by various officers who had been at the Front, drills and very little flying, Charlesworth was pressured by his colleagues to put pressure on the CO to find them a permanent base.

The base at St Omer was the vast clearing house for replacement pilots, the starting point for all squadrons, newly out from the UK to receive their assignment bases in France. All spares for all the aircraft of the UK in France were forwarded from this complex. Ground crews assembled here for onward transit to their units.

The general atmosphere was one of orderly chaos. Nobody seemed to know anything. Charlesworth came into the mess one evening, waving a piece of paper, smiling, his face exhibiting great excitement.

"We're off tomorrow, gentlemen!" he announced, cheerfully.

"Where?" was the universal question.

"Mailly, near Albert," said Charlesworth.

There was a cheer, sheet pleasure at being released from the anonymity of the base at St Omer.

On the 19th September, they left for Mailly, the ground crews and mechanics leaving a day earlier in order to be in situ and have everything ready for when the aircraft arrived.

It rained heavily on the morning of the 19th September, making the airfield soggy and tacky. One of the FEs of 'A' Flight hit a deep rut in the field and almost toppled onto its nose, despite the long forward wheel projecting on a strut under the nacelle. Mechanics rushed out and restored the aircraft to its rightful position, and eventually all of 'A' Flight got off safely. 'C' Flight under Captain Anderson, and then 'B' Flight under Jones with Bob in the left of the 'V' formation.

They managed the fifty-odd miles in just under an hour against a headwind. Clouds were piling up in the east and they had barely landed when a heavy shower developed. Men rushed around trying desperately to get the aircraft under cover. Pilots, ground crew and transport drivers were all pressed into assisting to get them into the hangars.

A farmhouse had been requisitioned to hold both air crews and ground staff. The attempts to dry sodden clothing were frustrated by lack of dry wood to burn. The smell of wet wool and khaki hung in the air for days after.

A week later some kind or order had been established and the squadron could consider itself operational.

Charlesworth announced on 27th September that the whole squadron had been ordered to support an RE8 spotter plane over the Front at Beaumont Hamel, the following morning at dawn.

Excitement was in the air. The squadron was actually going over the enemy lines!

Bob found it difficult to sleep that night, and had just fallen into an uneasy doze when his batman, Corporal West, awakened him at 6 a.m. with a cup of tea. The next moment there was the ear-splitting roar of a Beardmore, followed in rapid succession by several more.

Hastily donning his Sidcot, he hurried out onto the tarmac, to find his observer, Second Lieutenant Mason, already in the cockpit, checking the twin Lewis guns and assembling the spare drums of ammunition, checking each cartridge for signs of bulges or snags.

Mason had only arrived with the rest of the observer personnel the day before and they had had no opportunity of getting to know one another. He was a small man with dark hair and close-set eyes, a small, mean-looking mouth.

Charlesworth led the formation.

They crossed the front lines at ten thousand feet. Mason tested his Lewis guns to warm them. The rattle startled Bob, who had been staring at the ghastly morass below them that was the Western Front. The mud and ill-defined trench systems of both Allied and German were fascinating to view from the air. The smoke that drifted over the nightmarish scene, and the flashes of artillery shells exploding, was like a frosting on some hellish cake. The shell-holes were like boils surrounded by a sea of pus, in which midget figures could be seen toiling at mysterious tasks.

Mason thumped him on the shoulder, pointing downwards.

Looking over the nacelle, he saw the dragon-fly outline of the British machine far below, circling over the German lines. The figures of the crew black dots on the green-brown colour of the machine.

Without warning, there came a blistering woof of an explosion close by the port wing, and a blossom of black smoke sprouted. It had a nasty core of orange flame. Then, in succession, there were others all around the squadron. Immediately, the planes lost formation trying to avoid the blasts of black smoke. This was the first experience of anti-aircraft fire. Jones and Anderson tried in vain to restore formation, but the petrified pilots were all over the place. By the time some semblance of order was maintained, the RE8 had vanished and the black blossoms had suddenly ceased as if by magic.

Bob saw Major Charlesworth rocking his wings and pointing upwards!

Bob's heart nearly stopped. His mouth dried in a fever of excitement. Three straight-winged monoplanes were plunging downwards out of a cloud formation. The semi-circular cowling left no doubt in the squadron's mind that these were the deadly Fokker Eindekker E111s.

Charlesworth seemed to be signalling something and turning his machine round to face the British lines. Unfortunately, the two raw pilots of his flight didn't interpret the signal in a similar manner. They continued on towards the east, their faces clearly visible over a half mile of thin air, staring bewilderingly at their leader.

Mason clapped him on the shoulder again, pointing. Jones was rocking his wings frantically and pointing westwards. Bob pulled the FE into a tight turn to follow Jones as the three Fokkers hit the two FEs of 'A' Flight.

Bob was horrified to note that all three were armed with twin Spandaus, not the single one they had been led to understand this machine was armed with. Even as he watched, two of the Fokkers went in behind the FEs, the harsh rattle of machine guns could be heard, smoke streaming back over the heads of the German pilots.

One of the FEs seemed to leap into the air, hang there for a moment before falling onto its back, and begin to spin downwards out of control.

The third Fokker flew directly behind one of the companions of Captain Anderson's flight. Again the harsh rattle of Spandaus and the FE suddenly erupted into flame as bullets found the petrol tank.

Horrified, Bob watched the stricken aeroplane plunge downwards, a long trail of flame and smoke pouring from it.

A leather-clad figure of a man floated from the burning machine to fall beside it.

The rattle of Mason's Lewis gun brought him to his senses. One of the Eindekkers was manoeuvring into a position behind and under his own tail. Bob stood the FE on its wing-tips, the deadly monoplane barely three hundred yards behind him. He knew that the Fokker was capable of 90mph in a shallow dive and this one was pulling out of one, lining his Spandaus up on his tail section. He also knew that the FE was slightly faster if he could but gain time to escape the clutches of the deadly enemy machine.

The rattle of guns behind him was heard and then a dreadful flack-flack of bullets tearing holes in the right wing. He threw the FE over in a tight turn to give Mason sufficient space to use his own guns. The Beardmore was howling in protest at the abuse of its power.

Mason gave the Eindekker a long burst as it flew past in a tight turn to come back underneath him. He flung the FE around in the sky in a desperate attempt to throw the German pilot from his aim, at the same time making towards the British lines.

The Fokker came in behind them again. Bob stood the FE on its wing-tips in a tight turn, Mason loosed off another long burst, the tracers missing the Fokker by a short distance.

Suddenly, the German aircraft were turning away, flying back towards their own lines.

Mason grinned at him and gave him the thumbs up sign.
Bob knew that he had wet his trousers.

****

Chapter 6

Three FEs had failed to return, amongst whom was Captain Anderson of 'B' Flight.

Bob tried to cover his embarrassing wet patch on his trousers as he got stiffly and shakily from the cockpit.

He felt shattered, his hands shook uncontrollably.

"You did alright, Spiers," said Mason, showing his uneven teeth in a grin.

"I did?" Bob thought his performance was dreadful.

"If you hadn't handled that crate as you did, we wouldn't be here, mate," said Mason enthusiastically. "I'm fucking glad I was with you!" He handed Bob a brandy flask.

They made their report at the Squadron office, confirming that they had seen two FEs go down, but they had not seen Anderson go down.

The mess was gloomy that night. Their first patrol and they had lost a third of their strength. Charlesworth attempted to restore morale, but it was a difficult and unenviable task.

Replacements arrived the next day from the base at St Omer, bringing new machines with them. Strange faces and new personalities.

The squadron went out again the next day, again escorting RE8s on artillery spotting missions. No enemy aircraft appeared.

At the end of a week, Bob had flown five missions over the lines and was feeling almost a veteran. Another brush with Eindekkers had occurred on the 30th September, and they had lost another FE.

Every day Bob took up his aircraft and practised manoeuvres over the aerodrome. Dives, turns, loops, hedge-hopping and throwing the FE about in a rough and brash manner.

The first week of October came and with it the loss of two more FEs by action via the deadly Eindekkers. By the middle of October, Bob noticed that one of his eyelids was given to an unnatural twitching and that he was drinking more than was good for him. He was only happy when in the air, and then fear seemed to be ever present. Mason was still with him, and he had become used to the man's taciturnity, appreciating the man's coolness under attack.

During the second week in October, he saw Captain Jones go down under a hail of bullets from a Fokker over the village of Serre, north of Beaucourt sur Ancre.

Jones's machine seemed to literally disintegrate as two streams of bullets from the twin Spandaus tore the centre section apart.

Charlesworth called him into his office that evening.

"Your promotion has come through, Spiers," he said. "It will be gazetted shortly. I want you to take on 'B' Flight for me. Think you can do it?"

"Yessir!" said Bob, saluting, forgetting where he was.

"Feeling under the weather, are you, Spiers?" asked Charlesworth, his face haggard and drawn.

"I guess we all are, sir," said Bob.

Charlesworth nodded tiredly. "Here you are, Jackson and Leigh . . . your two men. Get them licked into shape, for God's sake, Spiers. We can't go on taking this hammering."

Leigh was seventeen and Jackson was eighteen, fresh out from the UK and full of enthusiasm, eager to get at the foe.

It seemed a hundred years since he had landed on the airfield at Mailly on the 19th September. It was barely four weeks before, and he had seen a dozen men die.

"We're going to fly until you are dizzy," he told his two flight members, grimly, feeling at least a hundred years older than they. In fact, Jackson was older than himself.

Over the next two days, between showers, he made the two young men fly and fly practising manoeuvres until they were exhausted. He pretended to be a Fokker and they had to avoid him.

The next day Jackson was killed as an Eindekker shot his FE out of the sky with a single burst from its twin Spandaus. Leigh followed two days after that. He never saw Leigh fall, but his FE never returned from patrol over the lines at Beauhamel.

One evening, just before dusk a lone Fokker was seen approaching the aerodrome at low level. It was too late to do anything about it and the Fokker merely flew over the aerodrome, dropping a message tin with a streamer attached.

In the tin was the identity disc of Second Lieutenant Leigh, and a message in English to the effect that Leigh had crashed behind the German lines and his observer had jumped. The body had not been found.

"Look, sir, could we not try something different tomorrow?" asked Bob of Charlesworth one night, early in November. "We are being used as Aunt Sallies by the Hun, sir."

Charlesworth looked at him. Bob was shocked to see that the CO looked an old man, a mass of nervous tics and twitches. "What had you in mind, Lieutenant?" he asked, his voice ragged with nerves.

"Let's sandwich our formation tomorrow, instead of flying over the line at one level. You, sir, remain at ten thousand feet, 'B' Flight at seven thousand and 'C' Flight at five thousand," said Bob.

"What's the object of that, Spiers?" asked Charlesworth, barely able to remain civil.

"We draw the Eindekkers down to 'C' Flight . . . decoys, if you like, and then we pounce on them from behind," said Bob, illustrating his ideas with glasses from the mess.

"Let's try anything rather than be knocked out of the sky in this fashion," said Charlesworth.

At dawn the next morning, there had been a frost the night before, and the air was bitterly cold. The nine Beardmores roared, and the air crews assembled in their aircraft. The plan had been explained to them and all were approving. Of the original 49 Squadron only four men remained.

They crossed the German lines to the accompaniment of the usual blasts from anti-aircraft fire, and assembled their formation in the approved plan.

At the end of half and hour's patrolling, it seemed that the Germans had seen the idea and were avoiding them.

As they turned back towards the lines, they saw three blobs above Charlesworth's flight, plummeting down towards the luckless 'C' Flight far below, doodling along at a bare five thousand feet.

Bob waggled his wings and dived after the three monoplanes, followed by 'A' Flight behind them. His two companions, who had been briefed carefully on what to do, followed him down.

The FEs of 'C' Flight had seen the menace bearing down on them and were streaking in shallow dives for the safety of the British lines. The Fokkers were intent on their kills and it appeared they hadn't even seen the tiered FEs above them. Or, if they had, considered them harmless.

The wind was a screaming demon in the wires of the FE as Bob headed towards the nearest Eindekker, Mason was crouched over his guns, his body hunched in anticipation of the fight that was to come.

Bob saw one of the FEs below him, stagger suddenly as one of the Fokkers poured in a burst. It fell out of line and began to dive, shallow at first, but steeper and steeper.

Cursing and snarling to himself, Bob aimed the FE straight at the Fokker. The German pilot had levelled out and was watching the downwards progress of the FE, oblivious of doom above him.

Mason, as they had agreed, held his fire until it seemed the FE would collide with the enemy machine. A stream of bullets from the twin Lewis guns went into body of the German. He thrashed about wildly, in agony in the cockpit for a brief moment before slumping into the shallow depression in the Fokker's fuselage.

It keeled over and didn't straighten until it hit the ground six thousand feet below.

He saw another Eindekker spinning downwards past them, and then he was desperately trying to pull the FE out of its downwards path. He levelled out a bare five hundred feet above the German trenches, seeing a thousand pale faces looking upwards at him.

He landed at Mailly ten minutes later.

Charlesworth came in a few minutes after, jubilant and delighted. "Two of the bastards!" he sang out, running over to Bob. "And the other one got such a hammering, he won't be around for some time!" He was pumping Bob's hand in joy. "It worked, it worked," he yelled, dancing Bob around.

There was a celebration in the mess that night, at the downing of two Eindekkers in one day. The loss of one FE seemed but a small price to pay for the destruction of the deadly monoplanes.

"Damn good work, Bob," said Charlesworth for the umpteenth time. "We'll try the same thing tomorrow . . . see how many more we can bag!"

Bob stared at Charlesworth, astounded. "But they'll have rumbled that now, sir, and they won't fall for the same trick twice!" he protested.

"Nonsense, Spiers," drawled one of the replacement Flight Leaders, Captain Foster. "The Hun is basically stupid and he wouldn't be able to think as clearly as that."

"Beg your pardon, sir, but I don't agree with you," said Bob, quietly.

Foster stared at him, as if hearing blasphemy. "Spiers, I know the Hun, and he is stupid . . . anyone who eats sauerkraut and sausage as a permanent diet, has just got to be stupid." Foster's voice had risen slightly. There was a steely glint to his gaze.

"If we run around believing that, sir, we shall never win this war!" said Bob.

Foster sat up straight. "Lieutenant Spiers, are you a member of the Higher Command?" he rasped.

"No, sir, but I believe that that kind of thinking is dangerous nonsense," insisted Bob.

"That will do, Spiers," broke in Charlesworth. Some of the euphoria had evaporated.

Bob shrugged and turned away, ordering another drink. Charlesworth came over to him. "What the hell are you into, Spiers? Foster is an ace, did you know that?"

Bob looked at Charlesworth's haggard features. "I just believe we would be utterly mad to try the same game twice in a row. We'll have to vary it somewhat."

"We are going to do exactly what we did today, Lieutenant," said Foster, loudly, so that everyone could hear him.

Bob shrugged and sipped his drink.

"Isn't that right, Major?" Foster challenged Charlesworth to deny him his opinion. Even the man's voice irritated Bob, high, almost a falsetto, a permanent smell under his nose.

"Yes, Captain," said Charlesworth.

From that moment, Bob knew that Charlesworth was a tiger made of paper. Foster and the Major began discussing the tactics to be used the next day, hoping to emulate this day's work.

Dawn broke on 8th November, chilly, with a fog over the ground, enough to reduce visibility to about forty yards, but not enough to preclude operations. Corporal West brought him his tea at six-thirty, put his Sidcot out for him, and boots, and then departed as soon as the sound of the first Beardmore shattered the stillness.

The light was eerie and flares had been improvised from petrol cans to mark the point at which take-off should normally occur.

'B' Flight had been assigned the highest role in the day's affairs, the top deck, whilst Foster took 'C' Flight into the middle layer, and the Major undertook to act as bait.

Disaster almost overtook them from the first moment. An FE from 'A' Flight ran off the prescribed runway and had to be pulled out of the mire. Charlesworth angrily told the young pilot to remain where he was, and took off with but one wingman. 'C' Flight went next, and lastly Bob's own Flight.

He looked round anxiously, as he burst into glorious sunlight at three thousand feet, to make sure his two subordinates were where they should be. The other two FEs swam out of the mist some distance away, but in order. Both were novice pilots with less than nine hours flying behind them.

Within minutes the mist cleared as if by magic, and the Front Line lay below with all its representation of hell.

German Ack-Ack fire broke out as soon as they cleared the front, the black blossoms making the raw pilots understandably nervous.

Bob looked down. 'C' Flight was still some distance behind him, and he could barely distinguish 'A' Flight because of cloud at around five thousand feet. They were farther back, still. He recalled Jessop's remarks about not flying in a straight line for more than a few seconds at a time. He had found over the past two months that advice the best he had ever received, with reference to combat flying. The pilots, usually raw, who flew in straight lines invited attention from the dreaded Eindekkers, made it easy for them.

As inexperienced as Bob was, he began to realise that this cretinous insistence on formation flying made it easier for the Hun flyers to knock them out of the sky. To attempt complicated manoeuvres whilst formation flying was like asking a two-year old to perform acrobatics.

He also had begun to realise that the toffy-nosed officers who purported to be leaders were idiots. His respect for most of them, like the straw-mouthed Foster, had dried up quickly. Most of them viewed the Germans with the same contempt they treated Pathans on the North-West Frontier of India, and with the same disastrous results.

He groaned, looked around to see if his cohorts were in position. His right-hand wingman was falling back, and the other on his left was drifting away, trying desperately to keep his FE in position.

Without warning the black blossoms ceased and the whoof-whoof of the explosions died. He searched the sky above his head, thumping Mason on the shoulder to make sure he understood the significance.

Mason had and warmed his Lewis guns in preparation. Whatever his private feelings about Mason, Bob had to acknowledge his skill as an observer and fighter.

He almost missed the silver streak that flashed in between them, making for his right wingman, who had been terrified on hearing Mason's machine-guns and had pulled away. The black Maltese crosses floated crazily before his eyes, and then the FE was lurching over onto its side, a pall of black smoke pouring from the engine.

He threw the FE into a tight turn, levelled out, looked round him. Mason tapped him, pointing.

Two Eindekkers were coming in at the remaining FE on his left from both sides. The German machines again were armed with twin Spandaus, and both were firing simultaneously.

The FE seemed to halt, as the converging streams of bullets hit the wings, then travelled like a sewing machine along the canvas to the nacelle. He saw the observer throw up his arms, slump down out of sight, and then the pilot was thrashing around like a fish on a hook. The FE keeled over on one wing, began to spin wildly. He couldn't see anything else. The sky seemed to be full of Maltese crosses and the Eindekkers seemed to be everywhere. Mason was firing almost continuously as the German Fokkers criss-crossed their path. Bob threw the FE around like a mad man, the smell of fear was in his bones. Any moment, he expected to feel the crunch of hot lead biting into him. Canvas ripped on the port wing, then something whanged off the engine cowling behind him, making him duck.

Quite suddenly, the controls seemed to go slack in his hands. At the same time he saw Mason fall backwards into the cockpit, blood pouring from his chest as a row of holes stitched themselves across his Sidcot. Then the machine was falling like a stone, just diving . . . straight down.

Wires screaming protest, the Beardmore howling in a weird cacophony behind him, the FE seemed to be going to plunge straight into the earth. He struggled desperately to restore some control to the plunging machine, lashing out at first with one foot and then the other to get some response. He yanked on the joystick into his thigh. Nothing happened, save the ground hurtling up to meet him with increasing force.

He felt an almost unendurable tiredness overcome him, a fatalism that paralysed all movement. This was the end as he had seen others go over the past three months . . . his Father, Mother, Barbara, Melvin, all seemed to be with him, watching his descent into oblivion . . .

****

Chapter 7

Slowly, his head thrust back against the headrest with the air pressure, the FE began to pull out of the dive. The earth was horribly close. He could see the explosions in No Man's Land, the pockmarked trenches, the wire stretching like evil decorations across the brown landscape. The white faces of the troops in their warrens, peering upwards at the careering FE, anticipating its point of impact.

The nose came up, agonisingly slowly. Mason's body was lolling on the coaming, blood running from the corners of his mouth. It rolled as the nose began to level out and the horizon assumed a normal aspect, his helmeted head hitting against the butts of the Lewis guns.

The FE flattened out a bare fifty feet over the British lines, lurching and staggering drunkenly. The controls still felt slack and without 'bite'. The trees, shattered stumps behind the trenches, loomed up just under the wheels of the FE. Treating it as if it were red hot, he eased the stick back, praying that the nose would rise. The Beardmore was clattering away behind him, as if some part was missing. He daren't look behind him.

A ruined house loomed up. The front skid wheel missed the crazy chimney stack by inches. He went just over the heads of a column of troops on the march. They scattered as the FE lurched over their heads.

A stretch of flat ground appeared between the stumps of poplars, tents at the far side. He knew he wouldn't have a second chance. Cutting the engine as soon as he passed the poplars, he pulled the stick back gently, hoping that the deceptively flat ground would prove solid.

The FE seemed to float for a moment before the undercarriage struck, bounced, then hit again, bounced yet once more, before the wheels became glued in the gunge of the flat ground.

Men appeared at the flaps to the tents, stared horrified at the approaching FE before running for safety.

The wing-tips touched the ground. The FE swung round in a vicious arc, before centrifugal force threw it onto the left wing-tip, the whole fabric crumpling into matchwood.

The force of the impact threw him forward, only the safety belt preventing him catapulting from the nacelle. The next instant he was buried in mud and there was an incredible weight on his legs.

Half stunned, he lay there, the mud oozing round his ears, into his mouth. He couldn't move anything, legs, arms or head. The weight seemed to be getting worse. He heard voices above him, and then the sound of axes chopping wood. He felt a thrill of fear run through him as he thought about the petrol tank somewhere behind him. If anyone was foolish enough to be smoking a cigarette!

The weight came off his legs, suddenly, and hands were pulling him from the wreckage.

He staggered upright, falling over again immediately. A hand held him, and a flask was thrust between his lips. He took a swig, coughed and staggered around like a drunken man.

Then he was in a tent, the sunlight illuminating the canvas, and his legs felt weak and rubbery. "Am I alright?" he asked, shakily.

"Few scratches, old boy, nothing worse," said a voice behind him. "Your aeroplane has gone, I'm afraid . . . caught fire."

Half an hour later, with smiling friendly faces around him, he felt a hundred per cent better. The officer had phoned the airfield at Mailly and a tender was being sent for him.

The tender arrived with Corporal West and a driver. An hour later, and after thanking the Artillery Officer and his colleagues for their hospitality, he was driven back to the squadron.

There were three FEs standing on the field, their wings torn with bullet holes and large starred holes in the nacelles. One had a central strut shot through and the whole structure seemed to sag in the middle.

Captain Foster greeted him, his face white with pain, his arm in a sling. The moustache over his lip had a stuck-on look, and the smell under his nose had faded leaving only the haggard facia of pain.

He seemed genuinely pleased to see Bob. "Good God, man, where did you come from?" he gasped, seeing the mud and blood on Bob's uniform and Sidcot.

Bob related his experiences, pleased at being able to unburden himself of the terrible sight of Mason's body in the back of the tender, torn and bleeding.

"We took a beating," confessed Foster. "Charlesworth's gone, and six others . . . we're down to those last aircraft!"

Bob suppressed the fury that rose inside him at the thought of all those men either dead or prisoners, because this comedian had been unable to credit the enemy with more than low intelligence.

It seemed there had been nine Eindekkers and they had attached the top layers of the squadron first, which had happened to be Bob's own 'B' Flight, then had moved on to 'C' Flight, Foster's, and finally attached the two FEs, one of which was the Major.

Vindication of his worst fears did not make Bob feel any better. He hated the pale face of the Captain who had been, more than anyone else, responsible for the deaths of nine men and the loss of their machines.

It was a week before replacements arrived, both men and machines. There were three of the new Sopwith Pups in the replacement aircraft. These were single seat fighters, the intention being to allocate these to the three Flight Commanders. The Sopwith was powered by an 80hp Le Rhone engine, in a nine cylinder rotary arrangement. With a total length of nineteen feet three and three-quarter inches, and a span of twenty-six feet six inches, it was small when compared with the FE.

Bob took his new machine up very gingerly. The difference in feel and performance was unbelievable. The little machine was highly manoeuvrable, had a maximum speed of 110mph plus and a ceiling of up to 17,000 feet.

After some rolls and loops, dives and sharp turns, Bob brought it down to a perfect three point landing.

The organisational problems created by the three Pups mixed with the six FEs were nearly insoluble. Beside the lumbering FEs, the Pups would race ahead and have to be pulled back in order to maintain even moderate formation.

After three days it was obvious to Foster, who had assumed temporary command, that it was an unworkable arrangement. The three Pups were made into a Flight under Bob and the remaining six FEs became 'A' and 'C' Flights.

After a morning of heavy rain, the squadron was ordered to escort some lumbering French Farman F40s, which were going to unload some bombs on a troublesome German artillery battery.

Foster insisted on crossing the line at under 9,000 feet, in spite of Bob's protests and those of the other single experienced pilot, named Robson. Bob and Robson claimed that they would be sitting targets for the Eindekkers.

The sky was cloud-laden, overcast and squally, a watery sun peered from behind cathedral banks of cumulus. It was bitterly cold, despite some of the heat from the Le Rhone rotary coming back into the cockpit.

At seven-thirty, almost precisely, nine Eindekkers dropped out of the sun onto the FEs, and sent two spinning earthwards.

Bob heard twin Spandaus chattering behind him, a row of holes stitched across the port wing, and then he thrust the Sopwith into a tight turn that had the German pilot goggling in amazement. Behind the Eindekker, he overhauled it rapidly with the Pup's superior speed. The head of the German pilot showed in the ring Aldis sight. He waited until he was less than two hundred yards from the Eindekker before squeezing the trip hammer.

The German pilot looked round as bullets from the Vickers with its Sopwith-Kauper interrupter gear, smashed into him. The Fokker nosed over and went straight down without pulling out. Bob saw it crash into a wood behind the British lines. He barely had time to whip the Pup round before another Eindekker was on his tail, bullets tearing holes in the canvas of the fuselage behind him.

He whirled the Pup virtually in its own length and the Eindekker went past, a look of utter astonishment on the face of the pilot. Bob was soon over and above him, the German pilot trying desperately to escape from the Pup's superior speed.

Bob again held off firing until the Pup was within a hundred yards of the Fokker. He could see the stitching in the canvas, the bolts in the semi-circular cowling. The Fokker banked wildly, but could not shake the Pup from its position on his tail.

Bob squeezed the trigger when the man's head came into the Aldis sight. At the last moment, the Fokker banked, and the tracer went into the Eindekker's engine. Bob saw sparks fly from the cowling, and then the Eindekker was keeling over, a long plume of smoke pouring from its engine, trailing backwards in a long curve.

By the time Bob had pulled out of the long climb and looked downwards, the mass of circling machines had drifted lower and over the German lines. He saw an FE spinning down out of control. There were two wrecked machines on the ground, one burning fiercely. Whether friend or foe, he could not tell.

The Eindekkers were pulling away now, leaving the British machines victors, but with another bloody nose, in charge of the field.

On landing, he saw only three FEs on the field and one Pup.

He made his way over to the Squadron office to find Foster fuming over the losses the squadron had again suffered, even with the new Pups. One was missing and the pilot was Robson, the only other experienced man in the squadron.

"We've had confirmation from Forward Ops . . . they saw two Eindekkers come down, Spiers, congratulations," said the Captain, his haggard face white and drawn. He made it sound as if he didn't want to congratulate anybody, least of all Bob.

"We lost five," he said, mournfully.

Bob felt the twitching at his eyelid again, more pronounced and violent this time. His skin felt like paper, and his fingers tingled with some nervous response to the stress he was feeling. He longed to be able to tell the horse-faced fool before him that his was the blame for the losses . . . the crazy insistence on crossing the line at less than ten thousand feet and the lack of any co-ordination of plans with the French Farman squadron.

The survivors went on a binge into Amiens that night, visiting the brothels and wine bars, and getting drunk. In a restaurant, they met the members of the French squadron whose Farmans they had been meant to escort.

The CO, a tiny little Frenchman with a square black moustache and brilliant black eyes, came over to them, leaving his companions watching him from their table.

He bowed in front of Foster, and spoke in clipped English with a strong accent.

"Sir! We lost four of our aeroplanes today to the Boche." He stood to attention, rigidly, as if delivering an address to troops.

"And we, sir, lost five," said Foster, saluting the little Captain, also standing.

"That is sad, sir. We offer our condolences to the RFC flyers," said the little man, struggling now with the English. "Why do you cross the line under ten thousand feet, may I ask?"

Foster flushed, the English pilots openly grinning, albeit well soaked in alcohol by now.

Foster coughed, cleared his throat, and muttered something about orders.

The little Frenchman's eyes glittered angrily. "You English are mad!" he spat. "You are brave but mad. My comrades would be alive now but for your stupid orders, and your own comrades would be alive, also."

"We don't question orders, sir," snapped Foster, furiously.

"You, sir, are a moron!" declared the little man, venomously.

Foster drew himself up to his full six feet, glaring down at the little Frenchman. "I will not be spoken to in this fashion!" he roared.

The estaminet was deathly quiet suddenly, all eyes on the two protagonists. The French pilots all stood up at their table, eyes angry, glaring at the English.

The RFC pilots in their turn were returning the compliment. Bob sat where he was, indifferently staring into his glass of red wine.

The little Frenchman suddenly switched his attention to Bob. "Why are you not supporting your officer, Lieutenant?" he demanded. "And stand up when you address a superior officer."

Bob staggered to his feet, saluted clumsily, nearly falling over. "Because he is a bigger bloody fool than you . . . sir!" he said, clutching the table.

The little man's eyes seemed to bulge with fury. "I will have you arrested, sir!" he screamed.

Bob shrugged. "Suit yourself, sir!" he said, flopping down again.

The Frenchman stood over Bob, as if about to strike him. "You insolent man," he screamed.

"Watch it, Captain," said one of the RFC pilots. "He shot down two Eindekkers today!"

The little Captain seemed confused for a moment, his anger melting away like snow in an oven. He threw his arms around Bob's neck and kissed him on both cheeks. "The hero!" he yelled. "Two Boche this man destroyed today!" he yelled at his companions. "Bring out the brandy!"

The French pilots all rushed over, holding out bottles of brandy to the English men. Before a minute was out they were all toasting one another and smiling, filling glasses, patting each other on the back.

"To His Majesty, King George of England!" yelled the Captain, raising his glass.

The English men responded by toasting the President, and then they were half drunk toasting one another.

The evening ended amicably with each CO giving out invitations to visit the other at their messes for dinner.

Foster was sour towards Bob for the next few days, and the relationship was on course for open conflict. Both were saved from drawn swords by an order, which arrived posting Bob to St Omer.

He found the sprawling base no different from his first visit. It seemed years since he had arrived on the long narrow aerodrome with 49 Squadron and Charlesworth, Anderson and Jones and his other colleagues. Now, all dead. There seemed to be even more chaos this time. Nobody seemed to know what to do with him and he was kept kicking his heels until the end of November, carrying out various duties and tasks, flying occasionally, but itching to get back to a line squadron at the Front.

On 10th December, a miserable day with snowflakes fluttering down from a leaden sky, he asked to see the CO Postings.

"What is it, Spiers? Getting itchy feet, are you?" asked the Colonel, leaning back in his chair, regarding the stocky young man in front of him. He had a few papers on his desk, but nothing else.

"Yessir. There just doesn't seem any point to my being here, when I could be doing something useful at the Front," said Bob.

"Understandable, Spiers, understandable. How long have you been in the RFC?" asked the Colonel, tall, close cropped hair, iron grey, lean with a monocle.

"June 1st, sir." Put like that it sounded like yesterday. It felt like ten years.

"Mere rookie, aren't you, Lieutenant?" said the Colonel, his face straight.

"How long does it take to become a veteran, sir?" asked Bob.

"Now that is a good question, Lieutenant," said the Colonel. He read one of the papers on his desk. "Have trouble accepting authority, Lieutenant?"

"I do get impatient with bad leadership, sir," admitted Bob, irritated.

"You consider you have bad leaders, do you, Lieutenant?" The Colonel's voice was soft.

"Some of them, sir," said Bob, wondering where this conversation was leading.

"Captain Foster one of them, Lieutenant?"

Bob stared at the map of France behind the Colonel's head . . . so the bastard had split on him . . . typical, thought Bob. He said nothing.

"Hmm." The Colonel sat up straight. "One of the indications of good soldiering, Lieutenant, is the ability to take orders, no matter how foolish they may appear at the time, to those of us in the ranks."

"I felt that my ideas should at least be given a try, sir, if winning the war is the objective of the experiment," said Bob.

The smell under the Colonel's nose grew pronounced, the monocle glinted. "All of us have pet theories on what should be done, Lieutenant. Fortunately for us, we aren't in a position to influence events or mayhap the war could be lost," he said, a chill in his tone. "You would agree with that?" he asked, after a silence.

"No, sir, I'm afraid I have to disagree with you," said Bob, stubbornly.

The Colonel sat up straight. "Now listen to me, Lieutenant. I will not tolerate barrack-room lawyers in the ranks . . . at whatever level. Is that clear?" he rasped.

"I'm not one of those at all, sir, I just feel that ideas at least should be given a hearing," said Bob, wishing he hadn't come into the office.

"This refers to your suggestion that Captain Foster should not have repeated the tactics you tried on 30th October, Lieutenant, when two of those Huns were shot down . . . these . . . er . . . ." He consulted the paper "Eindekkers, eh?"

"Wasn't that, sir," said Bob, doggedly.

"What was it then, Lieutenant?" The Colonel's tone was abrasive, harsh.

"The Captain called the Germans stupid, sir," said Bob.

****

Chapter 8

Two days later on the 12th, he was given seven days' leave of absence, with orders to return an FE2C to Farnborough on his way.

He took off with snowflakes dazzling the view to the front. His kit had been lashed into the front cockpit. With a south-easterly wind behind him, he made good time and landed at Farnborough some two hours later.

He caught a train to Guildford, changed and was at Alton station by five p.m.

His kit he put into the left-luggage office, walked the half mile or so to his parents' home.

"Bobby!" gasped Mrs Spiers, astonished when he walked in the door. She hugged him, kissing him with moist kisses. "How long have you got?"

Bob winced. Jesus, already! he cursed. "Seven days," he said. "Any tea?"

"A little, dear," said his mother, leading the way into the house. She looked older somehow than he remembered. Lines at her eyes and rings round her neck. She was only forty-odd.

He had to tell her all about his experiences in France, where he'd been and who he had met. "What's the matter with your eye, Bobby . . . it keeps twitching," she said suddenly.

"Bit of strain, Mum," he said, trying to head her off.

"Shouldn't you have it seen to?"

"Nothing anybody can do about that, Mum."

His mother immediately went into a long diatribe about hospitals and medicine and the neighbours who had operations.

When his father came home, he had to repeat his story again, and again for Melvin. His brother was still morose and bad-tempered and listened with ill-grace to Bob's story of life at the Front.

Over tea, his father went on about why the British Army had failed at the Somme and why the Hun was still virtually where he had been six months before, only having inflicted enormous casualties on the British.

Bob listened silently whilst his father went on and on, lack of training, lack of morale, lack of initiative . . .

"It wasn't that at all, Dad," said Bob, suddenly, when he could take no more.

"Oh?" Mr Spiers sat up. "What was it, then?"

"The men at the top, if they're anything like those in the RFC, are useless and don't know what's happening to men in the trenches."

"But they're born to lead, my boy, trained from birth," protested his father.

"Well, something's gone wrong with the strain," said Bob.

"What's the matter, Bob, you weren't like this before you went into the Flying Corps?"

"I hadn't seen it first hand," said Bob, sourly.

"You must never question your superiors, my boy, they know what they're doing," said Harley Spiers.

"Dad, they don't," said Bob, quietly. "They're sending men in against machine-guns with bayonets, just like they did at the Alma and Balaclava."

Mrs Spiers stopped any further argument. "Bobby was always arguing with his teachers at school," she said. "Looks like he's going to do the same with the officers."

Down at the Station Hotel that evening, the locals stared at his 'Wings' afresh as if trying to find a reason why he shouldn't wear them. The flicker in his left eyelid came in for some ribald remarks.

Back at home, he sat in the chair by the fire, listening to the rising wind and the flurries of snow beating at the windows. He went to bed early. His bed had a hot water bottle in it for hours and was snug and warm. The bedroom itself smelt damp and cold.

He was up early and went for a walk down Anstey Lane, his greatcoat up around his ears. He collected his kit from the station and walked home in time for breakfast. The home-made bread smelled delicious, the fresh farm butter was a treat after the margarine in the mess. The bacon was from a local farmer and was cooked with his mother's usual skill.

"What are you going to do with yourself, Bobby?" asked his mother after Harley had left for work.

"I'll go and see what Barbara's doing," he said, casually.

His mother's mouth went tight into a straight line. "I wish I'd never suggested you go and look her up," she said, bitterly. "That young woman is too forward by far."

"Depends on what you mean by forward," said Bob, picking up his greatcoat and hat.

"You know what I mean, young feller-me-lad," said Mrs Spiers. "And don't you go bringing shame on this house!"

He hurried out of the house.

He knocked at the Wellands's front door, his heart beating rapidly.

After an interval it opened, and a strange woman looked at him, questioningly.

"Young Miss Welland is in the QAIMNS now, young man, and Mrs Welland is in the WRVS. Both are away from home now. I'm just caretaking the house."

His heart went into his boots. " Do you know where Miss Welland is stationed?" he asked.

"Guy's Hospital, London," said the little woman, anxious to close the door.

"Could have told you that before you went," snapped his mother, peevishly, on his arrival back home.

"Why didn't you . . . could have saved me that long walk," snapped Bob, angrily.

His mother's mouth went all tight again, with imagined insult.

The next day, he was up early, caught a train to London, and arrived at Waterloo at ten a.m.

An ambulance train had just pulled in from Dover and they were unloading the wounded. There were hundreds of them, stretcher cases, amputations without arms, legs, and other hideous wounds.

He stared horrified. Close proximity to the results of the fighting on the Somme gave a new dimension to the war.

"If it isn't Spiers . . . How are you, Robert?" came a voice from behind him, as he stood gazing at the horror of the train.

Charles Martine stood there, a Captain's three pips on his shoulders, a smile of welcome on his face.

They shook hands, exchanged stories, experiences.

"I say, come home with me, old boy, have lunch with Mater and Sis . . . come on . . . we can't let you get away without having a chinwag. Congratulations on your full Lieutenant pips, old boy." He wouldn't take no for an answer, and soon they were in a taxi being driven to Bayswater.

Bob decided that in all probability, Barbara would be on duty until later, so he welcomed the opportunity to fill in time.

The Martines lived in a massive four-storey Regency terraced house in Westbourne Terrace. Martine's mother met him in the large drawing room. A tall woman with features similar to Charles. Her hair was greying in large badger streaks on either side of the severe bun she wore, but a good-looking woman.

"Well, the hero returns from the wars," greeted Michelle as she came into the room. "And a real, live Lieutenant . . . Bravo!"

Bob knew that Michelle and Barbara had much in common in their attitudes towards femininity, and their role in the world. The only difference being that Barbara was more aggressive and forthright, whereas Michelle seemed to take a lot for granted. Her social standing seemed to advance this attitude without undue strain. She came up and kissed him, much to his embarrassment, and secret pleasure.

"Welcome home, Lieutenant Spiers!"

She linked her arm with his, led him away and then questioned him closely on his exploits in France. He was flattered, but the close comparison with Barbara's personality was uncomfortable. Despite this, he opened up to her, his uneasiness at the leadership he had encountered in the RFC . . . the overbearing brashness, the inability to adapt to new ideas, and above all the conceit of the higher ranks, who considered their viewpoints unassailable, their decisions correct. He found himself telling her of the incident with the Eindekkers over Bertincourt, and Foster's insistence that they repeat the manoeuvre the next day.

"Why didn't you protest?" demanded Michelle, after hearing him out.

"Is that a joke?" he said, truculently.

"Robert, don't get on your high horse with me . . . I am on your side, you know," she said, gently.

"Sorry," he muttered, shamefacedly. "But I did protest, but Foster told me to shut up and mind my own business, in as many words."

"And what about the CO . . . didn't he support you?" she asked.

"That's what I'm getting at . . . he went along with Foster . . . got himself killed for his pains."

"You can't do more than that, Robert," said Michelle, sympathetically.

"We lost seven men that day through his stupidity," said Bob, angrily. "Because he believes the Germans to be idiots, incapable of thinking it out."

"We heard all about that at Army Command," said Charles, behind them. "Created quite a stink, old man. Foster was all set to have you court martialled for disobeying orders, questioning a superior officer's orders."

"Do they do that sort of thing, Charles?" asked Michelle.

"For a mere Lieutenant to question orders at that level is tantamount to treason," said Charles, his face serious.

"Even when the order is palpably idiotic?" demanded Michelle.

"If everybody started questioning orders, we'd never get anywhere, Sis . . . there'd be chaos," said Martine.

"I realise that, but if there's an intelligent alternative, surely the correct thing would be to investigate it?" said Michelle. "Seven men killed because of that man Foster's idiocy, it doesn't bear thinking about."

"I don't think you're in a position to judge the pros and cons, Sis," said Charles.

Michelle's eyes flashed. "In other words, a woman is not capable of understanding the problem, is that it?"

Before he knew, brother and sister were having a flaming row over the merits or otherwise, of women's contributions to events.

"Hey, stop it, you two," he cried. "It's not worth quarrelling about, it's my problem, not yours. So, please, stop arguing."

They ignored him, tearing into each other hammer and tongs, Michelle taking his side and Charles putting forth the High Command's viewpoint.

As suddenly as they'd started, they stopped, both grinned at one another, and made up.

"Take no notice of us, Robert," said Michelle. "We're always having a go . . . I'm all for votes for women, Mrs Pankhurst and all that. He gets too big for his boots on occasions . . . have to take him down a peg."

They had lunch and everything seemed normal again. Vincent Martine, Charles's father, asked him questions about the flying at the Front, the kind of machines they were flying and the standards of workmanship and a host of other questions. Bob, sensitive to the explosive atmosphere surrounding his views on command, kept his comments to himself, concentrating on organisational and mechanical problems.

"You managed that very well, Robert," said Michelle after they were sitting down drinking coffee in the drawing room. "Avoided the prickly issues very adroitly."

"I didn't want to spark off another session," he grinned.

"Oh, we don't mean anything by it . . . we often row like that, part of the Martine's Latin ancestry . . . Huguenots and all that." She smiled at him. "There's some Shakespeare on in the Strand . . . Charles doesn't want to go . . . do you fancy escorting me? Two tickets in the circle . . . good seats?"

He thought of Barbara at Guy's Hospital, and then he thought that since she hadn't bothered to let him know about her move away from home . . . there was always another day. How did he know she'd be pleased to see him? Probably engaged to some handsome officer, well up in the ranks.

"I have to catch the last train to Alton," he said.

"Nonsense, we can put you up here for the night . . . Charles can provide you pyjamas and the wherewithal." She smiled at him, appealingly.

During the afternoon they walked in Kensington Gardens and talked about all the things that had been burning him up for so long regarding the RFC. He felt better after it, grateful for Michelle's silent sympathy.

Again, he was struck at the strong likeness between Michelle and Barbara, in personality terms. He might have been talking to Barbara, as he had done during the occasion of his last leave in the summer, in the fields around Chawton, save for the fact that this was London and this young woman had more self-assurance than even Barbara.

They had tea at a small restaurant in Knightsbridge, and then walked back to Bayswater across the park once more.

He found that the double-breasted tunic of the RFC attracted a lot of attention from both soldiers and women alike. They stared, unabashed at the wings on his left breast, and at the young woman by his side.

they took a cab to the theatre in the Strand.

"You like Shakespeare, Robert?" asked Michelle, as they alighted and he paid the man.

"I've never read, or seen it," he confessed, shamefacedly.

"Well, it will be an experience for you, won't it? I like it . . . but it's not everybody's cup of tea."

The play was Macbeth, and Bob found it tedious in the extreme after the first half an hour. The language left him cold and the plot seemed overly complicated and stretched.

"Aren't enjoying it much, are you, Robert?" she said, as they went into the bar during the interval between Acts.

"I'm afraid it goes over my head, most of the time," he admitted, sorrowfully.

She squeezed his hand. "It's an acquired taste. After you've seen one or two, you begin to get the message."

He stuck it, silently squirming, and wishing he'd gone to see Barbara instead.

After the theatre, they went for dinner at a restaurant in Piccadilly.

"Poor Robert, made you suffer, didn't I?" she murmured as they sat down.

"I didn't get much out of it," he said. "Perhaps next time I'll be able to enjoy it more."

"Do you fancy risking a next time, Robert?" she asked, softly.

He blushed. "There must be thousands of young men all wanting to take you out and able to give you a good time . . . rich young men . . . like de Vinguind or Launcey-Moore."

"Vyvyan is a crashing bore . . . so full of himself that I could scream, and as for Bertie . . . well, he's a stuffed shirt," she confided.

"But there must be thousands of them . . . a beautiful woman like you, rich, plenty of money, intelligent and caring," he said.

It was her turn to blush. "That was a nice compliment, Robert . . . your first. Not very adept with women, are you?"

"I haven't had much experience," he said, his face colouring.

"I'm glad," she said.

He was open-mouthed. "But I thought . . ." he began.

"That we sophisticated women like the suave, man-of-the-world, knows everything, been everywhere and is conceited and full of themselves?" she finished for him.

"Welll . . . yes," he said.

"I suppose some women do, Robert, but men like de Vinguind and Launcey-Moore bore me with their airs and graces, supercilious lot."

"But I'm not much different," he said.

"You're modest, save when something upsets you like this business of leadership, and you're quiet, not gabbling all the time . . . I like it." Her eyes were on his, luminous and entreating.

He didn't know what to say, he stammered and stuttered, finally coming to a stop.

"Don't try to emulate men like Vyvyan and Bertie, Robert, you have your own brand of individuality . . . let it grow, come out, and don't be put off by men like them."

Martin Jessop's words came back to him, on his posting to Gosport . . . "don't get a chip on your shoulder over men like Martine." He smiled to himself over the other ribald comment of Jessop's.

"What are you smiling about?" she asked.

"Something my first flying instructor said to me," he said, openly grinning. "Not repeatable to ladies."

It seemed as if the tension that had been between them during the Shakespeare and the dinner suddenly evaporated and they became at ease with one another.

they arrived back at Bayswater at 11 p.m.

the house was silent, no sign of either Charles or his father.

"Afraid to be alone with me, Robert?" she whispered, as she poured coffee from the percolator left on the gas hot plate.

"Where is Charles?" he asked.

"Out whoring, I shouldn't wonder," she said, in a matter-of-fact voice.

He was mildly shocked.

"Oh, dear, have I said something terrible?" she asked, giggling.

"Took me back a bit," he said, candidly.

"Not used to it, are you . . . the modern, sophisticated woman?" she said, still laughing.

"Not really," he said, wonderingly.

She leaned over and kissed him. Not in the way she had greeted him earlier that morning, but softly, lingeringly.

He grabbed her, fiercely, passionately.

"Wow!" she breathed later. "Not all iron, are you, Robert?"

Later, in bed, he wondered whether he had been dreaming it all. He felt elated and depressed in turns. It hadn't been at all difficult, as he imagined it would and he felt confused and troubled. "Don't bring trouble home, Bobby," his mother's words came to him.

She was subdued at breakfast the next morning. Again, neither Charles, nor the father or mother were present.

"Where's everyone?" he asked, surprised.

"Mummy's gone to Chelmsford for the day, and Daddy works in the War Ministry and works all hours. Charles, well, I can guess where he is," she said.

"What will you do today?" he asked her, shyly.

"Be miserable, Robert," she said, her face downcast. "Probably cry when you've gone and give the lie to my sophisticated airs."

"I don't have to go back," he said, feeling guilty over Barbara and his mother and father missing him. We could go to Richmond or somewhere."

"How lovely, Robert. Are you sure your parents won't be upset?"

"Probably will, but they'll have to put up with it, won't they?" he said, with more aggression than he'd intended.

"I wouldn't like them to be unhappy about you," she said.

"They won't," he assured her, with bravado.

"Send them a telegram telling them where you are," she suggested.

"My God, they'd never open it for a day, fearing I'd been killed or something," he said.

"If you're sure," she said.

He spent the day with her and the next day, and the next.

Barbara faded into the background. His parents were just a vague nagging responsibility at the back of his mind. The RFC, the problems, the nagging fears, all dispersed. He felt renewed. Every night they made love in his room, and every morning, just before dawn, she left him to go back to her own room. He never saw Charles, her mother or father. There were two servants, old and decrepit, who didn't bother about anything very much.

On the morning of the fifth day he knew he had to go back to Alton. His seven days were up the day after that, and he would have to report to Farnborough or some such place.

It was a wrench, leaving Michelle, and she clung to him crying unashamedly on the platform at Waterloo. "Write to me, won't you?" she begged.

He promised, and waved to her from the moving train, until she disappeared from sight, just as Barbara had done on the last night of his leave the previous August.

The journey back to Alton was all too short. He indulged fantasies of marriage and home, but realised the futility of that dream as soon as he considered the facts. He had no job, no income, no prospects . . . there was only the war, and if he wasn't killed, the war had to end sometime, and then what?

His mother was all reproachful and tearful at his long absence and began to berate him for his lack of consideration. His father was a little brittle tempered also, something unusual for Harley Spiers.

There was a letter from Barbara on the mantel. It had been posted two days before in London, asking him to come and see her on his next leave.

He felt stricken with remorse and guilt . . . his mind full of Michelle.

There were also orders for his reporting to Farnborough, but his leave had been extended by a further seven days to include Christmas.

"Perhaps we can see a bit more of you now?" said his mother, bitterly, on hearing the news. "Or are you going gallivanting off again?"

Harley attempted to remonstrate with his wife, but she turned her fury upon him.

He wrote to Michelle every day, and she to him. Letters full of passion and love. Taking them up to his room, he devoured every word and longed to be able to see her again. He was sorely tempted to go up to London and see her, but every time his mother seemed to be prescient about his feelings and would turn on the waterworks at any suggestion of his leaving.

On Christmas Eve, Harley and Melvin and Bob went to the Station Hotel for a celebration drink. "Go and see your girl if you want to, son," said his father. "Never mind your Mother . . . women all get jealous and bitchy about their sons . . . think they don't need other women, only them."

"Oh, come on, Dad, that can't be true," he protested.

Harley Spiers sipped his pint, looking at his son over the glass. "True, son," he said slowly. "At least, it is in your Mother's case."

"Too late now, Dad," he said. "I have to be back at Farnborough on Boxing Day."

Christmas Day was a sombre affair. Nobody felt festive and his mother would occasionally break into a bitter denunciation of his four days in London.

He was glad when he had to report to Farnborough

****

Chapter 9

"Ah, Spiers, Lieutenant, isn't it? Good, good, come in man, please, sit down, smoke?"

The Colonel of the RFC section of the Royal Aircraft Factory hooked his heels behind the chair legs, leaned backwards to look up at the stocky young man before him.

Bob sat down, refused the cigarette, held himself upright in the chair, almost to attention.

The Colonel looked down at the paper on his desk. Bob saw with a feeling of apprehension it was the same paper that had graced the desk of the Colonel at St Omer. "Well, Lieutenant, two Eindekkers to your credit, in one day . . . very good. Not many RFC pilots can claim that distinction."

"Luck, sir," said Bob, diffidently, wondering where the conversation was leading.

"Nonsense, makings of a good scout pilot, Spiers . . . aggressive, action-man, aren't you?"

The Colonel teetered back and forth, as if the whole episode was a boring chore he had been lumbered with.

"I like flying, Colonel, sir," said Bob.

"Just as well, Spiers," said the Colonel, referring to the paper again. "You're one of the few people that can't take orders, aren't you . . . you can take them, but you need to know why . . . is that right, Spiers?" The Colonel's voice had a supercilious drawl.

"I don't like stupidity, sir, if that's what's implied," said Bob, feeling his irritation rising.

"Humble background, haven't you, Spiers . . . Father works on the Southern Railway . . . trades union man, isn't he . . . Bolshevik?" said the Colonel, his face a mask of distaste, the moustache drawn up like puckered washing on a line.

"Everyone has humble beginnings, sir," said Bob. "Even Napoleon was not born an emperor."

The Colonel's codfish eyes flickered. "My family have been in Worcester for four hundred years, Spiers. What do you think of that?"

Bully for you, you snide bastard, thought Bob." Impressive, sir," he said.

The Colonel stared at the impassive young face before him, searching for signs of insolence. Finding none, he dropped the chair on all four feet, leaned forward.

"Born to lead, Spiers, people like my Father and others like him, reared for leadership . . . come to it as naturally as a bird flies, when it's ready, never looked back. Others are meant to follow. The line is never crossed, you know, Spiers . . . never . . . The day it is will be a bad day for England."

Bob kept his face straight, wondering whether he was hearing correctly. He'd read a summary of the casualties on the Somme for the past six months only the other day. And this bastard was a leader of men?

"Well, Spiers, what have you to say to that?"

"I understand that ten of Napoleon's sixteen marshals were all of humble origin, sir, including Ney, Soult and Lannes. They conquered Europe between them."

A glitter entered the Colonel's eye, then vanished.

"Historian, are you, Spiers? Learnt it all from the books?"

"No, sir, I put it into practice, learned the hard way . . . being of humble origins there's no other way." Bob stared over the Colonel's head, face impassive.

The Colonel leaned forward to study the paper before him. "Says you questioned the orders of a superior officer last month, eh, Spiers?" He tapped the paper.

"If Captain Foster had listened to what I had to say, seven flyers would still be alive, including Major Charlesworth, sir," said Bob, coldly.

"Know better than your superiors, eh, Spiers?" The Colonel's voice was harsh.

"No, sir, but if you insist on believing the enemy to be stupid, you are bound to get a bloody nose," Bob said, staring straight at the Colonel.

The officer swept the papers into an open drawer, impatiently. "Very well, Lieutenant," he said, his voice a rasp. "You are being posted to No 77 Squadron RFC, at . . ." The Colonel consulted a piece of paper, "Lourconter." He glared at Bob. "You will be taking a replacement Sopwith Pup with you . . . your kit can follow you." The Colonel stood up.

Bob stood, saluted smartly, about turned and walked out.

A door at the side of the Colonel's office opened and Charles Martine walked in.

"See what you mean, sir," he said, slowly.

"The man is a confirmed Bolshie, Martine . . . useless for officer material. We'd be asking for trouble giving him a command situation," said the Colonel. "I've followed your recommendation, only because it is you, and you know the man, but if I had my way . . . I'd reduce the whippersnapper to the ranks!"

****

Lourconter was located on a bend in the River Somme, south of Bray. The village, if it could be dignified by such a name, consisted of a cluster of cottages and a farmhouse. The inhabitants had long since fled the shelling and noise of artillery, and the village now housed 77 Squadron RFC, the officers, pilots and ground crews.

There were nine Sopwith Pups in the Squadron, most of them new. Bob discovered this the day of his arrival. The reason was not easily discerned until later.

Major Briggs was the CO, and Major Landers the Adjutant.

"Welcome to Lourconter, Spiers," said the Adjutant. "I don't think you'll enjoy the experience, but you never can tell."

"That's a little enigmatic, sir. Why is that?" asked Bob, standing to attention, looking over the Major's head.

"I believe in allowing the officers here time for reflection, Spiers, before I give them the bad news," said Landers, his face set.

The door opened. A short man with crinkly black hair and a bulbous nose came in. Brown eyes stared at Bob for a long moment from a narrow face. His lips were compressed permanently.

"Ah, you must be Spiers?" said the man. "Briggs, CO of this shower, for my pains." He grinned, his eyes crinkling like his hair, held out his hand. "Time enough to become disillusioned later."

Bob gripped the man's hand, felt his hand crushed. "What's the bad news, sir? I'd sooner be told now rather than later, or find out for myself," he asked.

Briggs looked at Landers, then back to Bob.

"Alright, Spiers, we'll give it you straight from the shoulder," he said, taking a deep breath. "There is only one reason for your presence in this unit. You can't take orders . . . at least the wankers in the higher command feel you can't, or you've crossed swords with one of the blue-eyed boys, or you have a criminal record or you've married the wrong woman . . . some such crime against civilised society, Spiers. I don't want to know what it is, neither does Landers. Nobody in this unit talks about the reasons for their presence. You're here, and we expect you to fight for His Majesty, just as any other Englishman does, with lily-white credentials . . . in other words, prepared to accept the chinless marvels for what they believe themselves to be . . . leaders of men. You've made a grave error, Spiers, if you believe you can buck the system, and you've ended up at Lourconter with the 77th."

Briggs stopped talking for a moment, regarding Bob to see that kind of effect his narration was having on the young man. "Another thing, Spiers, casualties are high in this unit, otherwise you wouldn't see so many new Pups out there. They are replacements for a mission we carried out the day before yesterday, and most of the lads are new . . . raw recruits, misfits, ne'er-do-wells, or whatever. We get the shitty end of the stick, every time, Spiers . . . anything nasty that needs to be done we get it." Briggs grinned, thumped Bob on the shoulder. "That's the bad news, Spiers. The good news is that comradeship in this unit is high . . .

higher than in any other RFC Squadron in France . . . it has to be . . . we stick together and nobody finds a chink in our armour. You get a warm bed at night, if you come back, and the food is above average . . . we have a Savoy chef at work for us in the mess, and there are plenty of women in Amiens prepared to soothe your ruffled feathers whenever you feel the need." Briggs looked at Landers. "Have I missed anything, Nigel?"

Landers shook his head. "I don't think so, Trevor," he said, his voice soft and without inflection, as if the timbre had been removed by some electronic process.

"Right, you can have Miller's billet, Spiers . . . top of the house at No 4. We'll get Corporal Matthews to be your batman," said Briggs, still smiling. "Can you fly a Pup, Spiers?"

"I flew one for several hours earlier this month, sir," said Bob.

Briggs looked at Landers, surprise in his eyes. "How many hours, Spiers?" he asked.

"Around a hundred, sir," said Bob. "Mostly on FEs, Farman and BEs," said Bob.

Briggs sucked in his breath. "How old are you, Spiers?" he asked, softly.

"Eighteen next birthday, sir."

"Jesus H Christ!" said Briggs, softly. "You're learning very young, Lieutenant."

"Sir?" Bob looked at the Major.

Briggs shook his head. "Never mind, Lieutenant," he said. "Go and find Corporal Matthews and tell him you're taking over Miller's billet."

Corporal Matthews turned out to be a Glaswegian with a thick accent. Short and stocky like Bob, with powerful shoulders, a massive head, and thickly muscled hands.

He took Bob up the tiny village street to Number 4, a cottage set back from the others with a small garden before it.

"This feller was killed earlier this morning, sir," said Matthews, pushing open the door to the attic room." I've cleared out his kit for you, and if there's anything else you want moving, just let me know. Best billet in the village, sir," added the little man, grinning, showing his poor teeth.

"Can you fix me up with a toothbrush and pyjamas, Corporal? My kit is still coming."

Matthews grinned. "Fix anything, sir, that's a promise," he said. "Just ask me. If I can't fix it, I'll tell you."

Bob grinned. "Thanks, Corporal Matthews," he said.

"If you'd like lunch, some down and I'll get Willy to fix it . . . he's a whizz . . . real clever fellow."

"I could do with something to eat," said Bob.

"You want it up here or down in the mess, sir?" asked Matthews.

Bob looked surprised. "Up here?" he queried.

"Part of the service, sir," said the Corporal. "Mr Miller always like his food brought up here . . . bit of a loner, sir . . . didn't mix well with the other officers!"

"I'll come down after I've had a wash," said Bob.

"You'll find hot water in the tap, sir," said Matthews, pointing to the wash-basin in the corner of the room. "Ginger fixed a hot water system up for us in the village," he added. "He's one of the Flight engineers."

Bob washed in the basin, found the water piping hot, and the room under the thatch was small, but private and very cosy. The previous tenant had left some pictures of a house in the country tacked to the wall, showing a family group round it posing self-consciously. There was a sepia-tone of a young woman in a leather frame on the bedside table. Young, fair and with fine features. The eyes were sad and held a faraway look.

Bob found the officers' mess in the farmhouse. The road had been filled in with brick rubble and was safe to walk on. There was no sign of the ubiquitous duck-boards that usually served as sidewalks.

There was a huge log fire blazing in the mess room, and several young officers were playing cards round a table to one side. Another was playing the grand piano that stood along a wall. Two more were asleep in armchairs before the fire.

The card players looked at him, nodded, and returned to their game without greeting.

A corporal in a white mess jacket, spotless and immaculate came forward. "This way, sir . . . lunch is ready for you."

He led the way into what had evidently been the farmer's lounge. There was a linen tablecloth and serviettes, shining silver cutlery, and a place had been set for him.

As soon as he was seated a plate of grapefruit was placed before him.

He couldn't recall the last time he'd seen a grapefruit. The waiter's face was impassive.

Real coffee was served with the bacon and eggs.

After lunch, Briggs came in, his greatcoat dusted with snow. He clapped his hands, introduced Bob to all the members of his new squadron. Most merely nodded, some shook hands, and then the close circle of card players all returned to their game.

Bob went down to the canvas hangars and looked over the Sopwith Pup that was to be his machine, different from the one he had flown in earlier.

A grizzled Sergeant with reddish hair came up, saluted. "Sergeant Williams, sir, Ginger for short . . . I shall be looking after your machine, sir. If you want any mods carried out, let me know and it will be done," he said, in a broad Lancashire accent.

"Just one thing right now, Sergeant," said Bob.

"Sir?"

"I want all my Vickers belts hand loaded by someone you can trust . . . no bulging cartridges, and no bent heads," said Bob.

"Will be done, sir," said Williams, standing to attention.

"OK, wheel her out, Sergeant, I want to see how she performs!" said Bob.

Williams looked at the lowering sky, the flakes of snow, the biting wind, he shrugged, shouted orders for the crew to wheel out the Pup.

Ten minutes later, after having gone over the Pup in minute detail, Bob took off.

The cloud ceiling was low, and the evening sky was darkening rapidly. He threw the Pup into several turns, dives and rolls, coming down low over the field and testing the Vickers machine-gun with its synchronising gear as he flew low over the hangar.

"Not bad, Sergeant," he said, on landing. "The engine sounds a little rough on take-off. Check it over, will you? I don't want it packing up over Hunland."

"Aye, sir," said Sergeant Williams, eyeing the young man with more respect after his exhibition over the field.

The ground crew watched Bob walk back to Number 4, phlegmatically. "Wotcha reckon, Sarge, a bullshitter or the genuine article?" asked one of the fitters.

"Well, he can fly better than most of the bastards we got on the strength," said Williams. "Even if he is just a kid."

Bob went to bed early after writing to Michelle and Barbara.

He was wide awake and dressed when Corporal Matthews brought him his early morning tea.

Matthews looked surprised but hid his emotion well.

Major Briggs looked over his assembled pilots in the mess. "We've got a nice one this morning, fellers. The Army Command want us to escort an RE8 on artillery spotting . . . over Combles. They've had a lot of bother from a Hun squadron just recently, and lost three machines and crews in the past two days."

Bob's Flight Commander was a Captain Phillips, a lean man with a sandy moustache, around thirty years of age. He had a wound stripe on his arm and an MC on his tunic.

The other member of the Flight was Shaw, a little youthful-looking man, with large white teeth and goggly eyes.

The whole squadron took off at first light. It was bitterly cold and the snowflakes came down in flurries.

Bob noted that Sergeant Williams had corrected the Le Rhone engine and it was now purring smoothly.

Over Quillemont the German Archie began its hymn of hate, the black blooms bursting all round the nine aircraft of 77 Squadron. The cloud ceiling had lifted somewhat, and a grey blanket of cloud covered the world to the horizon at five thousand feet.

The RE8 was far below them turning, endlessly circling the new front line established after the fierce battles of the summer, around Sailly and Rancourt. He could see the observer peering through binoculars at the Hun batteries that were firing fitfully in the grey winter morning at targets behind the British lines. Occasionally the wireless aerial would glitter in the rancid sunlight that gleamed now and again, its lead plummet swinging below the aircraft's nacelle.

They circled over the RE8 for a good fifteen minutes before Bob saw Briggs waggle his wings and point upwards.

Out of the lowering sky seven planes with Maltese crosses were plunging. All were biplanes of a design Bob hadn't seen before. A coxcomb exhaust travelled upwards over the leading edge of the top wing, and the fuselage tapered away to a thin pencil line at the tail section.

They came down rapidly, the leading machine opening fire as the Pups climbed to meet them. He saw a lion's head painted inside a circle on the fuselage under the cockpit on one of the machines as it came at him, twin Spandaus blazing. The Pup avoided the tracer easily, and as the German passed him he was on its tail in a trice.

The German flyer was no amateur and could fly. Up and down they went, first on the tail of the German, and then the roles would be reversed. At the top of a loop Bob suddenly missed the enemy machine. Instead of where it should have been, under his guns, the biplane was above him coming in for the kill. He could see the head of the pilot framed between the menacing Spandaus, goggles glinting in the brittle air.

He waited until the last moment, before the German opened fire, before standing the Pup on its tail, the 80hp Le Rhone howling protest. The German shot by underneath. Throwing the Pup over in a whip-like turn, Bob stared through the Aldis sight at the German machine. The cockpit grew larger as the Pup overtook the enemy machine. He waited until he was less than a hundred yards from the German machine before opening fire.

He saw the tracers enter the pilot's toehold in the side of the machine, and the bullets were shattering the coaming around the cockpit. The German seemed to leap up in the cockpit, thrashing about in agony, and then the biplane tipped over, beginning to spin.

The rattle of Spandaus behind him made him jerk into wakefulness. Another of the strange machines was behind him, bullets stitching holes along his fuselage. He jerked the Pup into a right-hand turn, turning ever closer until he could see the grim face of the enemy pilot across two hundred yards of space. The man had a black moustache in a semi circle above his thin lips. His teeth were bared in a stressful indication of the tension he was feeling.

The turning circle of the Pup was proving too much for the enemy biplane. At the last moment, the German pulled out of the circle, and Bob was on his tail. Ten seconds later, the German machine was spinning below out of control.

Pulling out of the dive, Bob looked above him. His compass was performing a Highland fling, and the altimeter read six thousand feet. A lone Pup trailing a long plume of smoke was turning end over end out of the sky. Another was spinning earthwards in a series of falling leaf gyrations. Even as he watched, the wings parted company with the fuselage, fluttering down like pieces of paper.

Above him two Pups were desperately trying to get away from a circle of four of the German biplanes.

He zoomed up in an attempt to divert the Germans from their quarry. It was hopeless.

First one and then the second Pup seemed to shudder, halt in the air, and then begin to fall, turning over and over as they went. A tongue of flame shot out from a Pup, and the next instant a human figure plunged from the cockpit into the murky void beside his aircraft.

There were no other British aircraft visible. The RE8 lay in a crumpled heap in Nomansland, the pilot and observer crawling painfully towards the British lines. A line of grey-clad infantry were trying to get at them.

He put the Pup's nose down, aligning the Aldis on the grey line, and swooped in low, Vickers gun chattering, the tracer hosing the German infantry.

He pulled up over the German trench system, turned and came back to repeat the operation on the return journey. The two British pilots waved to him as he flew low over their heads at less than twenty feet. A group of Tommies were crawling towards them, dragging a stretcher.

He made several more passes at the German lines before his ammunition ran out and he flew once more, low over the British lines before making off, hedge-hopping towards Lourconter.

****

Chapter 10

"You'll be delighted to know, chaps, that our leaders, military and political, have decided they are to strike the final blow that will defeat the Central Powers and give us victory," said Major Briggs to his assembled flyers in the mess at Lourconter.

There were some raspberries and catcalls, then silence as Briggs glared at them. He unrolled a linen map onto a blackboard facing them. He pointed to Arras. "This is where the dagger is going to strike, gentlemen, at the heart of German armies."

"Christ," said a voice. "That's only a few miles up from the old Somme battlefield. How do they hope to break through there?"

Briggs grinned. "The High Command, in their wisdom, tell us that since we've had a succession of hard frosts throughout France, the earth will be packed solid and enable them to use our new secret weapon with confidence."

"They're joking!" said another voice, disbelievingly.

"What secret weapon . . . the 77th?"

"If we know it, you can bet your boots the Hun knows all about it as well," said another pilot, tall, long-legged, his Sidcot oil-stained and worn.

"True, my fine-feathered friend, but as you are all aware, the High Command only gives the orders . . . they don't have to do the fighting," said Briggs, acidly.

"What's our part in all this glory?" asked another.

"I was coming to that, Legge," said Briggs.

There was silence. Every man in the room felt the tension, as Briggs paused.

"We have to keep the Hun out of the skies for at least a month, gentlemen. Every RFC Squadron will be concentrated in this area to sweep the Hun from the skies so that he can't find out what's going on."

"Aw, for Chrissakes, Major, that wouldn't fool my fucking cat . . . the minute the Hun sees all this hardware up there, he'll jump to the right conclusion in about two minutes flat," said Legge, caustically.

Briggs nodded. "Couldn't agree more with you, Legge, old man, but ours is not to reason why . . . "

"Fuckinghellfire!" yelled another. "Those Jerry bastards'll mince us . . . they've got these new crates they didn't have last year and they're gonna have a field day. What do those bastards want? . . . a few hundred wrecked Pups all over France?"

Briggs nodded his head like a donkey, looked at Bob. "Anything to say to that, Bob?"

Bob shook his head. "Everything they say is true, sir, the Hun has the new Albatross, Fokkers and the Pfalz scouts and they're fast and dangerous . . . even the SE5s can't touch them."

"Makes us being here in this squadron a vindication of what we all feel, doesn't it, Major . . . that those clowns in the High Command don't know what the hell to do next, they're bankrupt in ideas," said the older pilot. "As soon as the Hun sees all this air activity, he'll be on to it in two minutes flat . . . and have you seen Arras, Major?"

Briggs nodded. "Yes, I've seen it, Cooper," he said, soberly.

"And they're going to launch an attack through that heap of rubble?" said Cooper. "They want their heads read . . . the Hun has pulled back from the old line and we know that he's been busy like a horde of bloody moles for the past three months building the Hindenburg Line . . . they'll mince any attack on that part of the Front."

"Alright, gentlemen, I am aware of the problems, but as I said before, ours is not to reason why . . . we go in and keep the Hun from the skies." Briggs was worried and looked it.

Bob felt the dismay creeping through him like a poison.

In the three first months of 1917, he had survived . . . by the skin of his teeth and intense hard work. He had seen the entire fighting strength of the 77th changed completely in that three months. Their casualties had been enormous, and now only he and Briggs remained out of the original complement of January.

He had, against all odds, been credited with an official 25 aerial victories, had been awarded an MC and DSO, and yet still remained a Lieutenant. Black despair filled nearly all his waking hours now, and he wanted only to get away from the incessant bombardment of his psyche by the demands of the air war. Every day he went out in his Sopwith, he knew his chances of survival were becoming reduced to a zero factor. It was inevitable. The remorseless logic of the casualty lists gave him food for more depression. It seemed only a matter of time before he too became a mere name on a list.

His letter writing had become sporadic and in the past few days had almost ceased. He didn't seem to have the mental energy to devote to putting on paper his black thoughts of death and disfigurement. Letters from both Barbara and Michelle continued to arrive with regularity. He could tell from the tenor of their responses that they were both aware of his mental condition. His sole thought now was survival, but not in a negative sense. He spent hours down at the hangars or in his billet at Number 4, Lourconter, either supervising the loading of the belts for the Vickers machine-gun, the performance of the Le Rhone engine, or merely staring at the ceiling from his bunk. He refused all invitations to go into Amiens for the usual drunken orgies, followed by visits to the local brothels. He had become completely withdrawn into a world of solitary loneliness of spirit that nothing seemed able to assuage.

In the air he was cold, determined, but not in an aggressive sense, but to survive through efficiency. He hated the whole idea of the killing of other young men who probably felt as he did about the war, the High Command, yet had to respond to the dictates of a war machine that ground on remorselessly to satisfy the paranoia of leaders on both sides. When he did act, it usually resulted in the destruction of an enemy machine and the death of its pilot. The after effects of victory beyond the temporary elation lay the deeper folds of black depression and thoughts of death.

Briggs allowed him a roving commission, and exempted him from all patrols unless directly ordered by the Army Command. He allowed his prima donna to do and go where he pleased, confident that it could only bring approbation from superiors who were at first inclined to come down with a heavy hand on this type of management. They could not gainsay the results, however, and since universal gloom attended all efforts on the Western Front from the Army viewpoint, glamour provided by this ace was welcome. They allowed Major Briggs to have his way. The Guynemers and Foncks of the French Air Force had no counterpart in the RFC, but for a select few like McCudden, Bishop, Ball and Mannock. The name of Spiers was a welcome addition for the glory-hungry press.

Briggs had offered him leave on several occasions but Bob refused. Whilst he wanted to get away from the treadmill of death, he feared that once away from it he would never possess the necessary spiritual reserves to want to return. He was terrified of becoming a 'flamer' . . . having seen so many of his victims fall to their deaths in burning machines . . . the roaring flames fanned by wind, eating them alive and roasting their flesh even before death overtook them.

Briggs called him into his office in the cottage nearest the canvas hangars, soon after the briefing. "I'm sorry, Bob, but you'll have to join the Squadron tomorrow. The Army are insisting that all available craft are in the skies at dawn," he said, without preamble.

Bob nodded to acknowledge that he heard, turning to go, his movements that of an old man. Briggs noted the streaks of grey in the young man's hair, the lines that graced the youthful face, and the twitch at his eyelid that had become pronounced over the past three months. Another had developed at Spiers's chin, where the taut skin reacted to bad news as if it were independent of any volition of the young man.

"Bob!" said Briggs, and waited until Spiers turned to face him. "I'm putting you on leave as from tomorrow morning . . . whether you like it or not." He held up his hand as Bob prepared to protest. "I don't want your death on my conscience, Bob, and regardless of how you feel now, I'm convinced that you'll feel better after a few days at home."

"But . . ." began Bob, feebly, his head aching.

"No buts about it, Bob, you're going, and that's an order, and if you feel like disobeying mine, I shall have no other recourse but to bring in

Colonel Danby's assistance to get you there." Briggs glared at the young man, without rancour. The criminality struck him more and more every day. A continuous procession of young men through his hands, who lasted days and then others came to replace them, a procession of youth into a crucible, that few of them understood until death or wounds overtook them.

"If you insist, Trevor," said Bob, dully.

Briggs watched the young man go out, slowly, as if in a trance, his eyes looking at something beyond the walls. He balled his fists and bashed the desk top in frustration.

Landers came in, saw his colleague's action, but pretended to ignore it. "Orders for tomorrow, mate," he said, softly, laying the papers on Briggs's desk.

"When is this stupidity ever going to end, Nigel?" asked Briggs, despairingly. "Three bloody years and no end in sight, and now those cretinous bastards are going in for another bloodbath at Arras . . . it'll be pure bloody murder."

"As usual," said Landers. "The price of the history book . . . you and me, and all those poor sods out there in the trenches . . . just face savers for some fucking politician frightened of losing his little seat of power."

"Is that how you see it, Nigel?" asked Briggs.

"The fact that the 77th exists is proof of it, mate," said Landers. "If we didn't disagree with the way things are being run, you and I would both be Colonels now, enjoying a back number with all the rest of the brown-nosers. We committed the cardinal sin of bucking the system, as you told Spiers when he arrived here and you dared question the basis of their decisions. That is the most deadly of all sins . . . you can't tamper with the ordained leaders . . . they get all bitchy and call you a Bolshevik. Look at Danby, a product of the system, Eton, Sandhurst and then fortuitously the war starts and he is now a full Colonel, and never heard a gun fired in anger, hands out orders to the underlings with complete detachment, oblivious to the misery he causes."

"What are we going to do about it, Nigel?" asked Briggs.

Landers stared at his colleague, amazed. "What can we do, for God's sake?" he demanded. "We're locked into the system like everyone else. Do you honestly believe that anything you said to Danby would get past his desk? Even you can't be that naïve Trevor."

Briggs plunged one fist into the open palm of his other hand. "There must be a way, Nigel, there has to be, of getting this to the notice of the people who count."

"They're all tarred with the same brush, mate, all belong to the same clubs, school societies. They can't afford to let the great British public see that their esteemed leaders are nothing but paper men . . . without substance, just seeking their own glory and edification in the books. Remember Colonel Watsonby at Farnborough, when he interviewed Spiers . . . how he howled at the bookish men in the ranks, incipient Bolsheviks . . . all because Spiers likes reading Napoleonic history, and quoted the ages of Napoleon's Marshalls to Watsonby, and how he told us what Spiers's reaction had been to Watsonby's four centuries in Worcester . . . his family, of course . . . Impressive, sir . . . Jesus, what can we do, Trevor? The killing will go on until some bastard in Westminster has had his fill of the gore and the nation has been bled white and then there'll be an end to it."

"We could get the Press in here, let them loose amongst the blokes," said Briggs.

"How long would you last after that, Trevor? A week, fortnight, before they found some reason to demote you, court martial you for treason or cowardice in the face of the enemy. What good would that do?" Landers looked worried by this suggestion.

"I'd have made my point to the world," said Briggs, earnestly.

"Bravo," mocked Landers, gently. "And what about your wife and kids . . . are they going to approve of your noble actions?" he asked.

Briggs thumped the table again. "Shit! Is this the answer for ever? Putting up with these morons with no chins?" he roared.

Landers said nothing for a moment. "I hear there's going to be a revolution in Russia . . . they're boiling up for it . . . perhaps that's the answer . . . like the French in the last century . . . get rid of the aristocrats and then we can have real justice.

"They got Napoleon," pointed out Briggs. "And he was worse than the bastards he replaced, I believe."

"There is no short answer, Trevor," said Landers, quietly. "It's going to take time."

"Meanwhile we see this procession through those doors going on and on . . . cannon fodder for the moronic leaders of men?" he roared. "I can't stand much more of it, Nigel . . . have you seen Spiers, recently? He's nearly eighteen years old and he looks like a bloody old man, haunted, depressed, and he hasn't started life yet . . . I tell you, Nigel, it's criminal."

"You can't do anything on your own, Trevor, you would be just compromising your family . . . they'd have to suffer for your heroic deed," said Landers.

"Bloody blackmail, isn't it . . . moral blackmail?" shouted Briggs.

"Yes, that's exactly what it is, mate," said Landers.

****

They met the nine Halberstadts over Bertincourt at six a.m. the next day. Before anyone realised it, the nine German machines were on them, plunging down from the sun and sending four Pups down out of control in the first ten seconds.

Bob shot down one of the fast, heavily armed German machines before he became involved in a fight for his life with three Halberstadts, the enemy determined to finish off this lone British machine before succour arrived. The enemy machines each had a lion's head painted on the fuselage in vivid blue.

He received repeated hits before he shot down another Halberstadt and the two remaining Germans were about to deliver the coup de grâce when five French Spads arrived. The Germans called it a day and flew off, leaving 77 Squadron to reform and turn back to the British lines.

The Spad formation flew alongside them, the leader waving to Bob in a cheery manner. Bob waved back, exhaustion sinking in after the hectic moments of combat.

The Spads landed beside them, and taxied up to the tarmac.

The first man from the cockpit of one of the Spads was a little man he vaguely recognised. The square black moustache and black eyes were vague reminders from the past, but he could not place the man.

"Lieutenant Spiers!" he called, advancing towards Bob. "My brother in arms . . . you got two more of the Boche today . . . you are a famous man in France, sir."

Bob stared, struggling to smile over the black depression, trying to place where he had seen the little man.

The little Frenchman saw his puzzled expression. "We met at a restaurant in Amiens last year. The big man, Foster, was your commanding officer . . . last November I believe it was, you had just finished two Eindekkers that day . . . after the Boche shot down our F40s."

Recognition dawned on Bob's face. He held out his hand. "Pleased to meet you again, sir," he said.

"Captain Lascalle, sir," said the little man, smiling.

"Come and have some brandy," invited Bob, as Briggs arrived, Landers and a few of the other pilots to greet the Frenchmen.

The mess waiters soon had brandy glasses filled and they were toasting one another, knocking back the brandy in large doses. Someone began to play popular tunes at the piano, and they all joined in standing round the instrument.

"Who got hit?" asked Bob of Briggs during the festivities.

"Adams, Cotton, Lambert and Joyner," said the Major, grimly, whilst smiling with his teeth at one of the Frenchmen. "If these lads hadn't arrived when they did, we'd have lost more."

The Frenchmen stayed for dinner and more singing and wine and brandy afterwards, departing only when the brandy ran out and the sun was at its meridian.

"Noisy bloody lot, aren't they?" grinned Landers, as the last of the Spads lifted from the airfield, joining the rest of the squadron in the air.

"Lascalle is one of their aces," said Briggs. "How'd you come to meet him, Bob?"

Bob recounted the incident in the estaminet in Amiens the previous November, when Foster had insisted on crossing the line below ten thousand feet and the Eindekkers had found them.

"Assholes," commented Briggs, succinctly. "Our command is full of them . . . leaders of men . . ." He saw Landers frowning at him and shut up.

A letter arrived from Barbara during the morning.

He retired to his billet in Number 4, lay on the bed, opened it.

Dear Bob,

You will have noticed the postmark on this letter by now! (He hadn't.) I'm in France at a hospital in Amiens. I've read all about your exploits in the papers. You are a very famous man now, and I admire you.

Can we not meet some time? I don't know the location of your squadron (censored) but it must be somewhere within striking distance of Amiens. I'd love to see you. Last summer seems a long time ago now. I hope you haven't forgotten me. Your letters are less frequent now. Does that mean I don't occupy a place in your list of friends any longer? Please write back soon and say that we can meet shortly.

Ever yours, Babs.

****

Chapter 11

He put down the letter, stared up at the ceiling, as he had done on countless occasions over the past months. Did he really want to see Barbara again? Michelle? Any of them? What point was there in all these relationships when they were so temporary and ephemeral. Nothing mattered any more, except survival, then perhaps he could begin thinking about other people.

Perhaps it would be good for him . . . to see someone not contaminated by killing and murder. Restore some sanity to his life.

Briggs had told him he was going on leave in the morning. Why not travel to Amiens? He didn't want to go back to England and his mother's nagging and his father's military assessments of events, Melvin's sulky distaste for him and his flying. He just wanted to be alone and think . . . do nothing except sleep and sleep. Why not look her up in Amiens?

He lay on his bed until Matthews awakened him at four o'clock with a cup of tea.

"Another patrol this evening, sir," he said grimly, noting the Lieutenant's drawn face and twitching facial muscles.

"Oh, no!" groaned Bob, sitting up, accepting the cup.

"Shall I tell 'em you're sick, sir?" asked the Corporal.

Bob shook his head. "No, I'll be alright in a minute, Corporal. Get my gear laid out will you?"

"Yessir. You want something to eat? I'll bring it up here?" The man hadn't eaten a square meal in weeks. He'd seen several men in the condition that Lieutenant Spiers was in . . . withdrawn, solitary, shunning company, wanting only to sleep and drink . . . usually alcohol, only this one didn't. They didn't last long as a rule. They just didn't come back from patrols and their manner of going was usually exceptional . . . head-on collision with an enemy, or diving into a melée, when they knew their chances of survival were remote.

"No, I'll be down in a moment. Where's the patrol heading?" Matthews knew everything, all the latest rumours, orders, troop movements, plans, and he was usually accurate.

"Bertincourt again, sir. Command want to know what the Hun are doing about the plans for the new offensive."

Christ, escorting another RE8 to its doom, moaned Bob to himself, throwing his legs over the bed, sipping the tea.

And Bertincourt it proved to be, as the pilots, the five remaining until replacements arrived from St Omer, heard Briggs out. It was to be an RE8 and it was going to report on enemy troop movements. 77 Squadron were going to take up message cannisters, see what was happening behind the main front and behind the old Somme battlefield. Intelligence reports indicated that the Germans were preparing a pre-emptive strike to upset the proposed Arras offensive plans and were aiming at the hinge beyond the end of the new Hindenburg Line and cut into the bulge or salient left by the British advance on the Somme the previous year. There had been reports of long lines of German reserves being poured into the area . . . artillery, munitions, men, horses, guns, machine-guns and endless activity day and night on the part of the enemy to extend the Hindenburg defences beyond the end at Queant through to Drocourt, a distance of some fifteen miles. By this means, the old defences of the Hindenburg Line five miles to the east of Arras now had a formidable defence in depth through which the British VII, VI and XVII Corps of the British Third Army would have to struggle before any hope of breakthrough could be attempted. The Nomansland between the old defences and the new line had been rendered a wasteland, with fields of fire, carefully sited machine-gun nests and mortar arcs, all planned for any British advance.

They crossed the Line at eleven thousand feet, five Pups, including that of Major Briggs. The sun was well down on the horizon and masses of cumulus cloud were arrayed in majestic cathedrals of vapour all over the German trenches, from five thousand to twelve thousand feet. It was a perfect hiding place for any proposed German ambush.

Over Le Sars, Major Briggs signalled for the three Pups who were to go down and investigate German troop movements, to commence their dive. He and Legge remained above them to protect them from surprise attack by marauding Halberstadts, and warn them to get clear. Their orders were explicit, not to attempt to intervene in any dogfight, but to fly for home by the best means possible. The lack of height would preclude the three Pups making any contribution to a fight above them. The time factor in flying them to a reasonable height, their vulnerability whilst climbing and the fact that other German machines might be waiting to pick them off if they attempted it, would merely be a waste of man and machine power. They would be sitting ducks.

Bob knew that his two companions were older men by RFC standards in 1917. Creasey was twenty-eight and Forbes was nearly thirty. Both were ex-infantry who had volunteered to join the RFC, preferring the personal duals in the air to the grisly mud of the infantry struggles where they were but faceless numbers to the distant higher command.

Both Forbes and Creasey were experienced pilots, who had been relegated to 77 for their outspokenness at official stupidity in other squadrons. He knew he could rely on their judgement and experience if it came to a fight.

Below him as he came down, he could see long lines of German infantry marching along the road from Bertincourt to Le Sars. Heavy guns were being hauled by horses, struggling with the heavy caissons and massive artillery pieces, howitzers and field guns of heavy calibre. Lorries carrying supplies were interspersed with the infantry columns.

As he came in low over their heads, he saw them all scatter like flies disturbed at the approach of a human. Some jumped for slit trenches, others merely raised their rifles and fired at him. Over the plunging horse-drawn carriages he went counting and evaluating the sizes of the guns and the numbers. The animals were going wild with unaccustomed noise, dragging their loads from the road into the ditches on the pavé roadside. The acute camber on the French roadways made it hard for any traffic to use anything but the immediate centre of the carriageway, and once the horses had pulled their loads off-centre it was hard for their drivers to urge them back on course.

As the ground flew beneath his wing-tips, he heard something whang off the engine cowling and go ricocheting into space. His wings had innumerable holes in them from lucky shots fired by the German infantry. Most troops were unaware of the fact that they had to shoot well to the front of the flying machine in order to compensate for its speed. The result was that very few bullets from rifles ever found their target. Tracer from machine-guns was a different proposition, since the gunners could correct their aim by watching the course of the bullet stream. He loaded his first cannister with his handwritten notes, freed the long ribbon and headed towards the British Line at Combles.

Dropping the message container in the map reference indicated, he turned and flew back towards Bertincourt, passing Forbes's Pup on his way. Creasey was still flying up and down the German columns creating havoc with his presence. He waved as Bob joined him, grinning, jabbing his thumb down towards the panic-stricken horses and infantry below him.

The German Archie gunners were depressing their guns as far as they could in order to be able to fire at the insolent British machines flying over their territory. Machine-guns were being set up to provide more effective deterrents to the Pups. Tracer lanced upwards at them. Invariably, however, the gunners forbore to allow for the hundred miles per hour speed of the flyers, and their aim was defective.

Without warning, Creasey's Pup disintegrated into a blossom of fragments of wire and canvas. Pieces of engine and wheels flew in all directions. The fuselage became a coffin of flames, which plunged down between two ruined houses and exploded in a ball of fire.

Bob saw it, registered the catastrophe, his mind cold and distant. It was a film in which he was but a spectator. It had no relationship to his own vulnerability. He could only conclude that a lucky bullet had found the Pup's petrol tank. He looked round, saw Forbes's look of utter horror at the disaster to Creasey, and the next instant Forbes's Pup was yawing crazily from side to side, an aileron hanging loose on his port wing.

Bob stabbed his fist towards the British Lines as Forbes looked up over the intervening space between the two machines.

For some unaccountable reason, Forbes turned eastwards, away from the Front and deeper into German territory. Bob cursed, swung the Pup round to pursue the errant British machine.

By the time he had caught up with Forbes, the other man was already over Bertincourt and headed north-east towards Cambrai. Bob waved frantically at Forbes, pointing westwards. The other man stared back at Bob, his goggles glinting in the sinking sun, incomprehendingly.

Bob searched the cloud-laden sky for signs of enemy machines, but couldn't see anything, not even the two Pups of Legge and Briggs who were supposedly protecting their heads from interference.

Weaving from side to side, Forbes's Pup was losing height rapidly, and a streamer of petrol vapour was pouring from the underbelly. Suddenly, he saw the propeller cease revolving, and then Forbes was desperately trying to find a suitable field in which to put the Pup down.

They were well behind the front now and before him he could see the outskirts of Cambrai.

Swinging like a drunken man, Forbes's machine was almost turning back on itself as the pilot attempted to correct the drag of the broken aileron by using his remaining device on the opposite wing.

Forbes's machine hit the turf in the field with a bounce that sent the Pup skyrocketing into the air, bounced again, then the tailskid dragged, and the Pup was heading for a line of poplars at the far side of the field.

At the last moment, the Pup swung round in its own length, the port wing crumpling like paper, and the wheels collapsing under the strain. He saw Forbes sit there for a moment, as if paralysed, and then scramble out of the cockpit and run from the machine. A faint haze seemed to be surrounding the Sopwith, and then suddenly it erupted into a dull whoosh of flame.

Eyeing the field carefully Bob flew round it, and approached it once more. There didn't appear to be any German troops within striking distance, and the nearest road was half a mile away.

He cut the engine and touched down, giving himself the longest possible space for a take-off. The Le Rhone spluttering and revving, he taxied over to where the lone figure of Forbes was watching his machine burn.

"On the wing! Grab the leading edge!" he screamed, as the man stared dully at him.

"Quickly, for fuck's sake!"

From the corner of his eye, he saw some German infantry burst through the hedge surrounding the field and were running towards him, their rifles held loosely in their hands.

Forbes stared up at Bob, his gaze vacant and dull, seemingly unable to think.

"Jump on, for fuck's sake!" bawled Bob, hysterically. "They're coming for us!"

Forbes still didn't seem to have heard him, and the Germans were now about four hundred yards away and coming at the double. An officer was yelling at them, giving some order.

"Forbes, for Chrissake!" roared Bob, giving the man five seconds to make up his mind. "Come on . . . jump on!"

One of the German infantrymen stopped, lifted his rifle and fired. The bullet hissed by Bob's head, the report coming faintly over the noise of the Le Rhone. It seemed to arouse Forbes, who jerked out of his trance-like state and stared at the advancing Germans horrified.

Bob revved the Le Rhone, and Forbes made a run for the starboard wing, threw himself across it next to the fuselage, grabbed the leading edge with his gauntletted hands and Bob swung the Pup round, opening the throttle wide.

The Germans were all kneeling now aiming at the Pup. A bullet went through the cockpit between Bob's stomach and the joystick, and then the Pup was lurching and swaying over the uneven ground, gathering speed.

The line of poplars seemed to be approaching at terrifying speed. Would the Pup be up to it with the double load wondered Bob, part of his mind detached and cold. He left the take-off until the last possible moment, pulling the stick back as far as he dared without stalling.

The tips of the poplars brushed the undercarriage and then they were lurching and swaying over the treetops, heading back towards the British lines. Compensating for the drag of the uneven loading on his starboard wing, Bob climbed slightly, but kept just at treetop height and passed over the British lines with barely fifty feet clearance.

They landed at Lourconter to a mass of running ground crew and admin staff as they saw the Pup approaching the field. Fitters grabbed the wing-tips and guided the lurching Pup towards the tarmac.

Forbes fell off, exhausted, to be pulled clear by willing hands.

Landers came up to Bob as he climbed wearily from the cockpit. "You alright, Bob?" he asked, anxiously.

Bob nodded, leaning against the side of the Pup, sucking in air as though he was asphyxiating. His heart was pounding away and he felt sick. "Where are the others?" he gasped.

Landers shook his head. "Haven't come back yet. Here, drink this!" Corporal Matthews handed Landers a cup of coffee laced with rum, who passed it to Bob.

He gulped the scalding liquid down in draughts. "Jesus!" he said, painfully. He looked over to where Forbes was being helped back to his feet.

"What happened, Bob?" asked Landers.

He told him, in terse sentences, still trying hard to get his breath back, for some unaccountable reason.

Landers's expression didn't change, but he merely looked at Forbes, wonderingly.

The other pilot was on his feet now, chafing at his frozen feet and hands, a dazed expression still in his eyes. He staggered over to Bob, holding out his hand. "Thanks, Spiers, that was really something to do for anyone . . . I was so bloody confused, I didn't know where I was . . .

the compass had gone haywire and I was trying desperately to work out what you were on about."

"Think nothing of it, Peter," said Bob, holding his chest, to ease the pain.

"I'm sorry to lumber you, Bob, but we've got an urgent one," said Landers, apologetically. "You're the only one who can do it."

"What is it?" Bob felt cold and ill.

"We have to drop someone over the Hun lines, mate," said Landers.

"Oh, no!" Bob felt drained. "When, now?"

"As soon as possible. There's an FE2B being delivered shortly, any minute now and you and your passenger will be in it." Landers thought about the tasks he gave people. Why should it always have to be him?

Bob nodded. "Alright," he muttered. "I'll get some food inside me."

Forbes and Landers stood together watching him walk away.

"I'd never have made it without him, Major," said Forbes. "Those Huns were taking pot-shots at him all the time, yet he didn't flinch . . . just kept yelling at me, and it wasn't until I heard that Hun's rifle go off that I came out of it."

"There are only a few like him, Pete," said Landers.

"What the hell did he do to qualify for this shower?" asked Forbes, quietly, still chafing his hands.

"We don't ask, you know that," said Landers.

"I'll take that passenger," offered Forbes. "That guy is killing himself."

"I'm not being funny, Pete, but you'd never make it. This is a tricky one and only someone like Spiers could do it, besides, you've never flown an FE, have you?"

"I could learn."

"You haven't time, mate. If my hearing isn't deficient, that FE is coming in now!"

The lumbering silhouette of an FE came out of the western sky, and plonked down like a duck on eggs.

"Where the hell are the rest of them?" asked Forbes, shading his eyes against the sun.

"They aren't coming, Pete," said Landers, quietly. "Ever."

****

Chapter 12

The man dressed in a fur-lined suit, hat pulled down over his ears, tied round with a scarf, and he wore dark glasses.

"This is your passenger, Bob. You have the co-ordinates. Best of luck." Landers smiled briefly at Bob.

"Let's go, mister," said Bob to the muffled stranger.

The FE2B stood on the tarmac, engine ticking over in the hoarse rachetty manner of the Beardmore. The passenger climbed the ladder into the bath-tub nacelle and strapped himself in.

Bob gave him a few seconds, then opened up the throttle. It felt strange to be flying the ancient FE again, ungainly and bulky after the light-fingered Pup. The plane waddled off the ground and into the air, as the first stars began to twinkle. The sunset was a thin line of aquamarine and blue, with a tinge of pink, like icing sugar.

Bob could just make out the head of his passenger as he headed by compass, directly east. He circled round until he was at ten thousand feet over Lourconter, and then and only then did he head for the lines. He passed over Comples and saw the poorly blacked-out lights of the village of Rancourt, where troops of the British Fifth Army were resting behind the new Somme salient. There were jagged explosions in Nomansland from bursting artillery shells, and the occasional Verey light but, apart from that, the universal darkness along the front was complete.

He calculated he was over Epehy a few moments later, and began his long glide downwards, the engine throttled back to lessen the noise. The featureless landscape beneath the nacelle was disturbing. If he had calculated wrong then he was in deep trouble, and the passenger in the front seat would also be in strife, having been put down far away from his planned descent. That was, if they didn't have an accident on landing and the field hadn't been wired. This was a device known and practised by both sides to prevent the kind of operation in which he was presently involved. A single strand of wire stretched taut over the ground at a height of three feet would satisfactorily wreck any aeroplane attempting to land by night.

His passenger tapped him on the arm and was pointing downwards, as they neared what he believed to be Le Catelet. He was now down to two thousand feet and trying desperately in the moonless night to distinguish landmarks. There was a church steeple marked on the map at Le Catelet, according to information received by British Intelligence. He had little faith in the so-called Intelligence work of the British Forces. Too many pilots had relied on this kind of information and had come to grief.

His passenger was pointing downwards, his arm barely visible in the blackness. Peering over the side he could just make out the vague outline of a steeple. At least, on this occasion, Intelligence sources had been correct . . . if this was Le Catelet, and not some other village. He prayed there weren't any foxholes or molehills on his landing path, that the Germans had not been warned of the possible landing of an agent behind their lines, if the French peasantry, fearful of German reprisals, did not wreck the plane, if there weren't any tall trees like poplars on his approach route, if there weren't any unindicated farm buildings in his path, if there wasn't a German Uhlan unit waiting for them in the bushes around the field. If, if, if . . . there were too many if's.

He cut the engine completely, put the nose down, and prayed there weren't any impedimenta en route.

The wind sang in the wires, the gloom below was profound. He could see the vague outline of trees and a farm out to his right. Then the square lozenge of the field showed vaguely ahead.

Christ, there were some dark blobs in the field! He could see the outline of something in front of him. What the devil were they? Fucking hell . . . cows! Jesus! If he was going to be killed hitting a bloody cow! Intelligence hadn't thought to suss that one out. It was too late now to change his mind. He just prayed that the animals would run like hell when they heard the weird sound of wind singing in the FE's wires.

The undercarriage touched, bounced, touched again, and then the tailskid caught. He thanked his lucky stars that he was flying an FE2B and not something unstable, like an RE8.

As soon as the plane had stopped rolling, the passenger tapped him on the arm, felt for his hand, shook it briefly, then jumped out, along with his suitcase. At least the field hadn't been wired. He could see the vague outline of a line of poplars in front of him about two hundred yards away. Looking carefully round, trying to pierce the thick gloom for signs that his landing had been detected, he paused for a few moments. The passenger stood below the nacelle waiting for his signal to swing the prop for him, his face a thick blob of deeper blackness, outlined by the scarf round his hat.

"Ready?" came the impatient hiss from his passenger.

"Ready!"

"Switches off?"

"Switches off!"

The man swung the propeller expertly. He'd done it before.

"Switches on?"

"Switches on!"

"Contact!"

"Contact!"

The 160hp Beardmore burst into ear-shattering life. He could see the vague outline of the cows running in all directions from the din. How he'd missed the animals on his approach run, he couldn't imagine. There seemed to be dozens of them . . . Fresians or Herefords . . . couldn't be Herefords, the French didn't have Herefords!

Without warning a searchlight blazed a shaft of light from the edge of the field. His eyes nearly collapsed after the prolonged immersion in darkness, under the impact.

A Spandau machine-gun chattered viciously, sending a stream of tracer towards the FE.

"Jump in!" he screamed at his passenger, sharply outlined in the shaft of intense light. "You can't wait now!"

The man leapt for the lip of the nacelle, grabbing it with his fingertips, swinging desperately, trying to gain purchase for his legs. Bob heard bullets ripping canvas as the FE began to move towards the poplars. His passenger was in the nacelle now and dragging the Lewis gun round, facing the searchlight. Bob could see vague outlines of infantry advancing, guns held before them. Only the inefficiency of the German officer ordering the Spandau to cease fire, for fear of hitting his own troops, saved him. Another second or so and the bullets from the machine-gun would have found either he, or some vital part of the aircraft.

He saw the passenger fire the Lewis gun at the searchlight, the tracer making straight for the light.

Bob tried not to look at the dazzling orb with its searing rays, and concentrate on the task of bringing the FE to the outer edge of the field before attempting a take-off.

Without warning, bullets from the Lewis found their target and the searchlight died, leaving the ground like a pit of utter gloom. Fireflies of flame from the muzzle flashes of the German infantry coloured the air some distance away, but they were firing blindly now.

The FE reached the outer limits, the poplars distinct against the skyline. Bob revved the Beardmore, swung the FE round into what little wind there was, and opened the throttle.

Bouncing and lurching over the uneven ground the FE was making heavy weather of the take-off. If there was a foxhole in his path, or a molehill, they were sunk. The FE would tip forward, despite the long skid projecting before the machine underneath the nacelle, and slew onto a wing-tip.

He felt the FE become light. His passenger was still firing bursts from the Lewis gun in the general direction of the advancing infantry, to keep their heads down.

He drew the joystick backwards, gently. The FE wobbled, then settled as the wings bit the air and the uplift began to take effect.

He felt something trickling down his chin, realised he had bitten into his lower lip. If there were trees in the direction he was taking off, they would be dead in a few seconds. The passenger ceased firing the Lewis gun. Whether he was changing ammunition drums or had just stopped he couldn't tell.

The altimeter showed a vague hundred feet, and the Beardmore was clattering away powerfully behind him. He began climbing.

He saw something in front of him, a dark slender shadow, and jerked the stick over, kicking out desperately on his left rudder. He was convinced he felt a shudder as the FE hit the weather vane on the church tower. Straightening out, he began a steady climb once more. His heart was thumping painfully at the fright he had received on seeing that tall shape.

He crossed the Lines at five thousand feet over Sailly, and began a gradual turn towards Bray-sur-Somme and Lourconter. His passenger was slumped forward in the front cockpit. What he was doing he had no idea and had not time to investigate. He needed to concentrate on locating Lourconter.

The shining ribbon of the Somme showed up before him, and he followed it until he estimated he was near the aerodrome at Lourconter.

A line of flares showed suddenly, almost directly ahead. Lander must have guessed the approximate time of his return and had put out the petrol tins to guide him in.

Several pairs of hands grabbed the wing-tips of the FE as he touched down and taxied towards the hangars.

Landers was there, his face anxious in the dim light of the flares which were being extinguished, one by one. "How did it go, Bob?" he called from the ground.

"The bastards had been tipped off," said Bob, viciously, climbing stiffly out. "They were waiting for us. I brought him back, the poor sonofabitch, they would have caught him easily."

"He's dead, sir" called Sergeant Williams from the cockpit above them. "Must have been hit by a bullet."

"Shit!" snarled Bob, aiming a kick at the FE's wheels. "All that way, and the poor bastard cops it!"

Several pairs of hands lowered the torn form to the ground. Someone shone a torch on the man's face, still muffled by scarf and hat, dark glasses. The man's clothes were soaked in blood.

The man's face, after removing the scarf, was peaceful in death, young, smooth and without a blemish. Only below his thorax was the sickening tide of red still oozing out.

In the mess, Bob stared vacantly at the wall, Landers by his side, drinking a glass of brandy.

"What a day," muttered Landers. "Only you came back this afternoon, Bob . . . the Major, Legge, Coombes, Forteith, Masters, Neville, Chaerters, Keene, MacIntosh . . . all gone . . . Christ! It doesn't bear thinking about . . . this fucking war!" The Adjutant's voice was harsh and brittle with strain. "Trevor was right, we have to do something about it . . . it just can't go on!"

"Eh?" Bob was lost in his own private world of sorrow, Landers's words not registering.

"Doesn't matter, mate," said Landers. "Your two kills were confirmed this afternoon."

"Kills," scoffed Bob. "I've murdered two more young men . . . just like me . . . who probably didn't want to fight me anymore than I did them."

Landers said nothing, watching the medical party taking the corpse of the spy on a stretcher towards the barn that did duty as a mortuary. He sighed deeply, looked round at the aerodrome in a despairing manner, then walked off towards the squadron office.

Bob dabbed at his lower lip, where the blood had congealed on his chin. It felt sore now that the tension had gone and he was aware of the cut.

Sergeant Williams stood there, watching him covertly. There was deep sympathy on his face. The crew pretended to be busy, but were also watching the young man via their tasks. Bob was aware of their faces in the gloom, but couldn't feel anything. He felt utterly drained of all nervous energy.

He walked across the sweet-smelling grass towards the mess along the village street. There was a mocking signboard on a wall 'Blighty – sixty-nine miles', an arrow pointing in the general direction of England.

He sat in the mess, alone, save for the mess staff, feeling like the sole survivor of some natural disaster. The usual evening mess sounds were absent, the piano, laughter, clink of glasses, boots on the bare boards . . . the warmth . . .

****

He found the 112th General Hospital located in a field on the outskirts of Amiens. The staff in the office all looked at him, curiously . . . at the RFC uniform, the ribbons of the MC and DSO on his breast, the grey streaks in his youthful hair.

"Sister Welland?" repeated the nurse on duty, staring awe-stricken at him. "I'll try to find her for you."

He paced up and down inside the tent whilst the staff entered, wounded were brought in on stretchers, medical staff attended their patients. The bustle of the hospital didn't seem connected with him at all. Two staff officers came in, red bands round their hats, swagger sticks impatiently tapping their darkly polished boots, their expressions one of a bad smell under their noses. They eyed him, appraisingly, the double-breasted RFC uniform and then their eyes went to the medal ribbons and thence to the pips on his shoulder. Their faces were dead pan in the light of the hurricane lamps.

"Robert!" came a voice behind him. "How lovely!"

She looked distant somehow, despite the familiar features, blue eyes and thick, heavy blonde hair, colder, more efficient than he recalled. The two staff officers looked all disapproving as if it was unfair that a mere Lieutenant could enjoy the company of such an attractive woman.

"Hello, Babs," he said, smiling, seeing her stare at him. "How are you?"

She stared at him, unblushingly, for a long moment. "What have they done to you, Bob?"

"Done? How do you mean?" he asked, self-consciously, suddenly.

"Your hair's grey!" she said softly, aware of the two officers staring at her.

"Old age!" he said, grinning. "Can you get away at all?"

"You bet I can, my love," she said, kissing him, suddenly. "Let me go and see Matron, tell her that I want some leave to be with one of England's heroic flyers!"

She left him abruptly, running out of the tent into the night.

"On leave, Lieutenant?" asked one of the staff officers, suddenly.

"Yessir!" he said. "Seven days."

"No Blighty?" asked the other officer. Both had plummy voices.

"My main interest is here, sir," said Bob, stiffly.

"Hmmm," said the first one, disdainfully. "What unit are you from, Lieutenant?"

"77th Squadron RFC, sir!" said Bob.

The two officers looked at one another. It was obvious they recognised the number, and knew the purpose of the unit.

"Can I see your leave pass, Lieutenant . . . er . . .?" asked the second one, his pencil moustache twitching.

"Spiers, sir!" said Bob, coldly, holding out his paybook and pass.

It was also obvious that they'd heard of Spiers too. Their manner changed subtly. Instead of officious and peremptory, they became almost friendly. The officer waved aside his paybook and pass. "Just a precaution, Lieutenant," said the man. "There are many deserters, you know. Your name is well known to us . . . Congratulations on your many aerial victories."

"Could do with a few more like you, Lieutenant!" said the first officer. "Show these dilletantes how to do it . . . cowardly, many of them!"

He was saved from further comment by the return of Barbara. She came into the tent waving a leave pass, excitedly. "Got it, Bobby!" she said, breathlessly. "Seven days!" She linked his arm, possessively. "Where do we go?"

"Let's go and have dinner, then I'll tell you," he grinned, nodding at the two officers who smiled obsequiously, and bowed to Barbara.

"Who are they, friends of yours, Bobby?" she asked, as they walked outside.

He felt all the familiar emotions come rushing back as she walked along beside him, the pain, the ache, the pleasure, the desire. "Hardly . . . staff officers don't normally talk to mere Lieutenants," he said, looking round. "Can we get a lift into Amiens?"

Barbara spoke to an ambulance driver, who immediately offered them both a lift.

****

Chapter 13

"Wasn't it lucky, us meeting that little Frenchman in Amiens . . . what was his name . . . Lascalle . . . the one with all those medals . . . we'd never have been so lucky with a place such as this . . . it's magnificent . . . and all free!" Barbara clapped her hands excitedly.

The river wound its way between lush banks of willows, cows grazed contentedly in the meadows, buttercups and daisies flowered profusely, insects buzzed lazily in the warm sun. They could see the vague outline of the house, perched on its rugged outcrop of rock above and behind them, and beyond the roofs of the village and church, nestling against the side of the tiny valley.

They lay in a tiny arbour they had found the second day after their arrival. Almost concealed from everyone, except the fish in the river, they lay in the soft grass, side by side, listening to the gurgle of the water as it passed by and the birdsong and insects, contentedly.

"That little twitch has almost gone from your eyelid, Bobby," she whispered, caressing his forehead.

"Shows the power of love-making!" he said, softly, tracing the line of her breast with his fingertips. "Cures all the screws and wrinkles out!"

"We've only another twenty-four hours, Bobby, and then we have to go back . . . it's awful how quickly it's gone . . . just flown by and now we have to part again!"

"Let's get married!" he said, suddenly, raising himself on one elbow, looking down at her. "Come on, now, let's go and get a priest to marry us." He tugged at her arm.

She shook her head, vigorously. "No way, Bobby Spiers . . . not for anything!" she said firmly.

"Why not? Don't you want to be married?" he rasped, nettled by this straight rebuffal.

"When all this is over . . . yes . . . but I'm not going to be rushed into something because times are unnatural . . . we'd both regret it!" She sat up, hugging her knees.

"Don't you love me?" he demanded.

"Do you honestly believe I'd be here, in this place, if I didn't," she said, hotly.

"Well, then, what's the hold-up . . . what don't you like about the idea?" he asked, angrily.

"Because there's a war on, and people do things in wars that they wouldn't do if there wasn't one . . . people get all emotional, distraught, out of focus, and then regret it when things get back to normal," she said, softly.

"How do you know all this, wise woman?" he demanded, lying back in the grass once more, hands behind his head, staring upwards.

"Because it's already happening . . . I've seen some of my colleagues rushing into marriage and then bingo, before they know it, they're widows and wondering what the devil it was all about." She was rocking gently back and forth as she spoke.

"And you don't want to be a widow, is that it?" he asked, bitterly.

"Too damned right, I don't, Bobby Spiers. A widow at eighteen?" She laughed, ironically.

He turned on his side away from her, sulkily. She leaned over him, her hair teasing his face. "You want to put your brand on me like those cowboys do, is that it, Bobby Spiers? Make sure your property is safe from all-comers?" She tried to turn his face back to hers. He resisted. "You've no worry on that score, I can assure you. I don't want anybody else."

"Then why?" he rasped.

"Because I'm not going to be blackmailed, Bobby, that's why," she said, sharply. "I'm, not that keen on a ring on my finger that I want to put myself, and you, in a silly situation that we can't extract ourselves from."

"What silly situation is that?" he almost yelled. "You think I'm going to be killed, is that it, and you don't want the embarrassment of becoming a young widow?"

"That as well, Bobby, but it's you I'm really thinking of," she said, softly.

"Fine, you're thinking of me," he mocked. "How does that tie in?"

"You'll be going back to your Squadron won't you, the day after tomorrow? How do you feel about that?" She sat back on her heels, rocking slightly.

Her words brought it all back with a terrible millstream of fear. The agonising minutes in the air, facing other men equally determined to knock him out of the sky, and the long nights waiting for dawn, and the first roar of a Le Rhone engine as the mechanics warmed them up. Each hour filled a kind of dread, hating the greyness when it arrived, forcing him out of his cocoon of silence.

"You don't feel good about it at all, do you?" she said, watching the struggle cross his features. "I can't blame you . . . I would be frantic with fear, and you want to compound that with worry about me? Does that make sense?"

He knew, deep down, that what she said was correct . . . it would paralyse him with an anxiety, yet a perverse feeling, irrational and hateful filled his mind . . . she wanted freedom of action . . . not to have to worry about him . . . fear of death, the telegram on the doorstep, wounds, loss of an arm, leg or even paralysis . . . she didn't want the problem in the future. "You don't care enough to want to marry me, is that it?" he groused.

"It's because I care that I'm saying 'No', Bobby . . . I wouldn't want you worried continually, all the time you were away from me, and it's no good you protesting that you wouldn't be, you would. Last August you were shy, diffident, unable to say boo to a goose . . ." She smiled fondly. "Now, you are already mature and hard . . . you've grown up in a few months, and I don't want to put additional burdens on you. That eyelid has stopped since we've been away . . . I don't want it to come back again, darling."

He was surly for the remainder of their last night together at Sainte Saveit d'Erve, withdrawn and contemplating the day after the next with something akin to dread.

They said their farewells to the concierge and his wife the next morning and made their way to Le Mans. They stayed their last night in Paris, and thence to Amiens the next day.

The roads were choked with men and matériel going up to the Front in preparation for the Arras offensive.

They both overstayed their pass time and had some awkward explaining to do to both their superiors.

" 'Bye, darling. Come back to me soon," said Barbara, tears in her eyes, as she waved him off when the tender came to take him back to Lourconter. "I'll marry you when the war is over . . . I promise."

He said little to Corporal Matthews who was driving the tender, an old Crossley tourer that had been converted to a van, sunk in thought and evil premonitions.

Matthews, if he noticed, said nothing about his officer's morose mien, but chattered away merrily, giving him all the latest news about the Squadron . . . the replacements, the new CO, a Major Riley . . . and news of the new Hun aircraft that had been seen in the skies over the Front and who were dominating the whole RFC with their skills and challenges. The Blue Lion Jagdstaffel had become one of the new German Jastas with a total strength of some thirty experienced flyers, and they were knocking RFC planes out of the sky at a terrifying rate. Losses were mounting and the turnover in pilots had become horrifying.

As they turned into the tiny village street of Lourconter, Bob felt a wild feeling of apprehension, mixed with pleasure at hearing an aero-engine again. He thought he detected a new note in the engines he could hear.

Dumping his single haversack in Number 4, he hurried down to the Squadron office to report in.

A tall sandy-haired man with a monocle regarded him from behind the new desk and chair. There was carpet on the floor and the litter usually associated with Major Briggs had all disappeared. All was neat and tidy, like the man himself.

"Come in, Lieutenant . . . Spiers, isn't it?" said the Major. "Riley's my name." He held out his hand in welcome. "Sit down, please!" He indicated a chair with a graceful flourish.

Bob wasn't sure whether he liked the man or not. The Major's eyes were cold and did not reflect the smile. The faint moustache adorning his upper lip looked painted on. His hair was thick, brushed straight back, was blond, almost white. A DSO and MC were across his left breast.

"I see you've been officially credited with twenty-seven kills, Spiers," said Riley. "That's an impressive record for someone as young as you evidently are. How old are you?"

"Eighteen in April, sir," said Bob, cautiously.

"And you can't take orders, eh?" Riley grinned. "Otherwise you wouldn't be in this flea-pit of a Squadron, would you?"

"I don't know what to say to that, sir," said Bob, uncomfortably.

Riley shrugged. "It doesn't matter, Lieutenant. What does matter is your expertise. I've had two lots of replacements in the last seven days. You've no doubt heard about von Dolin-Berensky's Lion Jasta from Corporal Matthews. Well, let me fill you in so that you won't be under any illusion about this man and his Jasta. He has been reported to have gained forty-two victories and there isn't a man in his Jasta that isn't an ace several times over. He flew with Immelmann and Boelke and has survived over two years at the Front. They are all flying the new Fokkers, Pfalzes, Rolands and their spotters are flying Halberstadt two seaters and Rumplers . . . dangerous even up close." Riley looked up at Bob, his face grim. "We're in for a hard time, Spiers, and I don't mean the 77th alone . . . I mean the RFC as a whole are going to suffer over the next few months." He waved his hands in a futile gesture. " We, naturally, are going to get the mucky end of the stick, as usual."

Bob listened with half an ear to this diatribe. What difference did it make whether he was with the 77th or some other militarily acceptable squadron? The end was likely to be the same. Riley had obviously offended the hierarchy in some way or he, too, would not be with the 77th.

"One piece of good news, Spiers . . . we now have the new Sopwith Camels . . . 130hp Le Clerget's . . . very fast and very manoeuvrable . . . ceiling around 19,000 feet, top speed around 115mph, twin Vickers with the new Sopwith-Kauper gear synchroniser and can climb a thousand feet in a minute . . . very quick on the right-hand turn due to the torque thrust of the Le Clerget rotary. You have to watch it, however, it handles very lightly and we've had two accidents already by people with little experience and I don't want any more. Is that clear, Spiers?"

"Yessir!" Bob tried not to sound too bored.

"Very well, welcome back to 77th Squadron and let's see if you can help me build this squadron into a first-rate combat unit. I need you, Spiers, I really do," said the Major. "By the way, your captaincy has come during the last two or three days. Been gazetted . . . which you wouldn't have known anything at all about, of course, being on leave."

Bob was surprised, and tried not to show it. Someone, somewhere must be watching his performance and seeing that he gained some reward. He got up, turned to go.

"You also have gained a DFC, Spiers," he said, almost casually.

"Thank you, sir," he said, stiffly.

"Major Briggs recommended you for it, just before he was killed," said Riley, softly. "Nothing to do with me."

Outside the office, Bob looked up at the sky. There were huge banks of cumulus like cathedrals moving across the hazy blue sky. Sergeant Williams greeted him, respectfully, showed him his new machine with pride. The clean lines of the Sopwith were a revelation when he related this new machine to the Farman back at Denham just under a year ago. The shining steel cowling of the rotary, the gleaming Vickers and the jaunty look of the little craft were pleasing.

"Got any artists amongst your blokes, Ginger?" he asked, grinning.

"As a matter of fact we have, sir . . . why do you ask?" Williams was looking at Bob askance.

"I want a tiger's head painted on the side of my machine . . . just there," he pointed to the spot just behind the red-white-blue cockades . . . on both sides," he said.

Sergeant Williams looked a little rueful. "Could create problems for you, Captain Spiers, sir . . . not being funny but there are regulations in the RFC against decorations of any kind."

"Sergeant, I don't give a fuck for regulations . . . just get it painted, will you? I'll take responsibility for any adverse comments," said Bob in a hard voice.

"Aye, sir," said the Sergeant, smiling.

"Is she ready, gunned and fuelled?"

"Yessir!" said Williams.

"Right, wheel her out, will you? I'll get my gear on."

Corporal Matthews had already stitched the third pip on his epaulettes when he got back to his billet and was busy stitching the DFC ribbon beside the MC and DSO.

He said nothing when Matthews looked up and grinned. "Couldn't tell you on the way from Amiens, sir . . . was told not to," said the Corporal. "We had a gent from Army Command down here whilst you were away . . . a Major Martine . . . talking to Major Riley . . . you were mentioned several times . . ."

Bob acknowledged the gift of intelligence without comment, just a nod of his head. So, Charles had been here. What the hell was the significance of that? No doubt Charles, with his father's connections in the War Office, had gained himself a staff appointment. Thinking of Martine brought Michelle back to his mind, having been obliterated by his liaison with Barbara for the past seven days. He was totally confused in his feelings about both women. Sometimes he thought that Barbara was the one he would enjoy a lifetime with, and then Michelle would interpose her easy charm and manner and then he would be back to square one again. Even the short time since he had left Barbara at the entrance to the 112ᵗʰ General Hospital he knew that she had been right in asserting that it would have been disaster for them to have married.

He didn't know his own mind, that was plain. He had merely been infatuated with the ecstasy of the moment.

He ponders on Martine's connection with 77th as he walked out to the waiting Camel.

Several of the replacement pilots were sitting in deck chairs in the mild March sunshine in front of the cottage that housed the mess. They eyed him curiously, waved a greeting, and a few comments of a ribald nature. Bob waved back but didn't introduce himself. He felt their eyes on him all the way down the street to the waiting Sopwith.

He checked out the Camel, going over every stitch and every strut, testing ailerons, elevators, rudder with meticulous care. Sergeant Williams and his crew watched him silently.

He swung up into the cockpit, after satisfying himself that all was in order.

He could feel the eyes of the replacement pilots on his back as he went round the Camel, trying wires and controls.

The view towards the front was a little restrictive after the Pup, but it had the same basic good layout of the Sopwith factory. The dihedral lower wing was sharper than that of the Pup, and he could feel the powerful forward weight of the Le Clerget after the Le Rhone, giving it a feeling of immense manoeuvrability.

Sergeant Williams swung the prop for him. The roar of the Le Clerget was satisfying and he began to feel at home again. It was as if the intervening seven days at Sainte Saveit sur d'Erve was but a distant memory.

The windsock was fluttering half-heartedly as he gave the machine half throttle finding that he had to continually correct the right-hand thrust of the Le Clerget, the tail of the Sopwith wagging as he took it across the turf and into the air. After a few lightning aerobatics over the field, rolls, loops and spins, he levelled out, gazing downwards. A haze of white faces were peering up at him from the ground. He flew off towards the Front, crossing the line at Clery-sur-Somme at twelve thousand feet and still climbing.

He was delighted with the Camel's performance, its rate of climb astounded him and the easy turns and complete mobility of the aircraft were a pleasure. He dodged round some massive banks of cloud, flying through immense valleys of vapour that changed constantly. On the occasions he emerged from the clouds German Archie sent up a few black bursts, before he was obscured again by the next bank of cloud. He was taken completely by surprise, when emerging from a cloud bank, to find himself in the middle of a group of three Fokker DR1 triplanes. Designed by Antony Fokker's brilliant designer, Rheinhold Platz, the Fokker DR1 was Germany's reply to the Sopwith triplane of 1916. Powered by the 110hp Oberusel UR11, the triplane was a formidable adversary as Werner Voss had already proven, as had Manfred von Richthofen. The twin, synchronised Spandau 7.92mm machine-guns gave it a punch that was equal to anything in the Allied air at the time.

The three Fokkers immediately dispersed into combat readiness, each taking a stance that would make an attack by the lone Camel on any one of them hazardous, if not suicidal.

Bob rolled upwards, completed an Immelmann turn into a cloud bank and swept through the damp layers, feeling the Camel bounce under the uneven air pressures and turbulence.

He emerged and found the wheels of one of the triplanes almost touching his head.

With chain lightning reaction he jerked the Camel upwards, waited until he was with a fifty yard range of the unsuspecting German and let fly with the Vickers. The triplane seemed to shake itself, stagger to one side, and then a gout of flame shot from the cowling as it plunged tail over nose downwards.

He barely had time to observe this before the rattle of Spandaus behind him were tearing fabric on the Camel's port wing surfaces, creeping closer. He jerked the Camel into a right-hand turn that had the Fokker pilot behind him, gasping. The third member of the trio had been waiting for this manoeuvre and brought his machine in on his flank. He was now sandwiched between the two Fokkers.

He ignored the threat posed by the third machine and levelled out on the tail of the second. He waited until he was two hundred yards away before giving the Fokker a burst. He found he had missed the pilot by a good twenty yards, and the third Fokker was now coming up underneath him. He caught sight of the blue lion on the side of one of the triplanes as he whipped round to face the oncoming triplane. The two machines faced one another, flying to mutual destruction at over two hundred miles an hour. Both pilots raked each other, before the Fokker swerved violently to avoid collision.

Bob saw bullets bounce off the Camel's cowling, a strut shattered and a wire cam drift with a loud twanging noise. Bullets were hammering into woodwork behind him. Splinters from spruce flew past from another shattered wing member and hit his tiny windscreen, which vanished into a million fragments, cutting his face.

The Le Clerget suddenly gave out a wild howling, followed by a horrid groaning noise, and the Camel seemed to falter in its tracks.

He dived and, as he did so, he saw the shadow of a triplane spinning wildly down out of control two thousand feet or so below him. The third triplane was heading away from him at speed.

Without warning the propeller came to a standstill, and smoke began pouring from the cowling.

A thrill of horror ran through him! He was about to become a flamer! He switched off immediately as the Camel began to flatten out of the dive. He headed for the British lines still some five miles away. His altimeter showed a mere seven thousand feet.

Three SE5s suddenly crossed his nose, banking and whirling around him. The flight leader waved at him, pointing westwards, and then at his own machine. They were going to escort him, keeping off any Huns that might be in the neighbourhood.

The right wing began juddering viciously in the wind, where the broken wing strut was held merely by the taut wire.

He eased off into as level flight as possible, and coasted down towards the British lines over Boucharesnes. The approach towards that desirable haven seemed painfully slow. He was now down to five thousand feet and still three miles to go.

The port wing was shaking like a leaf in the windstream. He felt a warm fluid issuing down his arm, saw the red tide flowing down from his face onto his collar and thence down his arm.

The Camel lurched suddenly, as if drunk, sending his pulse-rate up in alarm. The German Archie were making things difficult, sending up salvo after salvo at the four British machines, hoping to cripple the Camel before it reached the safety of the front line.

He felt the Camel lift suddenly as a high-trajectory howitzer shell passed under the plane. The sound of the wind in the wires and faint roar of the Hispano-Suiza engines of the SE5s was a steady dythramb to his predicament. The British machines were asking for trouble flying this low. They would provide easy meat for any roaming Fokker.

The German front line trenches were before him now, a few hundred feet under his wheels. The infantrymen joined in, firing their rifles at him as he passed over their heads.

A violent explosion in Nomansland made the Camel swerve with the blast, sending it lower. With a gasp of relief he saw the British trench system pass under his wheels, and then he began searching for level ground in which to put down the Camel.

Stumps of trees were like teeth in some muddy maw. Shell-holes dotted the landscape. Communication trenches lined with duckboards, filled with water and evil-looking scum criss-crossed his path.

The Camel's wing caught a tree stump, whirled, bringing him facing eastwards, then the wheel went into a shell-hole and he was pitched forward on his face. Mud filled the cockpit . . . !

****

Chapter 14

Major Riley glared at him, his pale features red with anger. "You've not only cost this unit a valuable aeroplane, you nearly caused a casualty . . . yourself, by your unprincipalled act of disobedience."

Bob switched off. The man's angry words passed over his head in a stream, not affecting him in any way, merely a torrent of abuse and fury that made no connection with his own emotions.

Suddenly, Riley, seeing the dead pan expression on Bob's features stopped his flow of denunciation and stared at Bob. "I do hope you are taking all this to heart, Captain Spiers," he said, coldly.

"Oh, yessir," said Bob. It didn't convince himself.

Riley bit his lip, trying to suppress the fury that rose up again. "Your arrogant disobedience of my orders lost us an aeroplane, Spiers. I don't like losing matériel without my knowledge, and I don't want my pilots put at risk through the ill-considered actions of subordinates. Is that clear to you, Captain Spiers?"

"Oh, yessir," said Bob, wishing to hell the man would get on with it, and let him go.

There was a knock at the door.

"Come in!" rasped Riley, irritably.

The Orderly Sergeant came in, saluted, placed a piece of paper before the Major.

His eyes stared straight over Riley's head.

Riley read the message, his lips moving as he read. He looked up, stared at Bob. "Seems like you got yourself two more victories, Spiers . . . just been confirmed by Forward Observation posts. Two Fokker DR1s . . . both from the von Dolin-Berensky's Jasta." Riley bit his lip. "Thank you, Sergeant."

The Sergeant sprang to attention, stamped his foot, about turned and marched out.

Riley sat there, staring at the sheet of paper, trying desperately to find a common fulcrum on which to opt out of his impossible situation, a face saver for himself and Bob.

"At ease, Captain," he muttered, throwing the paper down. "Now then, I want to make it plain to you, Captain, there are to be no unauthorised flying jaunts over the German lines, is that clear?"

"Yessir."

"Damn it, man, is that all you can say?" he rasped, furiously.

"Not much else I can say, sir, is there?" said Bob, after a silence.

"For Chrissake, Spiers . . . are you completely bloody crazy? You are the only experienced man in this squadron right now. I have seven men out there, all with less than twenty hours under their belts . . . some of them have never flown a Camel before and you go and put your neck at risk . . . do you understand me?"

"Tell you what, sir," said Bob. "I'll make a bargain with you."

"Well?" Riley's lip was being chewed by his upper teeth.

"You allow me to fly my own sorties, whenever I feel like it and I'll knock the rookies into shape for you."

Riley looked as if he were going to explode. "I make no bargains with subordinates, Spiers, now or ever," he snarled.

Bob shrugged. "Very good, sir," he said, coolly.

"You may go, Spiers. We have an evening patrol and that commences at 1700 hours. Is that clear?"

"Yessir." Bob stood to attention, saluted, turned on his heel and left.

The pilots were still sitting in their deck chairs outside the mess, reading, sleeping. The news of the two Fokkers had already gone the rounds. The young men looked at him with awe in their eyes.

Bob went into the mess. The Orderly Sergeant was speaking to the Mess Sergeant.

"Thank you, Sergeant Blomford," he said, quietly.

The Sergeant smiled. "Any time, sir," he said.

"Join me in a drink, Sergeant. You have my permission," said Bob.

"Thank you, sir, a beer, Gary, please."

The sergeant felt ill-at-ease in the Officers' Mess. Bob led the way outside. He and the sergeant drank their beers together, in silence.

Blomford finished his quickly, placed the glass on one of the wooden trestles, and thanked Bob, before marching off, a clipboard under his arm.

Bob went inside the mess. "Sergeant," he called to the mess NCO. "Take a crate of beer down to the hangar to Sergeant Williams with my compliments, will you?"

Carter looked at the new pips on Bob's shoulders, smiled, nodded. "Right away, sir."

Corporal Matthews was putting the finishing touches to his uniform. The DFC and the other two ribbons looked smart and neat on the breast of his tunic.

He lay down on his cot, put some Chopin on the gramophone and sat listening to the wailing sounds of the piano playing a nocturne.

At 1700 hours the eight Camels of the 77th Squadron were all spluttering away contentedly on the tarmac, like eight gees about to fly. They were to fly over the Epehy sector of the German lines and report on any unusual activity on the ground.

Bob left it until the last minute before walking across to his Camel.

"Thanks for the beer, sir, and congratulations on the two Fokkers and your promotion, sir," said Sergeant Williams, as he began his customary walk round his aircraft, examining ailerons, and controls, engine and wires. "Private Billings will paint the tiger on your aircraft, sir, when your new crate arrives. Says he will be delighted."

"Thanks, Sergeant." Bob climbed into the cockpit, settled down, strapped his safety-belt round his middle.

Five minutes' later, an impatient Major Riley gave the go signal. Eight Sopwiths ran down the field and into the air. Two nearly came cropper, as in the inexperienced pilots treated their machines as if they were Avros or Farman biplanes, not correcting the vicious torque as they went down the field, tails in the air.

Riley took them up to twelve thousand feet, and crossed the lines at the precise point that Bob had crossed it earlier that day.

He could see his Camel, nose down in the mud, just behind the British lines at Clery-sur-Somme. He marvelled just how he had got out of that shell-hole into which the machine had tumbled without drowning. He had slid down into the awful gunge three times before a stretcher party had arrived, held a pole down for him, pulled him out. He stank of shit and urine, and God alone knew what else. The medical detail, led by a Corporal, stood well away from him, grins on their faces. After enquiring whether he was fit enough to walk, they had taken him to an Advanced Field Dressing station, where an orderly had played a hose over him, washing the dreadful filth from him. He had dried out before a fire in an improvised boiler-house, and then cadged a lift from an RASC driver back to Lourconter.

At fifteen thousand feet over Bertincourt, the Jasta of Freiherr von Dolin-Berensky was waiting to exact revenge for the loss of two of their number earlier.

A mixed bag of Albatross, Pfalz, Halberstadt and Fokker triplanes plunged out of the clouds into the eight Camels like bats from hell.

Inside fifteen seconds, four Camels were on their way earthwards, twisting and turning, out of control. Even as Bob switched his machine into a right-hand turn and jumped on the tail of an Albatross, painted white and yellow in jazzed stripes, the blue lion's head on the fuselage, he saw another Camel plunge from the sky, a plume of smoke racing out behind it, engine screaming as the dead pilot fell into the floor of the cockpit.

He fired a burst at the Albatross, but it slid away beneath him and two triplanes were on his tail, bullets ripping canvas behind him. He could hear the tell-tale flack-flack of torn doped fabric. A wire sprang with a wailing twang, and then his windshield vanished as if chopped by an invisible axe. A strut came apart on his left wing, and then he was glued to the tail of a black Pfalz that was shooting hell out of a lone Camel. He fired a long burst before the Pfalz swung away from the Camel. German machines with Maltese crosses seemed to be all round him. The lion's head dominant on their fuselages. Diving, rolling, looping, spinning, the last Camel went out of the sky, a wing sheering off as it fell earthwards, the loose plane fluttered down like an autumn leaf.

He made for the nearest cloud bank, fear gripping him like a paralysing disease. He tried to suppress the feeling of panic that began to seize him as the avenging Germans came after him, guns blazing.

The shattered strut was beginning to thrum, and a loose wire was thrashing the side of his cockpit like a steel whip. Bullets whanged off the engine cowling and then he was in the choking vapour, concealed and temporarily safe.

He stood the Camel on its tail, the Le Clerget howling frantically to maintain speed.

He emerged from the cloud to find a group of three German aeroplanes waiting to pounce. He was through them before they realised what was happening and into another cloud bank.

When he came out of it, he was totally confused as to his whereabouts. He didn't recognise the terrain six thousand feet below. A hill, a village, a church and a large factory-looking building, followed by the thin thread of a railway line. He glanced swiftly round, searching for the avenging German planes. The sky seemed empty. He knew it was a treacherous sense of security. At any moment planes could come out of the dying sun to blast him out of the sky.

He flew on, turning and twisting to confuse the aim of any possible concealed enemy springing out at him from the cloud banks.

Ten minutes' later he noticed a steeple below him that looked vaguely familiar. His compass was still gyrating madly and was virtually useless for a direction finding. He circled the tiny village until, with a shock, he recognised Le Catelet and the Escaut running through the village. The memory of that night just under two weeks before came back to him . . . the searchlight, and the glittering fire from German infantry rifles and the hideous tracer from the Spandau . . .

Scanning the sky for the millionth time, he turned, headed westwards, having fixed his position on the map.

Keeping to the massed cloud banks, the setting sun lighting up the blue-white edifices in glorious colour, he flew at fifteen thousand feet until he crossed the British lines.

Less than ten miles from Lourconter, the Le Clerget suddenly cut out. He checked the fuel gauge instinctively. It was indicating zero. A bullet hole in the tank was the explanation.

He followed the silver snake of the Somme to Bray-sur-Somme and then, still with plenty of height in hand, made a dead-stick landing at Lourconter.

He sat in the cockpit unable to move, hands shaking, the need to urinate and vomit nearly paralysing him. Sergeant Williams and Landers were all running towards him. Willing hands almost lifted him bodily from the cockpit.

"You alright, Bob?" asked Major Landers, anxiously.

He nodded, pushing past the assisting hands. "Must pee or I'll have an accident!" he muttered.

Nobody laughed.

He was half way to the latrines when he heard the sound of a Le Clerget, choking and spluttering in the eastern sky. A black dot appeared over the poplars and Bray-sur-Somme. It was a Camel, of that there was no doubt. It was lurching and staggering around, crazily. A trail of smoke was disfiguring the azure sky, coming from the tail.

He paused, watching the antics of the aeroplane awed, his urgent call forgotten.

The Camel bounced on the turf at the end of the field, rose like an antelope, then hit again. The Le Clerget was still going at full blast and the Camel was heading straight for him in gigantic grasshopper leaps.

He ran for the village street, his mind blowing with fear. The Camel appeared to have a life of its own, following upon his heels, as if alive.

Suddenly, the undercarriage collapsed and the crazy machine was hurtling along, dragging up earth and grass in a huge gouge on its underbelly. The propeller disintegrated into flying fragments, the wings crumpled like paper, and the Camel came to rest less than twenty feet from him.

A cloud of petrol vapour was pouring from the underside, and the smell of aviation fuel was strong in the evening air.

Jumping at the cockpit, Bob leaned over, released the safety-belt from the slumped body of the pilot, and began dragging him over the coaming. A flicker of flame was licking at the engine cowling. As he struggled, Sergeant Williams came up and together pulled the unconscious form from the vicinity of the smoking aircraft. With a dull whoosh and thud, the Camel caught fire and began to blaze furiously. The fire crew trained their hoses on the burning craft.

"Who is it, Bob?" asked Landers, coming up, breathless, with the other ground crew members.

"Major Riley, sir," said Bob, pulling the helmet from the lifeless face of the pilot. His hand came away bloodstained, dripping with the evil-smelling sticky fluid. "Dead, I'm afraid!"

Landers cursed horribly, beating his fists impotently on the side of the fire tender. "Jesus Holy Christ!" he moaned. "When is this killing going to stop?"

"We didn't stand an earthly, Major," said Bob. "They were waiting for us over Bertincourt . . . the whole Jasta . . . so it seemed, and they jumped us . . . I saw them all go down before I made my escape into the clouds . . . they were hunting for me for some time, trying finish us off."

"Come and make your report, Captain Spiers," said Lander, his arm round Bob's shoulders. the heat from the burning Camel was blistering.

"Sorry I wasn't here to greet you on your return from leave, Bob. I had to attend a conference over at Amiens . . . General Snow's Seventh Corps HQ. I hear that Riley let you have it for going up alone?"

Bob nodded, miserably. "I feel responsible for this debâcle . . . if I hadn't downed those two tripehounds, then this wouldn't have happened."

"Rubbish, my friend," snapped Landers. "It could easily have been planned and could have happened any time. Riley came from a Naval squadron at Portsmouth, flying seaplanes . . . Shorts . . . Type 184s . . . did some sterling work for the Navy . . ." Landers held up his hand. "I know your next question . . . what the hell was he doing here? The answer to that one is that Riley upset a senior Naval Officer with some caustic comments on what the Navy expected of his men. His feet never touched the floor."

"When is this stupidity going to end, Nigel?" asked Bob. "Are they going to get shot of everyone who disagrees with this maniacal war plan . . . bombardment, over the top, cut the wire, break through, send in the cavalry to finish them off? And the same with us . . . tactics stupid, sending lads out here with no experience of aerial fighting, no time spent at gunnery in the air, not on the ground . . . Christ! It's pure bloody murder!"

"We are on the same side, Bob," said Landers, quietly, motioning Bob to a chair.

"Sorry, Nigel . . . I just get madder and madder," muttered Bob.

"What would have Napoleon done?" asked Landers, humorously.

"Even he was a bit of a twat towards the end. He was offered a hot air balloon just before Waterloo, for observation purposes. If he'd taken them up on it, he'd have seen Blucher's Germans beyond Ligny, and he'd have swept Wellington into the Channel."

"I believe you, Bob." Landers picked up some papers from his desk. "You, my young friend, are temporarily CO of the 77th as from this minute!"

****

Chapter 15

The staff car screamed along the dusty road, swerving and turning to miss a French farmer driving his solitary cow, or a woman and her pram. On approaching Lourconter the Sergeant driver slowed down, marginally. The VII Corps pennant on the bonnet of the Armstrong Siddeley open tourer was a rigid square of cloth.

The driver narrowly missed a group of ground crew exercising in the tiny square under the watchful eye of Sergeant Carter. Carter bawled at the driver for being a stupid sonofabitch, and realigned his men in their calisthenic rows, ready for a knees bend operation.

The staff car jerked to a halt outside the Squadron Office. The Sergeant jumped out, ran round and opened the passenger door.

A tall, lean officer with a Colonel's crown and pip on his shoulder epaulettes stepped out, jerked his uniform jacket down, straightened his tie, adjusted his red-banded hat, slapped his swagger stick on his polished boots, then marched smartly into the office.

Nigel Landers was not expecting visitors, and when Sergeant Blomford knocked on his door he had his collar open, his tunic unbuttoned, he was smoking his pipe and had his feet on his desk, tilted back in his chair.

"What is it, Sergeant?" he asked, irritably, welcoming the moment's peace and relief at no responsibility. He could vaguely hear the sound of Le Clergets in the air somewhere, apart from that all was silent.

Sergeant Blomford attempted to give the Major warning of what was impending, jerking his thumb over his shoulder at something behind him.

"Never mind the warnings, Sergeant," drawled the Colonel, pushing past him, standing over Landers, eyeing the disarray and the untidy office with disgust.

Landers stood up hastily, attempting to button his tunic and collar, and trying to salute at the same time.

The Colonel languidly poked his swagger stick across the desk and pushed Landers gently back again into his chair. "Beastly mess in here, Major. Open a window, will you, Sergeant, if it's possible to open the damned thing . . . My God, look at the cobwebs. What kind of an outfit are you running here, Major?"

The Colonel pulled out a chair, dusted it lightly with a handkerchief, sat down as if expecting it to collapse under him. He lifted the leather briefcase onto his knee, opened it with fingers finely manicured, laid a bunch of papers on the desk before him.

"Right, Major. My name is Blawford . . . Croxley-Blawford, actually, I'm on General Snow's staff . . . with special duties as liaison with the RFC under his command. He asked me to come down here specially today, even though it is dashed inconvenient . . . got a dinner date in Amiens tonight . . . and talk to you about the activities of your squadron over the past seven days." The Colonel pushed a monocle into his left eye, wriggled it around by screwing his face up, sighed, and referred to some of the papers before him on the desk. "Well, Major? What have you to say about that?" he lisped harshly.

Landers thought Oh, Christ, no, it would have to be one of these ponces, wouldn't it, not someone who has seen service, but a chinless fucking marvel who's never been nearer the front than Thiepval. "Activities, sir? I'm not with you, sir," said Nigel.

"For God's sake, man, don't prevaricate with me. The squadron has been virtually non-operational for seven days. How do you suppose we can win this war by this kind of cowardly reticence?" The Colonel smacked his stick against his boot impatiently, anxious to be off.

"You must know, sir, that I'm not responsible for the operational activities of the 77 Squadron. I'm merely the Adjutant . . . a paper man," said Landers, swallowing.

"Ah, yes, I was coming to that, Major . . . a junior ranking officer . . ." He hummed and hawked, turning over paper. "Leave that window, Sergeant!" he rasped at Blomford, who was still trying to lever open the window behind Landers. "It's quite obvious that the damned thing hasn't been open since the Revolution." He waited until Blomford had withdrawn. "Captain Robert Spiers, an ace, I believe you call them in this service, 35 accredited victories in the air over the Hun. Is that correct?"

"Yessir," said Landers. "Five of those in the last seven days."

"He is temporarily executive officer of this unit, Major?" rapped Croxley-Blawford, adjusting the monocle.

"Yessir, until a new CO has been appointed . . . I understand Army Command are having difficulty in finding an officer with the relevant experience?" said Landers, uncomfortably, knowing what was coming.

"I met this Spiers . . . last November, in St Omer . . . Bolshevik, isn't he? Thinks he knows how to win the war all by himself, is that right, Major?" demanded the Colonel, brushing imaginary dust from his tunic.

"I believe that Captain Spiers has some sound ideas, Colonel Blawford, and the fact that he has downed 35 enemy aircraft is an earnest of his ability as a flyer," said Landers.

Croxley-Blawford consulted his papers, looked up at Landers, his expression hard and vicious. "For seven bloody days, Major, this Squadron of yours has not flown over the enemy lines once, despite repeated requests from VII Corps that you keep enemy activity to a minimum bearing in mind the importance of the forthcoming offensive at Arras. Now, what the hell is going on, Major? General Snow is becoming very impatient with your repeated denials of readiness for combat. Every other squadron on this sector of the front has had heavy loses, but they are not refusing to do their bit to win the war. What have you to say to that, Major?"

"Captain Spiers is the only man who can state when the squadron is ready for combat, Colonel. With respect, the RFC is not an infantry regiment. It is composed of highly trained men, using expensive machines . . ." said Landers.

"Major, I'm well aware of the fact that these prima donnas don't have to put up with what we land-based types have to endure . . . in the trenches, cold, wet, hungry, going over the top." The Colonel's eyes wobbled slightly at the last statement. "I do expect them to fight, however, and your men have not, I repeat, been over the front lines once in seven days. Now what the hell is going on here, Major, and where is Captain Spiers now?"

"He's in the air with his men, sir," said Landers, stolidly.

"Over the German lines I hope, Major?" said Croxley-Blawford, sniffing, preening his moustache.

"I don't think so, sir," said Landers, coolly.

"You don't bloody well think so, Major Landers?" roared the Colonel. "Are you, or are you not the senior officer of this unit?"

"Yessir."

"Then why don't you know what Captain Spiers is doing with these men?" screamed the Colonel, his face red.

"I didn't say that I didn't know what he was doing with them, sir. I said that I didn't think they were over the German lines," said Landers, his face pale.

"Then what in God's name is he doing with them, Major?" bellowed the Colonel.

"Training them, sir," said Landers, quietly.

Croxley-Blawford's face went purple with fury. "Training them? What the hell does he think they need training for? They learned to fly, didn't they . . ." He consulted the papers before him. Blake, nine hours, Thompson, ten hours, Chessman, nine hours . . . it's all down here, Major . . . they've been trained and now you're telling me that Captain Spiers is training them further?" Croxley-Blawford's face was magenta with fury. "I want an explanation, Major, and I want one now. Do you hear me?"

"Certainly, sir," said Landers, shaken but unmoved.

"Well? I'm waiting, Major," roared the Colonel.

"If you'll refer to those records again, sir, you will notice that only two of those men have ever flown a Camel before this week . . . Chessman and Holliday, and that was only four hours actually in the air . . . no experience of aerial gunnery and none of manoeuvre at all."

"Camel? What the devil's a camel, Major? I thought they were animals with humps? What the hell are camels doing here at Lourconter. Have you gone stark raving mad, Major?"

"That's a Camel, sir," said Landers, pointing to a sectional drawing of a Sopwith Camel on the wall behind the Colonel. "130hp Le Clerget engine, sir, top speed 115mph, ceiling 19,000 feet . . ."

"Yes, yes, I can see that now, Major . . . all this bloody stupid technical data . . . don't know what the Army's coming to . . . in the Cavalry, we don't have to bother with such pettifogging detail. What's this got to do with these new men flying sorties over the lines, eh?" Croxley-Blawford's discomfort was hidden behind bluster at being caught out, showing his ignorance of the facts.

"I'll explain, sir, if you'll permit me," said Landers, and proceeded to give the reasons why young men just out of flying school were not necessarily ready for fighting in the air. He told him about von Dolin-Berensky's Lion Jasta and the kind of opposition the 77th were up against and every reason that he and Spiers had discussed over the past few days.

He had barely finished before there was the roar of a Le Clerget, seemingly just over the roof the cottage. The Colonel ducked, involuntarily, then cringed as another screamed low, followed by others in swift succession. He heard the rattle of Vickers machine-guns and then for the next five minutes all speech was impossible by virtue of the noise of the aircraft overhead.

"What in hell are those bloody maniacs doing?" bellowed the Colonel, apoplectic with frustration.

"Captain Spiers is training them to avoid being shot down . . . he's using live ammunition . . . his theory is that if they can't avoid being hit by him, then their chances of lasting more than one patrol against Dolin-Berensky are remote, sir," said Landers.

The Colonel arose, walked swiftly out into the village street, staring upwards, just as a Camel screamed down at roof-top level, closely followed by another, which was firing its Vickers at the machine in front. Bullets ricocheted off the chimney pots. The men performing calisthenics all dived for cover as the tracer lanced down into the street, chewing up chunks of earth and wood from the houses. Colonel Croxley-Blawford threw himself full length on the dusty street, his hands covering his ears. Landers watched, calmly and dispassionately from the doorway. He hadn't budged an inch.

Four Camels came down, all firing at one another in deadly earnest. Others were locked in mortal combat higher up in the blue vault of the sky. The rattle of gunfire could be heard continuously.

The Colonel was assisted to his feet by Sergeant Blomford. The officer threw his arm off angrily, his face white, dusting himself down. The Sergeant driver from the staff car rushed over with a clothes brush, began brushing the dust from the Colonel's serge tunic.

Suddenly, as if at a given signal, the Camels began to land, one by one, taxiing noisily up to the hangars, in short bursts of snarling power from the Le Clergets. Even at this distance, the Colonel could see fabric hanging from two of the Camels.

"That man is a raving lunatic!" roared the Colonel, pointing to where a young man, stocky and thick-set was talking towards the Squadron office, after consulting with a Sergeant fitter briefly, and pointing to his machine. The young pilots all came running after the stocky young man, thumping him on the back and laughing, pointing and miming aerial combat with their hands, demonstrating manoeuvres enthusiastically. Spiers halted when he saw the staff car and Colonel Croxley-Blawford standing with Major Landers, stiffened, changed direction, then walked into Number 4, without acknowledging anyone.

"I want that officer down here at once!" screamed the Colonel, pointing at Number 4.

"Sergeant!" said Landers, quietly.

Blomford snapped to attention, saluted, ran off towards the billet.

The young flyers were all chattering excitedly amongst themselves around themes, describing in lurid detail aspects of their mock combat. There was a lot of laughter and ribaldry.

"Get those fucking machines re-fuelled, Sergeant!" yelled one of them at Sergeant Williams. "We're going up again in ten minutes!"

The Sergeant drilling his men in the street suddenly gave the dismiss order and the group of men all ran past the two officers, heading for the hangars, where they immediately swarmed round the Camels, performing their various tasks.

Captain Spiers emerged from Number 4 after at least five minutes, accompanied by Sergeant Blomford. He had changed from his Sidcot into uniform. He turned on passing the young men outside the mess. " I want those machines in the air in ten minutes, Lieutenant Chessman!" he yelled. "You take charge if I'm not back. I want to see someone shot down!"

The Staff Sergeant had finished brushing the Colonel down as Captain Spiers arrived.

"In here, Captain!" choked the Colonel, pointing to the office.

Inside the airless squadron office the Colonel faced the young Captain. "Remember me, Captain Spiers?" rasped Croxley-Blawford.

"Yessir, you were postings OC at St Omer last year, sir," said Spiers.

"So you are aware that I know your record . . . and I don't mean combat record, Captain?" asked the Colonel, his voice had a harmonic of acute irritation.

"Yessir!"

"Good! At ease, Captain, sit down!" ordered the Colonel.

"I have to be gone in ten minutes, sir, if you don't mind, I must press on with the training schedule."

"Precisely, Captain, that is what I'm here for," said the Colonel.

"You want to know why the squadron has not been operational for seven days, sir, I take it?" asked the young man.

The Colonel nodded, barely able to contain his temper. "I . . ." he began.

"If you don't mind, sir, I'll fill you in on the reasons why," offered Spiers.

"Captain Spiers, I'm not interested in excuses . . . training, and I've heard it all from the Major here . . . I want you over the German lines, and I mean within the next twenty-four hours. Is that understood? I will brook no more prevarication, and tolerate no more excuses. I will check with our

Ops on this sector tomorrow morning to verify that it has been done. Failure to comply with this order, Captain, will result in your court martial at an early date. Am I coming over clear to you?"

"Oh, yessir, and let me assure you, sir, the FOPs will observe the 77th over the German lines at dawn tomorrow, sir. You can rely on it!" Spiers looked hurt and innocent at the same time.

The Colonel regarded the greying hair, the twitch at the eyelid with something akin to fury.

Landers nearly had heart failure at this dumb insolence.

"You're a Bolshevik, Spiers, a rebel and a maverick. I hate men who can't keep in step, Spiers . . . you're the odd man out . . . and there's always one bastard who can't keep time or obey simple instructions. We're fighting a war for survival against a vicious foe, Spiers . . . they want to dominate the world, and we aren't going to permit them to do it. Men who can't obey orders are a liability, Spiers, they prejudice the whole fabric of command. If you want to play it that way, Captain, you'll find me well prepared to make you toe the line. Is that clear, Captain?"

"Crystal, sir," said Spiers, his young face wooden.

Colonel Croxley-Blawford stood up. "I told you last year, Spiers, that I don't tolerate barrack-room lawyers or Bolsheviks and, by Jingo, I mean it. I don't like fancy ideas either . . . all these new-fangled tanks and tactics . . . utterly ridiculous and they're all the work of indisciplined comedians like that Colonel Fuller and his gang of pie-in-the-sky music hall turns. What I'm not going to do, Spiers, is permit such communistic ideas to permeate this command. Understood, Captain?"

"Yessir!" said Spiers, expressionlessly.

"Good! Tomorrow morning then . . . over the German lines, Captain. You are a witness, Major Landers, and I'm holding you responsible. You will both be charged with cowardice in the face of the enemy and court martialled, if my orders are not obeyed. Moreover, I will personally see to it that you both face a firing squad!"

The Colonel picked up his brief-case, swept the papers inside, snapped it shut, planted his hat firmly on his patrician head, stormed out. Landers and Spiers heard the Armstrong roar away before they relaxed.

"We don't stand a fucking chance, do we, Nigel?" said Spiers, quietly. "Can you honestly imagine this bloody country of ours getting anywhere whilst fucking nutcases like him are free to roam around the world?"

"Alright, Bob, for Chrissake keep your voice down!" said Landers, urgently.

"Don't worry, Nigel, the whole squadron will be over Clery at dawn tomorrow," he said. "Can't have the only decent officer we've ever had getting court martialled can we now?"

Landers sat there, sliding the pencil between his fingers, end to end, long after Spiers had gone.

With a sudden vicious movement he hurled the pencil at the sectional drawing of the Sopwith Camel. "Fuck 'em . . .!" he cursed. "Fuck 'em all!"

****

Chapter 16

"I'm getting the Press in, Bob," said Landers, after Bob had made his report.

Bob looked at Landers, amazed. "You crazy, or something, Nigel? That Croxley-Blawford will crucify you. He'll be on that phone in a moment, telling you that the FOPs saw us over the German lines at dawn this morning, and congratulating you on your wisdom and rationality," said Bob. "You tell him that you're getting the Press in to tell them what we're doing about reducing casualties in the RFC and he'll have kittens."

Landers looked at the young-old face before him. "Bob, just before Trevor copped it . . . just three weeks ago, we sat in this office . . . he sat where you're sitting and we talked about the war . . ."

Bob grinned, the skin round his mouth taut and greyish-looking. "Everybody does that, mate . . . doesn't get us anywhere," he said.

"Exactly, and I've seen over forty men come through those doors in the past two months . . . over a hundred since Christmas . . . and most of them I never saw after the first day over the Lines . . . they were dead, and their machines lost forever. Now, whatever you feel about the war, there's nothing, but nothing, that says we have to keep on doing the same old things just to satisfy those ghoulish bastards at Army Command that we're being aggressive and taking the fight to the Germans. I haven't read Napoleonic history like you, Bob, but I did read Roman history and I seem to recall there was a bloke by the name of Pyrrhus, a Greek, who fought the Romans before the Punic wars. He won three battles, but lost so many men that although he won the battles, his losses were more than the Romans, and in the end he had to jack it in . . . he was finished. It seems to me that that's the position the RFC are in right now, and it's going to get worse . . . unless we make a gesture."

"What were you thinking of, Nigel?" asked Bob, curiously, amazed at this new side to Landers, never before revealed.

"You are insisting on training your blokes to fight, Bob, before you expose them to von Dolin-Berensky's Lions. I agree with you, and this morning you proved it. You came back without any losses at all. I want to bring one of the big names in the Press in, ostensibly to take photos of you as our leading ace, but at the same time tell them what you are hoping to achieve by this rigorous training programme."

"Nigel, there's something you should know before you have any more flights of fancy," interrupted Bob.

Landers looked at him, unsure of how far he could trust even Spiers to assist him.

"What is it?" he asked.

"I took those blokes over the lines this morning, as that creep, Croxley-Blawford, ordered. He was looking for a fight and didn't get one, because he thought I'd given in to his brow-beating . . . seven days without being operational and Arras coming up . . . just not cricket, Spiers, you know," mimicked Bob.

"And you brought nine men back with you, counting yourself, of course," said Landers. "That's a vindication of your theories about training."

"Nigel, it is nothing of the sort," said Bob.

"What the hell are you getting at, Bob? You did go over the Line, didn't you?" Landers was appalled.

Bob nodded. "We went over alright . . . at eighteen thousand feet and that's where we stayed, mate," he said. "No observations, no aggressive interdiction of the enemy, not a damned thing . . . I just took them over, let 'em have a taste of Archie and see what life on the other side looks like . . . then I brought them back again . . . in one piece it is true, but we did fuck-all."

Landers looked horrified. "But for Chrissake, Bob . . . how long can you keep that up?" he gasped. "It won't take Croxley-Blawford long to figure that one out and then he'll be down here again . . . shouting his head off, and threatening you and me."

"That's why I'm warning you, Nigel, today was a vindication of nothing . . . yet . . . it will be, but I'm wondering if I'll ever get that far before I'm court martialled for cowardice in the face of the enemy."

"It's about time you levelled with me, Bob, don't you think?" asked Landers. "I'm the one who's going to take the brunt of it first, being the senior officer . . . and I know you'll get it also, but if we are in this thing we may as well be back to back . . . I can't keep that man off you unless you tell me what you have in mind."

"If I tell you that, Nigel, you know as well as I do what'll happen . . . nobody would believe it possible, and I'll be arrested, and so will you . . . or at the very least they'll bring in some toffy-nosed bastard to take over from me, who'll play by the rules of the Top Brass, and I'll never get a chance to try it out," said Bob, bitterly.

"Bob, unless you take me into your confidence, completely, and this is where we have to trust one another . . . to the bitter end, there's no way I can support you. Believe me I want to . . . when Trevor and I talked in here, he said there must be a way of bringing what's going on in the RFC to the notice of the people who count . . . I didn't want to know on that occasion . . . told him he was a nut and he'd end up before a courts martial . . . achieve nothing . . . that was before we lost those eight blokes last week . . . eight in one day . . . then I knew Trevor was right . . . I had to do something, and I want to . . . I believe this is our opportunity, Bob, you and me . . ."

"And end up in the glasshouse . . . for what, Nigel? Bloody martyrdom . . . do you honestly believe it will alter anything if we expose ourselves in this way?" Bob shrugged angrily.

"You want to go on this way, do you, Spiers?" he rasped angrily. "Look at you . . . how old are you, Bob? Eighteen? I'll tell you, you look thirty and older, and your chances of survival become smaller every day . . . you know it, I know it . . . one day, sooner or later, one of von Dolin-Berensky's fellows is going to wipe you out . . . even the great man himself . . . and then what? Yes, you'll be dead, won't have to worry about what goes on any longer, but will that be any satisfaction to you . . . just to give those bastards at HQ something to talk about for five minutes, and then quietly forget you . . . after pinning a posthumous VC on your coffin of course . . . if they every find you, that is . . ."

"Thanks very much, Nigel, I didn't know you cared," sneered Bob. "Makes me feel great knowing how much confidence you have in me."

"Bob!" Landers came round his desk. "I didn't mean it that way, and you know it . . . but it doesn't make it any the less valid . . . you'll be just another number on an unknown grave somewhere in France . . . and you can imagine the crap that's going to be plastered over every village in England when this lot's over, can't you? Gave their all for their country . . . and what about the widows and fatherless kids . . . quite frankly I'd sooner end up in the glasshouse, or shot for cowardice than continue this fucking stupidity for ever. What will the widows and orphans get? What did Wellington's men of the Peninsular get for their wounds and loss of limbs . . . sure, they erected a statue to Wellington, for being a stout fellow, and made him a Duke, but I don't remember seeing a memorial to the fellows that fought at Waterloo or Quatre Bras, do you?"

"Alright, so this Press man arrives with his photographers, and takes pictures of me and the others out there . . . what do we achieve by that? As soon as Croxley-Blawford gets to hear of it, you and I will be on our way . . . our feet won't touch the ground."

"You heard what he said, Bob," said Landers desperately. "He doesn't like fancy ideas . . . new-fangled tanks, and still believes in the cavalry . . . communistic ideas permeating the ranks . . . can you really have faith in men like him, Bob?"

"I wouldn't be here, in this Squadron, if I believed in their ability to lead men, Nigel, but that doesn't help us if we're in the glasshouse awaiting a firing squad," said Bob.

Landers sighed, wearily. "I thought we had something special between you and I, my friend, apart from a common command . . . something that went deeper. When you arrived here last December, I thought you were something special, apart from your youth and experience . . . even when Trevor laid it on the line for you about the reasons for being in the 77th . . . and if you recall what he told you about esprit de corps? Comradeship? Nobody finds a chink in our armour . . . the shitty end of the stick . . . anything nasty to be done, and the 77th get it?"

"Alright, Nigel, you've made your point, but how does that alter anything? That bastard yesterday was mean as hell, and he meant it . . . He's got to mean it, otherwise those blokes in the trenches who think they're fighting the vicious Hun, who are raping women, eating babies, to save England from the Kaiser, are going to start thinking. And if they think, then Croxley-Blawford and his ilk are lost, their mystique has gone . . . no longer born to lead . . . Worcester and four centuries of in-breeding. Oh, no, Nigel, I'm not going to be some martyr on the altar of aristocratic privilege . . . I just want to end this war in one piece and live to a ripe old age . . . I probably won't . . . as you say, the odds against it are high, but no way am I going to be a martyr . . . not for anyone . . . there's no Jean d'Arc in me, or Giordano Bruno."

"That was quite a speech, Captain," said Landers, softly, his voice hard, his face set.

"Is that all, Major?" asked Bob, standing up.

"Not quite, Captain," said Landers.

Bob was startled. Landers had never before come the heavy hand on any officer in the 77th. As Adjutant, he couldn't, but being the senior officer in the unit gave him authority he did not normally enjoy. "Sir?" He stood to attention.

"This training of yours comes to an end, right now. Is that clear, Captain Spiers?" rasped Landers. "You get those flyers of yours over the German Lines and you bring back the information HQ needs . . . and since you've kindly told me how you managed to bring all your men back this morning, and the methods you employed to achieve that desirable end . . . I hereby warn you that any further attempt to avoid what you are paid to do, I, personally, will charge you with cowardice and have you put under close arrest. Have you received the message, loud and clear, Captain?"

"Nigel, what the hell are you doing to me?" gasped Bob.

"Major Landers to you, Captain," snapped Landers, harshly. "And this evening's patrol will be over the German Lines, and I shall give you specific details of the kind of information I need, Captain. Failure to bring back that information will result in your arrest forthwith. Got that?"

"Yes, sir!" Bob spat. "Anything else, sir?"

"Briefing will be at 1700 hours, Captain, in the mess!" Landers turned aside. "That will be all!"

Rage suffused Bob's heart as he stamped out of the Squadron Office. What the hell had got into the Adjutant? Did he really believe that he was going to become a martyr for Croxley-Blawford and his gang of upper-class nits, just so that Landers could fulfil a vague promise to the dead Major Briggs? He could hardly see, so black was his rage.

"All filled up, Sergeant? Ready to go?" he rasped at Sergeant Williams, as he got into the hangar.

"Yessir!" Williams gave his men the sign. No monkey business, the Captain was in one of his moods.

They wheeled the Camel out, watched whilst Spiers went all over it, with penetrating thoroughness. Satisfied, he donned his Sidcot, boots and goggles, swung into the cockpit.

A mechanic swung the prop for him.

The Le Clerget roared smoothly. The Captain took off in a series of gigantic hops and flew over the aerodrome, climbing steeply.

Over Clery-sur-Somme he saw a Rumpler below him at five thousand feet. The observer was bent over his camera, fixed to the side of the machine, unaware of the danger above him. the pilot also was peering over the side, oblivious of danger above. Bob felt numb with fury at Landers, and his suggestion, the way he had turned on him at the end, cold, hard, calculating . . . he'd been wrong about Landers . . . believing him to be on the side of the Just . . . he wasn't, he was just another half-assed wanker thinking about his position in the hierarchy.

He was confused, mixed up. Nothing seemed valid any more, if Landers, that rock of steadfastness, could turn in that manner, then nothing could be relied upon.

He searched the cloud-banked sky above him, holding his thumb against the sun to see if there were any black dots hidden there, using the Rumpler as bait. It was a CV11 and the observer had twin Parabellum machine-guns on a fixed mounting. The Rumpler CV11 was a formidable opponent in the hands of experienced crews, and many an RFC pilot had come drift believing the German machine to be a pushover.

With another swift glance at the sun, he pushed the stick over. German Archie had seen him, and put up a salvo to attract the German pilot's attention to his danger. He was a thousand feet above the Rumpler before the pilot awoke to the peril of the Camel.

Bob saw him thump the observer's shoulder, pointing to the approaching Camel and then the pilot was headed homewards.

Coming down on the eastward side, under the nose of the Rumpler, avoiding the threat of the Spandau synchronised machine-guns, he waited until he was a bare hundred yards before opening fire. He saw his tracers hit the engine of the Rumpler and sparks and smoke pour out immediately. Then the observer let fly with his twin Parabellums, shooting holes in his right wing. The Rumpler turned steeply to allow the gunner full field of fire, as Bob came in from the opposite side. Smoke was still pouring out of the Rumpler's Mercedes engine, blinding the pilot.

Bob gave the Rumpler another burst, which shot off the enemy machine's right aileron.

The Rumpler staggered, and slipped over, as the observer gave him another burst from his Parabellum. The machine, to Bob's surprise, was heading westwards, smoke pouring from the engine nacelle.

He was about to give the Rumpler the coup de grâce, when something held his hand. This could be himself . . . the two benighted Germans in that burning machine, desperately trying to save their lives, and escape from the terrible savagery of the twin Vickers guns on the Camel. He, Bob Spiers, could be Dolin-Berensky in his Fokker triplane, and that stricken Rumpler could be his Camel. Visions of death by burning, Landers's angry face, Croxley-Blawford's mean and vicious expression came before him.

The pilot was looking up at him, the twin Parabellums had evidently jammed and the observer was trying desperately to free the bulging cartridge that blocked the drums. There was a horrified expression of abject fear on his features.

Bob jabbed his finger westwards and down, keeping a steady pace alongside the Rumpler, watchful for any signs that the observer was ready to use his guns again.

The observer suddenly held up his hands in surrender, tipping the Parabellums downwards.

Bob was surprised. There had been stories of air crews of various sides surrendering to victorious fighters, bandied around the mess. He had never before witnessed the incidence of this.

At first, he suspected a trick, and hovered over the crippled Rumpler, menacingly.

the pilot was having great difficulty in keeping the machine airborne, fighting to prevent the Rumpler sliding sideways into a spin.

Over Bray-sur-Somme, he indicated that the German pilot turn northwards. The man obeyed, and a few moments later they were over Lourconter, the ground crews and air crews standing in the field, gaping at the incredible sight.

The Rumpler landed badly, but managed to stay upright. There were a dozen hands all round the enemy machine before the pilot could set fire to it, and had dragged the two Germans from the machine.

He landed himself, some short distance away, taxied the Camel towards the hangars and then walked to meet the two prisoners. The Sergeant was pointing a Lee-Enfield at the two men, who held their hands above their heads.

"That will do, Sergeant!" said Bob, sternly. He motioned for the two young Germans to lower their hands. He held out his hand to the pilot. "Captain Spiers, RFC," he said.

The young man was blond and blue-eyed, and appeared barely as old as Bob himself.

His observer was older, and dark, but with a merry smile. They were both trembling still from their ordeal.

Bob waved Sergeant Blomford away, and his two men with guns, leading the two young Germans into the mess. He gave them two brandies, sat them down and offered them cigarettes.

The observer took one, the pilot refused, indicating that he didn't smoke.

"I am Hauptman Blasczik, and this is Feldwebel Meinvoller," said the young pilot in halting English.

"Robert Spiers . . . Bob, for short," said Bob, wishing he could speak German.

Their names turned out to be Hans and Emile.

Landers came in at that moment, paused when he saw Bob talking to the two prisoners, came over, introduced himself. "HQ have been on the blower, wanting to know when they can interrogate these two," said Landers, his manner still distant and cold. "They're sending two staff officers over immediately to take them away."

"Oh, no!" said Bob, firmly. "They stay for dinner this evening as our guests. They can have them in the morning!"

The young replacement pilots of 77 Squadron all came in, curious to see what their adversaries looked like close up. After introductions, and more drinks, the ice was broken, and the whole mess was soon dancing, and singing, and drinking together. The two young Germans were singing a duet accompanied by one of the British pilots on the piano, when the two staff officers arrived.

****

Chapter 17

Bob recognised the two men immediately. They were the pair who had intercepted him in the reception area of the 112th General Hospital at Amiens, whilst he had been waiting for Barbara Welland.

Both had loud, overbearing public-school voices, bad smells under their noses and waxed moustaches. Both were very tall, and their uniforms immaculate.

They stood in the doorway of the mess, their noses wrinkling at the smell, the fug of tobacco smoke, and the noise. The two Germans were executing an Austrian dance in the middle of the floor to the accompaniment of the piano and hand clapping. Even as the two staff officers glared, disbelievingly, two RFC pilots joined in, slapping knees, then hands, until the whole room resounded to the sound of boots and slapping, whilst the pianist played some unorthodox Austrian Laendler. The young men not dancing were holding brimming pint pots, and swaying them to the rhythm of the dance, clashing their glasses every so often, spilling beer all down their uniforms.

Major Landers called for attention. Nobody paid any attention to him, until he bawled out "Atten-shun!"

The singing and dancing gradually died away, the piano ceased its ump-pah-pah rhythmic thumping, all eyes swung to Landers and the two staff officers. The two young Germans stood to attention, clicking their heels, and bowing to the two officers, stiffly from the neck.

"Fun's over, lads!" called Landers. "These two officers have come to take out prisoners for interrogation."

"Like hell they are, Nigel," said Bob, swaying slightly from too much drink. "They can come for them in the morning . . . tonight, they're our guests!" He turned to the two Germans, bowed and clicked his heels, nearly falling over in the process. He gave the names of the two men to the staff officers, each German bowing and clicking his heels as he did so.

"Now, listen to me, Captain . . . Spiers, isn't it?" wah-wahed the taller man, stepping forward importantly. "We need information from these two enemy officers, and we need it quickly."

"Tomorrow, dear chap, tomorrow!" hiccoughed Bob, swaying close to the finely dressed officer. "Tonight, these gentlemen are the guests of the RFC. That right, you blokes?" He appealed to the air crews.

There was noisy approval and roars of dismay, mixed. "Tell 'em to piss off, Bob!" said a voice from the rear.

More noisy approval. "Yeah, go get fucked, you stuck up bastards . . . tomorrow we're deader than mutton, so tonight we enjoy the company of our friends!" yelled another.

"From the look of 'em I prefer the Jerries!" shouted another to the red-faced staff officers, waving a pint mug in the face of the taller man.

"Yeah, piss off you fellers, go back to your chateaux and get laid. These blokes are with us tonight!"

"Play up, Higgins!" yelled Bob. "Some more of that Austrian Laendler . . . let's get busy!"

He began prancing up and down, first one knee and then the other, slapping his open palm first on one knee and then the other. "Come on, Higgins, what the fuck are you waiting for?"

Higgins began playing uncertainly, and soon lustily as all the young men began prancing and slapping, the two Germans following suit.

"Now, see here, Major Landers, are you going to permit this insubordination?" wah-wahed the tall staff officer, indignantly.

Landers shrugged. "It's accepted RFC practice, gentlemen, all prisoners are the guests of the air crews until the next day," he said, as quietly as he could.

"But you're the senior officer here, order those two Germans released to us at once!" demanded the shorter man, his moustache twitching furiously.

"Just remember who is the senior officer, Captain!" said Landers, coldly. "I cannot go against tradition . . . it would harm the RFC's reputation with our German opponents . . . we try to fly a decent war, even if we are killing one another tomorrow morning!"

"Are you serious, Major Landers?" rasped the first officer. "We must have those two Huns tonight for interrogation . . . we have our orders!"

"Let's take them, Bruce!" said the shorter man. "General Snow will be expecting us to return with them, and now these young fools think they have some God-given right to their rituals!"

"They're Captain Spiers's prisoners, gentlemen," said Landers, a frosty smile on his face. "I suggest you approach him. I'm going back to my office!"

"Aren't you going to order Spiers to release those men, Major?" screamed the taller man, trying to make himself heard over the din.

Landers shook his head. "I suggest you come back tomorrow morning, gentlemen. You've got no chance tonight!" Landers exited without another word.

The two staff officers looked at one another, bemused, then at the prancing young pilots, the drink, the smoke, the noise, then stepped forward in the best British tradition, stiff upper-lips, not shooting until they saw the whites of their eyes. They seized the two Germans, and began dragging them towards the door.

The music ceased, the dancing stopped. All eyes were on the two staff officers and the struggling young German officers. It was deathly quiet.

The bang of the Webley Service revolver shattered all their ear drums. The bullet missed the ear of the tall staff officer by an inch, and ploughed through the mess door.

The four men froze into a tableau, shocked.

Bob held the Webley in both hands, the muzzle rocking slightly, but pointing at the two staff officers. "Let them go, you bastards!" he snarled, thickly.

"Now see here, Spiers," said the staff captain, stepping towards Bob.

The Webley went off again, the floorboards splintering at the captain's feet an inch from his boot.

"Piss off, you snide bastards!" snarled Bob, his eyes bleak. "The next bullet goes through your kneecap, and if you think I'm kidding, try me!"

The two staff men were staring horror-stricken at Bob, the Webley and the bullet hole in the floor. The mess was deathly still, all eyes on Bob and the two staff officers with their red-banded caps.

The man stepped forward again, and another bullet went into the floorboards an inch from his toe. "I'm being reasonable . . . up to now, fuck-face . . . you've outstayed your welcome . . . Piss off!" snarled Bob. "Release those men at once!" The Webley went up, the barrel pointing at the officer holding the two Germans. "Over here, Hans and Emile!" ordered Bob, gesturing with the Webley.

The two Germans did as they were told, horrified at the rank murder in the young Englishman's eyes.

"I'm warning you, Spiers!" rasped the officer.

The Webley cracked out again and the lobe of the staff officer's ear vanished in a welter of blood. "Out!" screamed Bob.

The two men ran for the exit, fear in their eyes.

Bob stood there for a long moment, the Webley held in his hands, wobbling, then he put it on the bar top, and laughed. "That's the first and last time they'll ever get wounded in action!" he roared. "Play up, Higgins, you bastard, let's have some more dancing!"

The young British pilots were stunned, and shocked by this evidence of ruthless determination on the part of their CO. They began dancing again, but with wonder in their eyes, appalled at the thought of the retribution that would follow on Captain Spiers's actions.

****

Landers came awake, his senses alert at the knock at his door. It was dark and the wind was getting up, whistling round the eaves of the cottage in which he had his billet. He glanced at his luminous watch hanging on a nail. Midnight.

"Who is it?" he rapped, irritably.

"Spiers . . . can I come in, Nigel?" came the voice from without.

"Do you know what time it is, Bob?" rapped Landers.

"It's urgent, Nigel!"

"Come in, then!" Landers sat up, his pyjamas hanging loose.

Spiers was still dressed, his tunic unbuttoned and his hair awry. He staggered in, sat on the edge of Landers's cot, rubbing his hands wearily over his face. Landers fumbled with a match to light the hurricane lamp beside his bed.

"What's the problem, Bob?" he asked, coolly, the memory of their row earlier that day still rankling with him.

"I'm sorry we had a slanging match earlier today, Nigel . . . I was an ass. I'm sorry!"

"Forget it, we're both under strain," said Landers, still not wholly contrite, but appreciating Spiers's gesture.

"I want you to get that Press man in, Nigel," said Spiers. "As soon as you can."

Landers's eyes opened wide with amazement. "Look, you don't have to do anything you don't want to, Bob," he said, quietly. "I'm not forcing you to go against your conscience.

"To hell with my conscience, mate," said Spiers. "Get him in and fast, and I'll outline my plan to you . . . why I've been holding these blokes off for the past week. I'm sure it will work, but I need your help to make it operate."

"Well, that's a turnabout, Bob," said Landers, smiling thinly. "What brought this on?"

"There are two Huns sleeping under this roof tonight, Nigel . . . the two from that Rumpler . . . I think you'll agree they are decent fellows, just as lost as we are and hating this bloody lot . . . perhaps even more than we do . . . They don't wanna kill us any more than we do them . . . they're just locked into it, like us . . . because of those bloody politicians wanting to save their lily-white faces and lose no power."

"OK . . . so you've seen the light, Bob, but it wasn't merely those two young Germans was it?" asked Landers, wide awake now.

"No, it wasn't just them . . ." mused Spiers, his hands on his knees, eyes vacant in recollection. "It was when I came over the top of those two in their crate over Clery, looking downwards at the deck, taking photos, and then their engine back spitting out smoke when my bullets hit them . . . I saw it all, then, Nigel . . . all of it . . . the whole stupid fucking mess we are in . . . that could have been me in that Rumpler, and I could have been von Dolin-Berensky . . . Spandaus lined up on my back . . . it was a nasty feeling, Nigel . . . oh, I know, there have been others, dozens of them, and I've never had any qualms, but that slanging match we had this morning and what you said about how I look, and my chances of survival getting slimmer by virtue of the laws of chance and averages . . . and as you said, just to give the toffy-nosed bastards like those two this evening, something to talk about for five minutes . . . good man, that Spiers, pity he had to go and get himself shot down . . . dashed bad luck . . . never mind . . . plenty more where he came from you chaps."

"Came home to you, Bob?" asked Landers, sympathetically. "I didn't mean to be so vicious . . . I was just angry . . . it doesn't have to happen that way."

"But it will, mate, look at Ball, Boolcke, Immelmann, Lanoe-Hawker, Rhys-David, and all the others . . . they no doubt thought they were immortal . . . until the last moment and then . . . presto, it was all over . . . dead as mutton . . . and gone for ever . . . and it is going to happen to me . . . I can feel it in my bones."

"You're just being morbid, Bob," protested Landers.

Spiers shook his head . . . "I can feel it deep down, Nigel . . . it's like a cloud hanging over my head . . . can't shake it off . . . I know I haven't much longer, and so let's get busy with the Press."

"You said you had a plan?"

Spiers nodded. "I'll give you the outline now, if you're not too tired, and we'll work out the details later . . . it's going to need the co-operation of Capitaine Pierre Lascalle and his Spads . . ."

****

Chapter 18

The British Press were present when General Honore de Jessuinde, Commander of the Ninth French Army in Flanders presented Captain Robert Spiers with his Croix de Guerre . . . for services to the Allied cause.

The silent ranks of recipients of awards, mostly Frenchmen, stood on the windy parade ground, awaiting their turn to march forward before the General and his aides. General de Jessuinde had been with Gallieni on the Marne in 1914, helping to turn the Boche line as they were about to enter Paris. His chest was full of decorations, and his breath smelled of garlic and wine. He also had an evening shadow that rasped as he kissed Bob on both cheeks.

Bob stepped back, saluted, then marched off to join Pierre Lascalle and four other flyers who had received the award of the Croix de Guerre.

"My friend! That was terrific . . . honoured by my country for valour and services against the Boche . . . fantastic!" Lascalle was full of emotion, hugging Bob as he joined the group. His little black eyes were shining with pride at his friend and the recognition accorded him by a grateful France.

"Dinner now, my friend, not snails, assure you, but something to suit your quaint English stomach . . . mince beef and cabbage, eh?" Lascalle clapped him on the back, and introduced him to the other Frenchmen.

In a fashionable restaurant, they all sat round a table for six, and drank and ate until they couldn't eat any more and were slightly drunk.

"Now, a nice mademoiselle for our English friend, eh?" roared Lascalle, posing for a photographer who had entered the restaurant on hearing Lascalle was there. The little French ace insisted that the photographer took one of he and Bob together and insisted that he publish them together. "Someone who will give him the full treatment . . . and leave him fulfilled . . . no low-class whores, but a fine young woman of good family . . . marvellous!"

Bob made his escape, excusing this latter offer by saying he was tired and would not do any woman justice. He made Lascalle promise to come over to Lourconter the following day. He had a plan he wished to discuss with him . . . that would bring glory to both of them.

He was walking along the long boulevarde, peering into the shop windows for want of something better to do, when he heard his name called.

"Robert! Robert Spiers!" shouted the voice again. "Over here!"

Charles Martine was standing beside an old taxi, beckoning to him.

"Charles, how nice to see you, my friend!" said Bob, shaking hands with the aristocratic looking man. He noticed the Colonel's crown and pips on his epaulettes.

"Congratulations on your promotion, my friend," he said, delightedly.

"And your decorations, Robert," said Martine. "Did he smell of garlic?"

Bob grinned. "And stale wine . . . needed a bath as well!"

Martine grinned. "Come on . . . join me . . . I have someone who wants to meet you!"

Bob was about to refuse when he thought of Colonel Croxley-Blawford and the incident in the mess with the two staff officers two evenings before. There had been a stony silence from General Snow's HQ over the incident. No reprimand, not a word of censure and still less about the threat from the Colonel with reference to his training activities. It had been over ten days now since he had commenced the operation, and his young flyers were becoming skilled and confident in the handling of their aircraft and weaponry. Landers, since their meeting in the Adjutant's bedroom the same night, had eased off his insistence on fulfilling the Army Command's request for full information. The plan he had evolved and explained to Landers was moving towards fruition, but the silence from VII Corps HQ was worrying. Surely they wouldn't allow his treatment of the two staff men to go unnoticed and ignored. If the award of the Croix de Guerre from General de Jessuinde had anything to do with it, then he had underestimated the Colonel. Croxley-Blawford was not renowned for magnanimity.

"Alright," he said, getting into the taxi with Martine.

Martine took him to a hotel near the station, paid off the taxi-man, and escorted Bob into the foyer.

For some unaccountable reason, the foyer was full of press men and they insisted on taking photos of Martine and Bob together. Bob had to given an impromptu interview with English, French, Swiss and American journalists on his life as a combat pilot on the Western Front. It seemed to be more than a mere coincidence.

In the bar, swarming with uniforms of all kinds, he faced Martine. For a man who had commenced his military career at the same time as Bob, his rise had been meteoric. Now a full Staff Colonel, in spite of his youth, it smacked of string-pulling in high places.

"You've had a hard time recently, Bob," said Charles, over brandy. "And you've given the General's staff a hard time as well, haven't you?"

"How did you know that?" Bob hardly touched his drink. He'd had enough with Lascalle and his comrades.

"My dear fellow, I'm on his staff myself, I should know. Fossett and Moran are very upset about the affair the other night in your mess, and are demanding your arrest for disobeying orders over those two Germans you captured," said Martine, seriously.

"Why haven't I been arrested?" asked Bob, directly.

"They can hardly arrest a man who has been decorated for bravery by our Allies, can they now? . . . picture in all the papers in Blighty . . . the youngest ace in the RFC and a man who has captured a German aeroplane, intact, together with its crew . . . very impolitic of them if they did." Martine sipped his brandy slowly. His face showed no signs of strain and was as smooth as it had been when they had joined the 9th FTS at Denham the previous June. There was now a definite bend in his nose that hadn't been present before their fight in the mess but, apart from that, Martine looked just as smooth as the day he had joined.

"But you think they will . . . when the moment is right?" he asked, slowly.

Martine looked at him, his voice barely distinguishable over the noise of voices around them. "Robert, the General is worried about this extensive training you're going in for with your replacements. We need every aircraft we can get over the Front just now, because of the impending offensive at Arras. The General's Corps is going to play a major part in the attack, and is the most southerly hinge of the Allied thrust . . . it's a crucial displacement and could mean success or failure for the British if General Snow's attack falters. We need information, fast, all the time, and the absence of intelligence gathering by one squadron can be vital."

"You know the reason I'm in the 77th, Charles," said Bob. "It's the dustbin of the RFC . . . I don't have to tell you that all the mavericks are in the unit . . . the misfits and the men who can't get on with others in orthodox units of the RFC. You must know the kind of casualty rate we've been having since Christmas, in men and machines. I want to break out of it . . . prepare them thoroughly so that when they do meet von Dolin-Berensky's Lions they can give them a good account of themselves," said Bob.

"I know your theory, Bob, and I know Boom Trenchard would approve, but we can't afford luxuries like withholding support at the critical point," said Martine.

"Charles, you know as well as I do that if we send those blokes out ill-prepared they'll last ten minutes against von Dolin-Berensky's Jasta, and then we'll be back in square one again, with more replacements and more machines," protested Bob.

Martine shrugged. "I try hard on your behalf, Bob, and whilst not over-estimating my influence with the Old Man, I can't keep him off your back for ever. He's screaming for results, and intelligence, and sooner or later will order me to direct you to do what you're supposed to do. Croxley-Blawford is bad news wherever he goes, but his father is on the War Council, has Lloyd George's ear and the Old Man can't afford to ignore him."

"Are you telling me this in an official capacity, Charles, or are you just dropping a hint?" asked Bob.

"Let's say that a word in the ear of the wise . . ." said Martine, leaving it unfinished.

"Alright, I understand, but I can tell you this, that if I'm allowed to complete my training plan and a new idea that I've been working on . . . I think even those dilletantes at HQ will be surprised," promised Bob.

"I'll pass your comments on, unofficially, of course," said Martine. "Anyway, let's forget the war for a moment, and come and meet someone," smiled Charles, patting Bob on the shoulder.

They walked into the wide lounge, the photographers' magnesium flashes blinding everyone, as they photographed their latest idol for the news hungry people in Blighty.

Thirty-five enemy aircraft shot down and still under eighteen.

He saw her before Martine could say anything. Dressed in a silken gown that showed her figure off to perfection, Michelle was even more beautiful than he recalled.

She came up to him, smiling, her hand held out. An enterprising photographer took a photo of them together.

"Robert," she smiled, and kissed him, in front of all the envious eyes of the officers present. "How lovely to see you again. Famous now, aren't you?"

"All in the mind," he assured her.

She reached out, touched his greying hair, ran her fingertips down his cheek. "My God! Do they have to make men out of boys, Charles?" she demanded, angrily.

"Hey, what's this boy business?" demanded Bob, amused, with an undertone of acerbity.

"Robert! They're making you old before you've even had your youth." she said, softly.

The memories of those nights in the Martine household came back to him, poignantly, their love-making in his room, and her slow departure early in the morning to go back to her own, and her face, stricken, and weeping unashamedly on the platform at Waterloo, begging him to write to her . . . the fantasies he had indulged in of marriage and home together, and the impossibility of it, bearing in mind their social status and position. He had no job, no prospects, no hope of being able to support a wife. Marriage to Michelle would be even more impossible than a similar proposal with Barbara Welland. It all came back to him in a kaleidoscope of emotions and recollections.

"I thought perhaps you'd like to have a chat together?" grinned Martine. "I have an appointment at HQ in a short while, so I'll leave you two together. Bear in mind what I told you, Robert!"

Then he was gone and he was alone with Michelle, feeling shy and diffident, despite the memory of their intimacy just before Christmas.

"Your letters were marvellous, Robert," she whispered, her eyes shining, as she leaned close to him. "I've kept them all . . . tied up with red ribbon in a secret place in my room in Bayswater."

He couldn't tell her that he'd had to destroy all hers, because of the prying fingers of Matthews, his batman. The stories would have been round the men's billets in no time at all, despite Corporal Matthews's fierce loyalty to him. "They were marvellous," he whispered, conscious of the eyes of all the military men upon them. "I read yours over and over again."

"We can't talk here, Robert," she said. "It's too public, and I want to hold you close."

"Where can we go?" he asked, anguished.

"To my room, darling," she said, softly.

"You're staying here?" he gasped.

"Daddy and I are over in France on War Department business, and I persuaded him to let me accompany him as his secretary," she giggled, laughing. "You should have seen the looks on the faces of the top brass . . . thought I had a sugar daddy!"

"Will it be alright?" he asked, unsure.

"Robert, this is France . . . not stuffy old England. There's been an English officer and his French mistress in the room next to mine for the past two days," she laughed. "I don't think they've been out of their bedroom all that time!"

"Tell me the room number and I'll come up in a few moments," he promised. "If you're sure it's going to be alright?"

"Of course I'm sure!"

She stood up, walked slowly over to the lift with its old-fashioned iron grill and shaft exposed all the way up, waved to him as she entered.

He arose, self-consciously, looked around the lounge at the military men sitting or standing in groups talking, and then walked into the foyer and out into the busy street.

He found the rear entrance to the hotel in a dingy back street, went up the fire escape stairs to the room number she had given him.

He passed two groups of officers on the way up. They didn't even acknowledge him so intent were they upon their own business.

He didn't have to knock, Michelle opening the door to him without a pause.

She was in his arms in a trice, kissing him hungrily . . .

Later he said. "I have to be back at Lourconter tonight . . . I only came to Amiens to get this medal from a smelly French General."

"Don't let's waste time then," she said, sliding her bare arms round his neck, pulling him down to her.

"What if your father should come back unexpectedly?" he asked, clasping her slim body.

"He has his own room, darling, don't be silly . . . couldn't sleep with his secretary now, could he? Everybody would be scandalised," she whispered, nibbling his ear.

"He'd be even more scandalised if he could see you now," he said, worriedly.

"Well, he won't, will he?" she said, sliding her hand downwards.

He sat up, holding her searching fingers in his. "What happens, afterwards?" he asked, seriously.

She stopped, looking at him, then sat up beside him. "We're going to be all self-conscious now, are we? Want to make an honest woman of me, is that it?" she asked.

"Is that so unimportant?" he asked.

"Right now, it is, Robert, darling," she said, trying pull him down again.

He resisted. "Tell me what would have happened if we hadn't met as we did . . . me in the RFC with Charles . . . if I were just ordinary Mister Spiers, instead of Bob Spiers with a captain's pips and all this notoriety, and we'd met in London . . ." he asked her.

She straightened up. "You want the truth, plainly . . . since all you men are something of a lot of masochists," Michelle's eyes were brittle.

"That's us, masochists," he agreed, sombrely.

"We probably wouldn't have got as far as a 'hello'," she said. "The social divisions would have prevented the opportunity."

"Exactly, so what happens afterwards?" he said, gruffly, irritated at her candour.

"After what? . . . the war . . . the Armageddon, holocaust, when the revolution happens, as it is going to happen in Russia?" Her eyes were wide now, a glint of hardness in them.

"The answer to that, Robert, is that I don't know . . . it's all a long way off, and a lot of things could happen in the meantime."

"I could conveniently be killed?" he suggested, harshly. "And then you'd be absolved the necessity of making a decision?"

She sighed. "Oh, dear, we are in a bitter mood, aren't we?" she said. "And the answer to that question is yes, you could be killed, and that's a reason I don't propose making any decision about anything, you, me, the future, anything . . . I'm just going to enjoy myself, and you should do the same, perhaps even more than me, Robert."

"Nice, isn't it?" he sneered. "I mustn't think about the future because I'm involved in the messy business of killing my fellow men . . . and the social divisions that would prevent us meeting under normal circumstances are going to operate again, when it is all over, and if I'm here to witness it. Doesn't matter about my social status whilst I'm useful to my country and King, of course, fighting the enemies of the politicians . . ."

"Robert!" she snapped. "If you really want to talk about the future, we can. Have you ever worked? Have you any skills? Any qualifications .

. . apart from being able to fly an aeroplane, well? How do you think you'll stack up in civilian life when the war is over? Will you be able to compete with Charles, and Vyvyan de Vinguind and Bertie Launcey-Moore?"

"I don't stand an earthly," he agreed. "They've got a head start on me, with money and influence."

"Alright, now, if you want to compete, and think about the great distant future . . . I'll help you . . . Daddy has friends all over the place, in business, civil service, banking. I'll speak up for you, help you get a position you'd be proud of. Will that do? Now stop this idiotic talk and make love to me again. If you really have got to be back at that aerodrome of yours tonight we haven't much time, and I love you."

"Just like that," he said, bitterly.

She sighed exaggeratedly. "Oh, God, you are a masochist, aren't you? Do you want to wallow in social differences, make yourself a martyr to class privilege? I had you catalogued as someone special, Robert, a real man, not like these fops that fuss around me most of the time . . . I know what they're after, apart from the obvious, and they think they're in the running . . . they don't stand a chance against you, darling."

Her voice changed to pleading, her eyes softening once more.

He left her at the last possible moment to be in time to catch the tender back to Lourconter.

She kissed him, tenderly. "I love you, Robert, always remember that," she whispered. "And keep writing to me, won't you, please?" Her eyes were large, luminous, lips parted.

Corporal Matthews met him with the Squadron Crossley outside the station.

He was silent all the way back to Lourconter, thinking of Michelle and his life. Had he really got a future? The black depression he had been in over the past weeks seemed to have lifted somewhat during the time he had been with Michelle. The omniscient feeling of ultimate disaster had not, however.

Landers met him upon his arrival, congratulating him on his receipt of the Croix de Guerre from General de Jessuinde. The Major's face was worried. "Orders for a dawn patrol . . . from Snow himself . . . and I have to acknowledge receipt of them," he said.

"Alright, I'll handle it," he said. "You can acknowledge receipt, Nigel. It will be carried out."

Landers looked relieved.

"I want to use your phone, please, Nigel," he said.

Landers indicated the instrument.

Lascalle answered almost immediately, and agreed to provide protection for his fledglings on the morrow, promising to return to Lourconter with the 77th to discuss Bob's plan.

****

Chapter 19

He was awakened by the ear-splitting roar of a Le Clerget.

Startled, he sat up, grabbed his luminous watch and peered at it. It was still dark and he was so tired he could hardly open his eyes wide enough to see the time. Five o'clock! What the devil . . . ?

He jumped out of bed, pulled his Sidcot on over his pyjamas and put his feet into slippers, ran down the stairs, into the bitter cold pre-dawn morning.

As he emerged from Number 4, a Camel, dimly outlined in the eerie light, staggered down the field and took off into the lowering sky.

"Who the hell is that, Sergeant?" he demanded of Williams, who was standing, shaking his head despairingly.

"Lieutenant Chesney, sir . . . ordered me to get his crate ready for five a.m., sir," said the Sergeant.

"Did he say where he was going?"

"No, sir, muttered something about getting his first Hun, sir," said the Sergeant.

"Shit!" cursed Bob, savagely. "The stupid bastard will get his ass shot off by a Lion and we'll be in the khazi again." He turned to Williams as the sound of the Le Clerget faded. "My compliments to all pilots, Sergeant, and tell them I want them all down here at the double. Wheel the rest of the squadron out, get them warmed up."

The Sergeant gave instructions to that effect as Major Landers came up, shivering, clad only in his dressing gown.

"Who, in God's name, was that, Bob?" he demanded.

"Chesney . . . gone to get his first Hun!" snarled Bob.

The first of the Le Clergets broke into sudden life, drowning all other sounds. It was followed by the others in quick succession, the smell of castor oil and aviation fuel stinging his nostrils.

A cold wind had already started up, making Landers shiver even more. Banks of cumulus cloud drifted overhead, blanking out the stars. The first greyness of dawn was creeping into the eastern sky. The silhouettes of the Camels could be seen now, against a grey-green background of grass and poplars.

The pilots began to arrive, nearly all with Sidcots donned over pyjamas. They all demanded to know what was going on. Bob told them tersely, his voice a snarl of ill-disguised bad temper.

"Now, listen to me, you lot," he choked. "I don't want any more bloody dead heroes, and if I catch one of you going down after something he thinks is easy meat, I, personally, will crucify the bastard, is that understood? We'll have enough on our plates finding Chesney . . . if he's still alive . . . When we find him we get back over the Line, is that clear?"

They all chorused their understanding.

"One more thing, we are meeting the French over Le Sars, who will protect our backs, whilst Lieutenants Shalter and Burgess go down with me to have a look at the Hun. Both of you know what to look for now, just make a note of anything you see you feel could be useful in the way of movements, guns, infantry columns, ammunition dumps, gas dumps . . . anything, put it in the cannisters you have been provided with, fly over the Thiepval co-ordinate, and drop them. You then fly back here. Is that clear? I want no heroics, no shooting up Huns and no fancy manoeuvring . . . just get the hell out of there as soon as you've done what's asked of you. You, Lieutenant Latimer, will be in charge of the rest of the squadron. You will fly at six thousand feet, under the protection of the Spads under Capitaine Lascalle, but if von Dolin-Berensky's lot appear, then you make for home as fast as you can make it."

"Do we leave the Froggies to the Hun, sir?" asked one young man.

"Those Froggies are all experienced pilots, with an impressive chain of kills to their credit . . . The Spad, as you know, is a fast machine and can outmanoeuvre most of the Hun machines and, what's more, there are more of them than us . . . fifteen of them who can handle the Lions if they show up!"

"But what if we are attached by the Hun, sir?" asked another. "Do we still run?"

"You get out as quickly as you can. Capitaine Lascalle knows this, I have already made out plans with him. He understands what is required of his men."

The young men he had so vigorously trained over the past ten days all looked at one another bewildered. They were raring to go and were being held back. They couldn't understand why.

They crossed the Line at eleven thousand feet over Clery-sur-Somme and turned north towards Boucheresnes and Etricourt. They saw nothing of Lieutenant Chesney, and the watery sun was plainly threatening rain shortly.

Sweeping westwards towards the rear of the German defences, they arrived over Le Sars in time to see fifteen Spads already arrayed over them at fifteen thousand feet. Masses of cumulus cloud were drifting eastwards, and offered a perfect hiding place for von Dolin-Berensky's Lion Jasta. The Spads of Lascalle's squadron were hidden from view for minutes at a time by the cloud banks, providing ample opportunity for the experienced German pilots to attack the Camels before aid could arrive.

He signalled for Shalter and Burgess to start down with him.

They arrived down behind the German lines to the accompaniment of Archie . . . black puffs of flame and smoke, making Shalter and Burgess swerve nervously. Bob could see Shalter and Burgess staring with awed curiosity at the disfigured landscape of tree stumps, shattered buildings and shell-holes, through which tiny insect humans moved painfully slowly.

He fired a warning burst from his Vickers to alert them to get on with the job in hand, waving at them frantically to press on. Every few seconds he gazed upwards to try to locate the protective Camels and Spads, but the cloud banks obscured much of the sky. Some black-edged clouds were gathering towards the west, and a faint rainbow was being etched against the light blue canopy of heaven. He groaned. That would be all they needed . . . a rain shower to completely obscure the view, and von Dolin-Berensky's Lions waiting, like their namesakes, for the kill, hovering on the rain shower's edge, waiting for their prey to emerge.

He and his two companions made several runs over the crazy terrain of shell-holes and shattered houses, seeing long columns of troops in field grey moving forward, long lines of horse-drawn artillery, wagons carrying shells and other munitions, convoys of heavy vehicles bringing in stores and food for the troops already in situ. He then signalled for Shalter and Burgess to make their run for Thiepval to the south-west of Le Sars, drop their cannisters and make their runs for Lourconter. As far as he was concerned, he had carried out his promise to Landers to do what they had been ordered by VII Corps orders. A sensation of anxiety cloaked all his emotions. He wanted this squadron, on whom he had lavished such care in training, intact for the denouement, as he saw it, of all the hours in mock aerial combat. Shalter and Burgess were zigzagging over the pock-marked ground towards Thiepval when he began his climb to rejoin the other Camels over Le Sars.

With a thrill of horror he saw the whirling, diving, rolling, looping specks far above his head. Even as the watched a long plume of smoke began to pour from one aircraft, whose identity he could not define. It plunged earthwards. Even at the distance he was from it, he could hear the ghastly whine of the engine. Another aircraft began to spin, pieces hanging from the wings like ruffled feathers. He was into a cloud and on emerging he found himself face to face with a motley collection of Fokker triplanes, Albatross and Pfalz scouts. There must have been fifteen of them.

They were as startled as he was, but reacted like veterans. In a few seconds the sky was full of whirling aircraft, diving, rolling, spinning. Machine-guns sounded and trails of cordite smoke poured back from cowlings as the Germans sought to eradicate this lone Camel.

A Fokker with green and black stripes along its sides, a blue lion inscribed along the fuselage, came at him, Spandaus yammering, simultaneously with another Albatross painted a violent pink with blue crosses all over it.

Pieces of the top plane peeled back, exposing the framework beneath, as he dived to avoid the converging streams of tracer. Bullets were hammering away at his back and his windscreen disappeared as if by magic. A stream of bullets shattered his dashboard, sending showers of splinters over this face and arms. The Vickers mountings suddenly erupted into potato peelings as a hail of Spandau tracer lanced along their lengths. The centre-section front strut went with a sickening crunch, leaving the wing shuddering in the slipstream. Oil stains were creeping over the cowling in long spiders' legs of black gunge, flecks of the burnt castor oil spotting his goggles.

He flew into a cloud, a black Fokker close on his tail. He switched off the engine with the automatic starting device on the joystick. Allowed the Camel to falter and turn into a spin.

At under five thousand feet he emerged, to find himself almost directly over the German trenches. Above him, the Fokkers, Albatross and Pflaz aeroplanes were puzzledly searching the skies for his Camel like a swarm of bees disturbed from their hive. Farther above them still he could see a formation of planes that resembled Camels and Spads flying in strict formation.

Flattening out, he flew low over the British trenches, astounded to see a hawthorn bush in full blossom amidst the horrific panorama of destruction. There were some underpants draped across the lower branches. A geyser of mud and debris was thrown up suddenly, a howitzer shell landed just behind the secondary British trenches. The underpants fluttered down from the tree.

British troops waved to him as he hedge-hopped over the garish landscape, keeping a wary eye out behind him for signs of pursuit from the Lion Jasta. His goggles were all fouled by the sprays of burnt oil from the cowling. Pushing them up, he gazed downwards for some landmark to establish his position. He recognised Combles out to his right, the valleys and hills of the Somme region were bursting into their Spring colours. Behind the front, greenery was paramount, and the warming earth promised renewal. From the stench, noise and decay of the Front Lines, sprang the inevitable thrust of irrepressible nature, daffodils thrust up from wasteland, crocii and cowslips burst into life behind the shattered stumps of trees in the forests.

As he flew low over the cattle and sheep on the farms of the Pas de Calais towards Bray-sur-Somme, it seemed that the depression hanging over him for months could be lifted in this resurgence of life from the earth.

The Spads of Lascalle's Escradille were lined up on the tarmac at Lourconter, along with seven Camels. He could hardly believe his eyes. Seven! Impossible, not after an encounter with von Dolin-Berensky's Lions. He rubbed his eyes, counted again. Seven it was.

He landed after flying low over the aerodrome twice. The shattered main strut was weakening every moment, threatening to discard the top plane completely. The oil slick coming back over the engine cowling had now completely smeared the front of the Camel's stubby nose. The Vickers mountings were like obscene flowers, opening up to the command of cordite and lead. The dashboard looked as if it had been vandalised by an axeman. There were large sections of the inner framework of spruce exposed where bullets had ripped away fabric and wood.

Mechanics grabbed his wing-tips as he taxied up to the lined up Spads and Camels. A mass of pilots, both French and British surrounded his aircraft as he switched off and sat back in his cockpit, wearily wiping his oil-smeared face with a cloth.

"My friend! What happened to you?" enquired Lascalle stepping up to Bob. "We search everywhere for you!"

"You OK, Bob?" asked Major Landers, his thin face concerned.

Bob nodded. "Who's missing?" he asked, climbing out.

"Chesney . . . I'm afraid," said Landers over the noisy greetings of Bob's men.

"Murchison downed a Hun and so did Clements," he added.

"Who else is missing?"

"Langley," said Landers.

There were noisy greetings from his young flyers, slapping him on the back, and then the Frenchmen.

"Your fledglings did well, my friend," said Lascalle. "We have all been hearing about your training methods and wondering what effect it would have on performance. It was good."

Over lunch in the mess, there were noisy toasts and greetings from all the pilots anxious to appear veterans after their first combat in the skies. Tales of narrow escapes, encounters with Fokkers and Albatross and Pfalz were retold countless times. The enthusiasm was infectious.

"Hush!" said Bob suddenly during their dessert.

Everybody ceased talking to listen, straining their ears.

They all heard it, the sound of a Le Clerget, faltering and roaring alternately.

All rushed outside onto the street, eyes shaded peering eastwards.

A lone Camel was swerving and fish-tailing over the eastern approaches to the aerodrome, executing crazy manoeuvres. The fire tender screamed into action, and then everyone was running to the anticipated spot the Camel would touch down.

It bounced once, twice, lurched onto a wing-tip, recovered, miraculously, then began a drunken path towards the hangars. there was something odd about the machine that Bob could not immediately determine, apart from the waltzing and lurching.

Mechanics grabbed the wing-tips, steadying the Camel, as the pilot switched off and the propeller gasped to a standstill.

****

Chapter 19

Lieutenant Chesney's pale face, twisted with pain, peered at them from the cockpit of his Camel. "Can . . . can someone help me out?" he gasped. "My leg!"

Willing hands eased him from the cockpit to the ground.

"It's bandaged!" exclaimed one of the British pilots. "And there's another round his chest!"

"Hey! Look at this!" shouted another excitedly, pointing to the fuselage. A large sheet of white cardboard had been pasted to the fuselage.

Then Bob noticed what was wrong with the Camel. The twin Vickers had been removed leaving only the grooved mountings.

"What's it say, Larry?" called someone, from the outer edge of the crowd.

" 'To the pilots of 77 Squadron RFC," read out the man, bending down. "We have returned your Lieutenant Chesney, who has been our guest for a few hours. He has been badly wounded, but expressed a wish to go back to England to convalesce. He is returned with our compliments and a medical report on his injuries will be found inside his flying suit. We salute the brave flyers of 77 Squadron, Sincerely, A von D-B.' "

"Jesus!" gasped someone. "That's the first time in history this has happened, I'll bet."

Lascalle's face was a study in consternation. "These Boche are diabolically clever swine," he muttered.

Chesney was almost fainting with the pain. Landers put his hand inside the Lieutenant's Sidcot and withdrew a large package, decorated with the German Imperial Eagles, opened it and nodded. "Medical report," he said, briefly, as the ambulance arrived to take Chesney away.

Landers pinned the envelope to Chesney's jacket, pointing it out to the medical orderlies, who placed Chesney on a stretcher.

It was a rather subdued company that reassembled in the mess a short time afterwards. Everyone talked about the incident, giving their opinions as to why the Germans had taken all this trouble to send Chesney back, and with his Camel, a prize the German Air Force must have dearly appreciated.

Bob stood on the table. His earlier fury at Chesney's ill-considered action in taking off without his permission had evaporated somewhat on seeing the Lieutenant's condition and the circumstances of his return.

"Gentlemen!" he called. "Your attention, please!"

All eyes were on him.

"I want to tell you about an idea I have that should compensate both of our squadrons for the humiliation we have suffered today at the hands of Anton von Dolin-Berensky's Lion Jasta. If someone could translate for those of our French allies who do not understand English, it would be helpful."

All eyes were upon him, including those of Major Landers, who had received the brunt of VII Corps staff demands for more action from 77 Squadron over the past four days. Colonel Croxley-Blawford had paid 77 Squadron yet another visit, the day before Bob's investiture at Amiens by General de Jessuinde, demanding that Major Landers's temporary squadron leader take up the men of the squadron and carry out the activity for which VII Corps HQ were asking. Today's affray over the German Lines had been an attempt on Bob's part to fulfill, at least in letter, if not in deed, the uncomplimentary requests by the Colonel. Landers's eyes were sunken hollows in his naturally pale face, and there was a tautness around his mouth that belied his outwards calm. Bob realised that unless he put his plan into action with despatch, the Colonel would summarily carry out his threat to remove Landers and he from command. His career would thus end in ignominious defeat at the hands of the establishment. All the new pilots were aware of the tension between the two senior officers of the squadron and the staff officers of HQ. Bob's action in the mess the evening of the capture of the Rumpler had excited but appalled them. Retribution, they were convinced, was only a matter of time, and their leader would be the recipient of exemplary disciplinary action of the most severe sort.

Conscious of these pressures, Bob looked down upon the faces of his comrades and the French flyers under Lascalle, who had agreed to co-operate in Bob's plan.

"We all know what happens after a dogfight over the Lines," he began, to the silent waiting assembly. "We become separated and we drift home in ones or twos or in small groups. We feel somehow safe once we are over our own Lines and over British . . . sorry . . . French territory . . . we cast nearly all caution to the winds, and just concentrate on getting home as fast as we can. Isn't that correct?" He paused to test reaction to this surmise. There were nods and murmurs of agreement. "How many of us even bother to glance backwards, or up into the sun for signs of enemy aircraft?" He paused again. More nods and murmurs. "None of us, because we all believe that since the Hun rarely flies over our Line and the wind is nearly always a prevailing south-westerly blowing over our trenches towards Germany, we feel safe, and free from interference." He knew he was addressing himself more to Lascalle than his own inexperienced pilots, but Lascalle's co-operation was vital to his plan. "I know that once over our Lines I have rarely, if ever, looked behind me . . . I am confident that there will be no Hun machines stacked up in the sun, watching me . . . and that, gentlemen, is really a terrifying thought."

Already there was a gleam in Lascalle's eye, an excitement that had not been there before, as if he divined the processes of Bob's thoughts. "Bravo, my friend!" he called out in French, translating for those of his men who did not speak English, the substance of Bob's message.

"Yes, gentlemen, terrifying . . . we feel safe and relaxed . . . no more fears about Fokkers and Albatross attacking us once we are over our own trenches. But let me put it to you, gentlemen . . . what would happen if, and I say, if, there were fifteen of von Dolin-Berensky's Lions waiting over our aerodrome for us to arrive in? Relaxed, comfortable, feeling secure?"

Lascalle could not restrain himself any longer. "Bravo, my friend, a fantastic idea! We wait for the Boche to arrive back at their aerodrome at Cussigny . . . safe, feeling well satisfied with events, having killed several of our comrades and looking forward to some Schnapps and an evening listening to Wagner on the gramophone . . . and then . . . pouff! The members of Escradille Lascalle jump on them from the skies and finish them off?" He could not contain his excitement any longer. He was literally dancing up and down. "It is brilliant, my friend! We carry the war to the Boche's own . . . how you say . . . backyard? Bang, bang, and it is all over for the Lion Jasta of von Dolin-Berensky?"

He translated rapidly for the benefit of his colleagues. Once they had grasped the essentials of the plan, were wild with enthusiasm. The British and French pilots all began toasting one another.

Bob held up his hand. "There is just one thing wrong with Capitaine Lascalle's evaluation of who does the killing," he said, into the sudden silence. "It is not the Escradille Lascalle . . . it is 77 Squadron who does the killing!"

There were furious protests from the Frenchmen and cheers from the British and, for a moment, it looked as if the allies were about to become enemies. Fists were brandished in faces and insults could be heard, cursing one another.

"Non! The Escradille Lascalle will do the killing, my friend!" shouted Lascalle, his black eyes furious. "We are better at it than you British . . . we are more experienced!"

"Shut up, you Froggy bastard!" roared Burgess, the big man who had shared Bob's mission over the German trenches. "It is our plan . . . we do the killing!" The two men squared up to one another, like tomcats, the burly Burgess towering over the diminutive Lascalle. One of Lascalle's pilots, a huge Frenchman called Houdinot, faced Burgess over the top of his little Captain's head. "I twist your roast beef neck off," he threatened.

Landers stepped into the melée smoothly. "Gentlemen, we are fighting the Boche, not ourselves!" he said, coolly. "There is an honourable way to settle this question!"

The two sides, squaring up to one another preparatory to having a punch-up paused and looked at Landers.

The Major held a French franc, diplomatically in his hand, tossing it up and down spinning. "We toss the coin . . . the side who calls the head of the President of the Republic . . . wins!"

There were some mutterings amongst the fliers, still glowering at one another over the table on which Bob stood.

"How about it, Pierre?" asked Bob, smiling. "Do we toss the coin, or do we have dogfight in the mess here?"

Lascalle's black eyes glittered angrily, weighing up the pros and cons of the offer.

Landers continued to idly toss the coin up and down into his palm, suggestively, tempting the little Frenchman with the obvious fairness of his mediation.

Bob held his breath. If Lascalle refused, then all his careful planning over the past fourteen days was all for nothing. Lascalle could quite easily refuse and then use French squadrons to carry out Bob's plan, independently of the British.

"What height do you propose crossing the German lines, my friend?" he demanded, grouchily.

"Maximum ceiling . . . over eighteen thousand feet . . . six thousand metres . . . otherwise we may lose the element of surprise if the Boche spot us," said Bob, cautiously, wondering where this line of reasoning was leading. "Your Spads can only reach five thousand metres, maximum, therefore it is imperative that we British do the work!"

"Aha . . . aha . . . wrong, my friend, you have not seen our new Spads out there, have you . . . they are not the S7 . . . they are S13s . . . with the 200hp Hispano-Suiza 8Aa . . . 8-vee engine . . . we can gain twenty-three thousand feet, outclimbing and outdistancing your old Camels . . . easily!" Lascalle was grinning impishly. His compatriots were all smiling now at this obvious technical superiority over the British.

Bob nearly fell off the table in surprise. The Spads lined up on the tarmac looked no different to the Spads Series VII that Lascalle and his compatriots usually flew. After a momentary examination, he could see some subtle differences . . . The air intake on the Spads on the tarmac were elliptical in place of the almost squashed circular grills behind the cowling of the Series VII, but apart from other minor details there was nothing to distinguish the aeroplanes on the tarmac from the previous aircraft of the Lascalle Escradille. "You want to test it out, my friend?" offered Lascalle, eagerly. "You fly your Camel and we see whose ceiling is the highest?"

Bob shook his head. "I believe you, my friend, I notice there are differences in the design of your new aircraft . . . we use the coin . . . despite your technical superiority over our Camels, another few thousand feet or so won't make that much difference." There were cheers from the British pilots.

After some more arguing and hassle, the French reluctantly agreed to a toss of the coin to settle the dispute, albeit with bad grace.

Both sides crowded round Landers, who stood in their midst, showing both sides of the franc to the two men to absolve any claim of unfairness. He then turned it over several times behind his back, eyes half closed, looking upwards.

"You call, my friend!" offered Bob to Lascalle.

Lascalle shrugged, nodded. The room was silent and tense, all eyes on Landers as he placed the coin on his thumb, the face covered by his hand. He flicked it high in the air. It flashed briefly before landing with a tinkle on the floor, rolling and oscillating several times before settling down, in a whir of metal on concrete.

All eyes waited for the coin to cease, everyone held their breaths.

It was the reverse side of the coin!

A British cheer went up. "We win!" they roared.

Lascalle held up his hand. "Non!" he cried. "It is the best of three tosses!" The Frenchmen cheered this time, booing their allies, derisively.

Landers looked at Bob, who shrugged "OK!" he said.

Landers tossed it again, after following the same routine. It landed, rolled, twisted and showed the head of the French President.

The Frenchmen went wild with glee . . .

All was still again as the Major picked up the coin, turned it over, tossed it high in the air. It landed, rolled, spun, and showed the reverse side!

Lascalle's face was a study in chagrin. The Frenchmen behind him began muttering about Perfidious Albion, and the eternal duplicity of the Roast Beef.

"Completely fair, sir," said Landers, holding out the coin for Lascalle's inspection.

Lascalle shrugged. "What do we have to do, Captain Spiers?" he asked, softly.

"You fly over the Line at ten thousand feet and make a nuisance of yourselves . . . shoot up balloons, trenches, artillery posts . . . any Rumplers or Halberstadts you see spotting for the Boche . . . anything to tempt von Dolin-Berensky's Lions out of their lair . . . and then we wait for them."

The Frenchmen began to murmur again about the unfairness of the arrangement, but Lascalle silenced his comrades with a wave of his hand. "It was all fair, and we all know the Roast Beef are fair, don't we?" he said in French, almost jocularly.

"This was fixed," snorted Houdinot, the huge man, glowering at Burgess malevolently.

"The Roast Beef have fixed this so that we . . . the Escradille Lascalle are the kitchen maids for them . . . look at them . . ." He pointed to the young British fliers. "All babes in arms . . . never yet seen the Boche in anger, and they expect to fight that Boche swine, Dolin-Berensky . . . it is stupid!"

"That will do!" snapped Lascalle. "The Roast Beef have to prove themselves some time and this may be the right time . . . the Escradille Lascalle are men of honour . . . we have gambled and lost . . . so be it!"

One of the young British fliers raised his glass. "To the great Captain Lascalle!" he shouted. "The greatest French flier . . . greater than Rene Fonck, or Guynemer! To his fifty-five victories over the Hun!"

The British all raised their glasses and drank Lascalle's health.

Lascalle bowed to the young man and raised his own glass.

The air of conviviality returned, more brandy was consumed, before the Frenchmen were more drunk than sober, announced their intention of departing. "Dawn tomorrow, over Cussigny!" shouted Lascalle, as the Frenchmen trooped out to the waiting Spads. He was halfway across the field when he suddenly asked to use the Squadron telephone, motioning his compatriots to go on without him.

Landers accompanied him back to the village, whilst the French fliers flamboyantly demonstrated the power of their new design Spads over the 77th aerodrome, looping, diving, turning, rolling, in mock combat.

"Those fellows can certainly fly, my friend," said Burgess to Shalter, watching the aerobatics enviously.

"I'm glad that they are going to be the bait tomorrow and not us," said Shalter heartily. "The Lions will crucify them!"

"As long as they don't crucify us, dear chap," said Burgess. "You reckon this is gonna work?"

Shalter, an Australian, looked thoughtful. "Seems daft that nobody's thought of doing this before," he murmured.

"We're all too chivalrous to play dirty tricks like that," said Burgess. "The RFC is still the only clean war, and that's what worries me."

"How d'ye mean?" asked the tall, lean, Shalter.

"Well, we might be setting a precedent . . . you know, shooting each other's fields up . . . and that could be nasty," said Burgess. "I know war's war, and nothing's fair, but it still worries me."

"He should know," said Shalter. "Who'd have thought that that little bastard has shot down thirty-five Huns . . . he's only a kid himself . . . under the hollow-eyes and grey hair."

"Looks a bloody old man, doesn't he?" grinned Burgess, nodding to where Spiers was inspecting Lascalle's Spad, admiring the clean lines and snub nose of the machine.

"You reckon that thing can top twenty-three thousand feet, or was the Froggy bull-shitting us?" asked Shalter. "Looks like any other Spad to me . . ."

"The Old Man was convinced, so it must be right."

The little Lascalle came out of the Squadron office, buckling his helmet on as he did so, closely followed by Landers.

They all watched the little man take off in a series of gigantic hops, the Spads' Hispano-Suiza lashing the tail like a fish. They all gasped as the Spad seemed to climb straight up into the sky.

"He was phoning all his mates for miles around," said Landers to Bob, as they dispersed after watching the Spad grow fainter and finally disappear.

"What was he saying to them?" asked Bob.

"He was talking in some patois that I couldn't follow precisely," said Landers. "But he was asking them to meet him at his aerodrome later today."

"That bastard is up to something, Nigel," said Bob, seeing the mechanics checking over Chesney's Camel.

"Of course he is, I saw him wink at that tall fellow . . . Houdinot, back there in the mess when the result of the coin tossing came out," said Landers.

"It wonder what the hell he is up to?" muttered Bob.

"I don't know, but you have your own problems, my friend," said Landers. "Croxley-Blawford is due any minute and his two henchmen, and I wouldn't be at all surprised if they aren't asking for our heads!"

****

Chapter 20

"I forbid it . . . do you hear me, Captain?" screamed Croxley-Blawford. "I have had enough crap from General Snow without taking any more on your behalf, and I am ordering you, here and now, to drop this ridiculous idea once and for all, is that understood?"

"But you wanted the air over our Lines cleared of enemy attention, because of the big offensive, sir," protested Bob in dismay. "This will ensure that the air is clear for days, perhaps months!"

"Poppycock, Captain!" yelled the Colonel, his face reddened with fury. "I've seen too many of these book-type soldiers . . . thinking they know better than their superiors how to win this war . . . and I heard all about your history reading and quoting, Spiers. Look what happened to that damned Frog at Waterloo . . . lot of balderdash talked about the French . . . the Duke had his measure . . . premier military nation in Europe . . . pooh! They haven't won a battle since Waterloo . . ."

"We're talking about the Germans, sir . . . and they won at Waterloo, not the Duke of Wellington . . . with respect!" said Bob, quietly.

He heard the two staff officers behind Croxley-Blawford gasp. Fossett had a bandage round his head under the red cap, covering his injured ear. Moran was sniffing disdainfully.

The Colonel's face turned redder. "Know more than your superiors, eh, Spiers . . . teach them history, can you?" he snarled.

"Yessir!" said Bob, calmly, ignoring Landers gesturing at him behind the backs of the three staff officers for him to quieten down. "I've said it before, and it will bear repeating . . . the Hun is not stupid, and will win this war, if we don't take note of what he is doing and can do."

"I don't want to hear any more, Captain!" roared the Colonel, furiously. "You are getting close to treason with that kind of despair and despondency." Fossett and Moran were nodding behind the Colonel's back, smug grins on their faces. The young upstart was receiving his just desserts.

"But the plan has the approval of the French!" insisted Bob, desperately. "The great French ace, Lascalle, is going to co-operate with us!"

"I don't care who is going to co-operate with you, Captain, I forbid this mad adventure totally . . . and what's more, Captain, to make sure you don't disobey my order, I'm relieving you as from this moment. You are no longer in command of this Squadron. Is that understood?" rasped Croxley-Blawford.

Bob held his breath, his whole world seemed to hang in the balance . . . surely not one of those two fops were going to be put in command. "Relieved, sir?" he stuttered, seeing Landers's stricken face momentarily, staring at him from behind the Colonel's back.

"Yes, relieving you, Spiers, and Major Landers also. This will take effect immediately. Major Landers will accompany me back to VII Corps HQ for reassignment, and you, Spiers, will make sure this Squadron is ready to receive your new OC . . . who will be arriving in a short time from now. All orders up to this moment are cancelled and any officer disobeying these instructions will be court martialled and I, personally, will see that he receives the just reward for refusing to obey an order."

"But who is to command the squadron, sir?" stammered Bob, aware that his world was about to fall apart.

"Captain Fossett here will assume temporary command until the new OC arrives, Captain."

"But what about Captain Lascalle and his men, sir . . . they'll be expecting us to be over Clery tomorrow morning . . . it could be a disgrace for the RFC to forsake our Allies. It would be looked upon as an insult!"

"There is nothing official about this arrangement, Spiers, and since you've made your bed, through ignoring instructions, you may now lie on it!" Croxley-Blawford was contemptuous.

"But let me inform Captain Lascalle that the arrangements have been cancelled, sir!" begged Bob.

"You may make your representations to Captain Fossett here after I've departed, Captain," said the Colonel, coldly. "It will be up to his discretion whether he feels this ad hoc affair deserves that much attention."

The Colonel picked up his black leather briefcase, swagger stick, jammed his hat firmly onto his square skull and turned to go.

"Blucher won Waterloo, and he was a German, sir," said Bob, softly, venomously.

Croxley-Blawford turned, his face a fiery red, the flush still travelling up from his collar.

There was a sudden noise outside in the street. Bob saw two Crossley tourers pull up in a cloud of dust. They were packed with photographers and newsmen. Someone hammered on the door imperiously, and a voice yelled out to be allowed in.

"Oh, my God!" muttered Croxley-Blawford, his fury swallowed up in the distraction of the arrival of the newsmen. "Get rid of them, William," he said to Fossett. He glared at Bob. "You are now a mere serving officer with no command other than that your rank confers upon you, Spiers . . . please remember that."

The Colonel departed with Captain Moran in tow, refusing to talk to the newspapermen despite their noisy clamouring for an interview. "Where's the star performer of this her squadron, Colonel?" bawled an American voice.

"Yeah . . . where's the Top ace Spiers?" yelled another, in the unmistakable accents of North America.

British voices added to the hubbub, the journalist and photographers attempted to push their way into the office, but Fossett barred their way.

"You the OC, her, Bub?" howled an irritated voice. "Why doncha let your stars shine?"

Bob saw magnesium flares flashing as photographers began taking pictures of the irritated Captain Fossett.

"Hey, Limey, how'dja git your wound?" called out the American voice.

"He ain't gotta wound stripe, Hank . . . perhaps it was self-inflicted!" called another.

"Naw, the Limeys shoot 'em for that!" said Hank, trying to push past Fossett. "Hey, you guys, Spiers is in there. Come on out, Captain, let's see the guy who captured a Hun crate and shot the guy who wanted to take the Huns away for questioning before they'd had their beano!"

Landers held out his hand to Bob, his face twitching in an effort to restrain his emotion. "Goodbye, Bob, pleased to have met you," he muttered, hoarsely.

A photographer caught the moment on celluloid at the moment the two men shook hands. "Hey, you goin' someplace, Major?" called out Hank. "You're Major Landers, aintcha . . . the Adjutant to this flying circus . . .?"

Landers nodded. "If you'll excuse me, gentlemen," he muttered, his eyes glistening, trying to ease past the mob of journalists towards the Colonel's waiting staff car.

"Hey, wait a minute!" cried out an English voice from the rear of the journalists.

"Major Landers is in command here . . ."

"So who's this toffy-nosed creep?" demanded Hank, a grizzle-haired, grey-faced American, tall, huge, hands like spades. "What's your function around here, Captain?"

"I'm in temporary command here," said Fossett in his clipped, lisping accent.

"You been relieved, Major?" roared an American of Landers, as he tried to make his way through the crowd of newsmen. "What for?"

"Hey, Colonel, what's going on?" demanded one of the Americans of the cold-faced Croxley-Blawford, who was waiting in the open Armstrong-Siddeley. "Why have you relieved Major Landers?"

"There's something screwy goin' on here, Hank!" said the second newsman. "You wanna make a statement, Colonel?"

The Colonel shook his head, vigorously, urging Landers to hurry.

"You would be advised to say something, Colonel," said Hank, leaning over the edge of the car, staring at Moran and the Colonel.

"Otherwise our readers are gonna git the situation all wrong, and that could be bad . . . for you!"

"I have nothing to say, to you colonial types . . . on your way!" snapped Croxley-Blawford.

"Hey, didja hear this blowfish . . . tellin' us ter git knotted!" yelled Hank, turning to face the newsmen behind him.

"Callin' us . . . colonial types . . . the two-faced bastard!" snarled another American. "We don't have to take this shit from any two-bit Limey . . .!"

"Do you mind, Colonel?" asked Landers, quietly.

"Make it brief, Major!" snapped the Colonel, angrily, his face a mottled colour at being insulted by the unruly Americans.

Landers turned to face the journalists, and in a quiet voice gave them the reasons for his departure and Bob's demotion, saying that an officer of higher rank was to take over, since Bob's command had been a temporary measure anyway. He, himself, was going to take up another appointment.

"That ain't the story we heard from Lascalle!" roared an Englishman.

"Yeah, what about this plan to throttle that Hun . . . von Dolin-Berensky . . . what's gonna happen to that, Colonel?" demanded Hank.

"I have nothing to say to you people," said Colonel Croxley-Blawford, haughtily.

"Well, now, that's too bad, Colonel," said Hank, softly, looking like a dinosaur bending over a cow. Hank's pale blue eyes were hard, chips of granite. "You are saying that the plan devised by Captain Spiers, and assisted by Captain Lascalle is to be called off?"

"I have nothing more to add to what Major Landers has already told you," snapped the Colonel, tapping the driver on the shoulder with his swagger stick.

"Hang about, Colonel," interrupted Hank, his large foot on the running board of the Armstrong-Siddeley open tourer. "We ain't finished with you yet, and I'd advise you to talk to us, or I promise you all hell will break loose when we git back to HQ."

The Colonel sighed heavily. "Very well, gentlemen, what do you wish to know?" he rasped.

"We all wanna know how come you want to stop guys like Captain Spiers here from doing what he can to win this goddamned war. Lascalle told us all about Spiers's plan to hobble this Jasta, once and for all. That's what it's all about it, ain't it, or have you bloody Limeys found some God-given formula that only the top brass know about for finishing it?"

"Look, I don't have to be spoken to in this fashion, sir," said the Colonel, testily. "And I'll certainly have words in the right quarters about your qualifications for wandering about in the war zone where you want."

Hank stared at Croxley-Blawford, his hard eyes on a level with the Colonel's despite the officer's elevated situation in the Armstrong. "Let me tell you something, Colonel, maybe it ain't crawled into your skull yet. I, and all these guys here, save for our Limey pals, represent the American people, who just got into this yere lil' old war on account of you Limeys and Frogs who can't win it by your own selves, and my rag is read by a lot of Congressmen and Representatives, and they ain't gonna take kindly to havin' one of their correspondents ripped off by some goddamn Limey Colonel giving us a load of shit about privilege and aristocracy knowing what it's all about, and calling us colonials . . ." Hank's voice could barely be heard over the sound of the engines being tested down at the hangars. Croxley-Blawford heard it though, loud and clear, and it lashed him as if from a raw-hide whip.

"You're dead right, Hank, give the bastard what he's askin' for," snarled another American. "Our doughboys are comin' over here to pull the chestnuts outta the fire and they're gonna know what kind 'o stoopid bastards are running this outfit, and if I have anythin' to do with it, no way are they gonna be run around by jerks like him . . ."

There were angry roars of approval from the American contingent, which formed, by far, the majority of the journalists present. The English and Frenchmen were more subdued, but nevertheless persistent.

Moran leaned over and said something into Croxley-Blawford's ear. The Colonel, red-faced and uncomfortable, listened, then nodded. The journalists waited in stony silence.

"Very well, gentlemen," said the Colonel in a strangled voice. "I can tell you that we, that is the High Command of the British VII Corps, General Snow, have not discounted entirely Captain Spiers's plan, but we need more time to examine it in detail before giving it our approval . . ."

"He's givin' us a loada shit, Hank," yelled Hank's compatriot, a smaller man with Italianate features.

"Yeah, wotcha gotta examine it for, Colonel? You frightened of fighting or somethin'?" roared another.

"Captain Spiers has proven that he knows what he's talkin' about . . . he's got thirty-five victories to prove it and a chestful of medals, so what's all this examination crap you givin' us, Colonel?" shouted another.

"He's stallin', fellers," roared yet another. "He ain't gotta fuckin' idea in his tiny skull and he don't want Spiers to show him how to do it . . ."

"Now that should make a good story, Colonel," said Hank, waiting for a Le Clerget to die down to acceptable levels. "How a Limey Colonel stopped a war-winning scheme because he was jealous of his subordinates . . . how about that?"

Colonel Croxley-Blawford was getting redder by the minute. He tapped the Sergeant driver imperiously on the shoulder. "Drive on, Sergeant!" he ordered, crisply.

The Sergeant, anxious to get out of the melée before the Colonel got any angrier, moved the car swiftly. Croxley-Blawford would take it out on him for days after this little fracas . . . that was the way these top brass operated.

The Colonel left a group of very angry journalists standing in the dusty roadway of Lourconter, shouting after his departing Armstrong.

In frustration they surged round Fossett, taking photos of he and Spiers with gusto and firing questions in a steady barrage.

Fossett was even redder than Colonel Croxley-Blawford, and less able to handle the noisy journalists. Used to the sedate and gentlemanly

English, his nerve failed when having to face the rough and brutal Americans.

"Come on, Captain, tell us how you got wounded!" taunted the Italian American, named Spiroetti.

"At the head of his men over the top," scoffed another.

"Is it true that Captain Spiers blew your ear off with a Colt 45, Captain?" asked another.

"Can you fly an aeroplane, Captain?"

"How many times you bin in the trenches, Captain?"

"How'd yuh git all them medals?"

"You gotta mater plan for finishing the war, Captain?"

"Gonna show Spiers how ter fly his crate?"

Bob was dismayed by the steady pressure from the journalists on Fossett, despite his dislike of the man and all he stood for.

He stepped forward, held up his hand. "If you don't mind, you fellows," he said, between the roar of the Le Clergets. "I'll answer your questions. Captain Fossett has just been pitchforked into a situation he probably didn't ask for, and he's making the best he can of it."

"Captain, that just ain't true," said Hank. "We appreciate just what you tryin' to do but let him talk for himself."

"Wait a minute, Hank," interrupted Spiroetti. "Let's hear from the Captain his version of the plan, to put von Dolin-Berensky outta business."

"Come and have a drink, gentlemen," offered Bob, indicating the mess.

"Hey, you guys, fer a goddamn Limey, he ain't bad!" roared Spiroetti. "That's the best news we heard today!"

****

Chapter 21

The news of Chesney's encounter with the Lion Jasta and its subsequent development were greeted with delight by the American journalists, and after drinking most of the Squadron's beer and spirits, they all rushed off to try to interview Chesney at the 112th General Hospital in Amiens.

"This war needs guys like you, Bob," Hank told him, the massive American towering over Bob's five-feet seven inches. "And we're gonna see that your name gets plastered over every Yankee paper Stateside. I don't know how you put up with shits like that fuckin' Colonel, and that creep Fossett. They don't know their asses from their elbows . . ."

"And to think they bin runnin' this little ole war for three years," said Spiroetti.

"No wonder you ain't winnin', pal," said another.

"The world's gonna hear about this outfit," said Hank, shaking Bob's hand in a grip that seemed to crush every bone in his fingers. "The maverick squadron . . . where the Limeys stick all those that wanna win the war and hope they git killed off damn quick!"

A massive American Packard drew up outside the mess, arriving without anybody noticing it. The half drunken Americans all piled in, singing and shouting and shaking their fists in the general direction of the German lines.

"Phew!" said Burgess, after the Packard had disappeared round a bend in the road.

"Let's hope we don't have too many visitations like that one."

There were murmurs of approval for those sentiments.

"Is it on for tomorrow, Skipper?" asked Clements, slightly drunk after victory over an Albatross from the Lion Jasta.

Bob shook his head. "The Colonel knocked it on the head," said Bob.

There were angry murmurs at this. "Jesus, anyone would think that we didn't want to win this war," muttered Murchison.

"We bin tellin' you guys that for years," said Shalter, the Australian.

"What can we do, Skipper?" asked Clements, his thin face sullen, dark eyes bloodshot.

"Lascalle will be pissed off, that's for sure," said Shalter.

"Think we got cold feet suddenly," agreed Murchison.

"Let's tell the Captain to go fuck himself and do it anyway," said Shalter. "What's it matter . . . we'll all be pushin' daisies up in a few weeks."

"Yes, what about it, Skipper?" said Burgess. "We're all with you."

"Who's gonna say anything after we finish the Lions off . . . they'll be so busy trying to justify their original decision that the Press will crucify them!" said Shalter.

All clamoured agreement.

"There won't be any flying until I give the orders, gentlemen!" said a voice from the doorway.

To Bob it was like seeing a ghost from some remote period in history. For a brief second or so, he had difficulty in orienting himself to the voice and face of the officer standing in the mess entrance. He had difficulty in approving what his sense told him was true.

The man was Major Jessop, burly, dark-haired still, but with streaks of grey and a pallor to his skin that Bob didn't recall being present at Denham. His nose, that magnificent organ that had dominated the school at Denham, seemed to have shrunk somehow. The moustache covering his hare-lip was bushier and ill-kempt from the tailored version Bob recalled. His eyes were shrunken hollows and he looked ill.

"Your new commanding officer, gentlemen!" introduced Fossett, standing next to Jessop.

The room sprang to attention.

"At ease, gents!" said Jessop's booming voice, the hectoring quality gone. Bob noticed that his leg seemed to drag more than it had done at Denham. He had evidently not had the member amputated.

Jessop walked into the room slowly, his face twisted with pain every time he put his leg down, staring at the young men around him, before leaning heavily on the mess table. "I'll have a whisky, Sergeant, and get these lads what they want!" he said quietly.

"Well, Captain Spiers . . . lasted more than a week, didn't you?" grinned Jessop. "Covered yourself with glory as well . . . never have thought it at Denham . . . nearly wrote off his first crate on his solo . . . didn't you, Captain?" Jessop grinned affectionately at Bob.

Bob grinned, feeling that somehow things weren't going to be all that bad.

There was more good-natured banter from Jessop, although he was plainly in a great deal of pain from his leg. The younger pilots stood round listening with awe and great interest.

Later, Jessop said "Come to my office, Captain Spiers . . . let's have a chat."

Jessop pulled out a packet of Players, lit one, inhaled deeply, breathing out a cloud of blue smoke through his nostrils. He regarded Bob through the cloud. "You are asking yourself, how I got into this outfit, aren't you, Captain?" he asked. "The Borstal of the RFC?"

"The thought had occurred to me, Major," said Bob.

"I'll tell you, then you can tell me how you got into it," said Jessop, his black brows meeting into a frown. "I told one of the top brass that they were bloody murderers . . . sending fellows like you out to France with less than five hours on the machines they were going to fly against people like Richthofen, von Dolin-Berensky, Voss, Udet, Goering." Jessop sucked on the cigarette again as is his life depended on inhaling the drug. Bob noticed that his hands were trembling. "I was a stupid bastard. I had a cushy number at Denham . . . could have sat out the war, playing at training blokes like you to fly crates like the Farman and FE . . . but I just had to open my big mouth." Jessop shrugged. "My leg hurts like fucking hell and should come off, I know that, but I believe that the Hun will do it for me sooner or later . . . and I just couldn't do that job month after bloody month, knowing that I was producing Hun-fodder for people like Richthofen . . . average life expectancy . . . two weeks . . . Jesus! I still feel like a fucking murderer when I think about it."

"With respect, sir, do you honestly believe it's any different here?" asked Bob, vaguely disappointed in Jessop. The big man had always been something of a hero to him . . . his first flying instructor . . . knew it all. In this situation, the Major looked uncomfortable, unable to command adequately, like a fish out of water. He seemed to have diminished in stature.

Jessop's deep blue eyes hardened, perceptibly, his lips under the black moustache curled. "No, I don't, Captain, but I expect you to support me and try to put that to rights," he said, softly.

Bob gave a short snort of disgusted laughter. "Do you think I haven't tried, sir?" he asked, caustically. We had the Colonel down here this afternoon, telling me that he forbids any attempt to cripple von Dolin-Berensky's Jasta by anything save the usual routine, telling me that training my blokes to fly was a waste of Government resources . . . ammunition, fuel and aircraft . . ."

"I heard all about it, Captain," said Jessop, softly, a faint smile on his thick lips.

"Your attempts to make fliers of those blokes before they became dog-food has reached the attentions of no less than 'Boom' himself . . ."

"You could have fooled me, Major," said Bob.

"Take my word for it, Captain Spiers," said Jessop. "I met Landers at HQ a few hours ago . . . he told me all about this plan for getting rid of the Lions . . . in fact I heard very little else . . . that bloke believes the sun shines out of your little asshole."

"Nigel and I reached an understanding," said Bob.

"There wasn't any doubt about that, Captain," said Jessop. He looked up at Bob. "I suppose you're expecting me to underwrite your plan, now that I'm here, on the old boy network routine?"

"That's up to you, sir," said Bob, stiffly. "If we aren't going out there tomorrow, we had better tell Lascalle that it's off . . . so he can start cursing the Roast Beef some more in the restaurants of Amiens . . . should do the RFC a lot of good."

Jessop lit another cigarette from the butt of the last, sucked on it sharply. "That bloody Frog can do what the hell he likes," he said, coldly. "From here on, this squadron does exactly what it's ordered to do, no more, no less. I don't propose dipping my head in shit for anybody, is that clear, Captain?"

"Yessir, routine only . . . never mind about winning the war . . . just don't shoot until you see the whites of their eyes . . . stiff upper lip, chaps," sneered Bob.

"When I want your opinion, Captain, on the best way of concluding this conflict, I'll ask for it," snapped Jessop.

"Is that all, sir?" asked Bob.

"No, it isn't, Captain." Jessop pulled out a fob watch. "It is now five p.m. You and I are going for a trip over the Lines . . . and you're going to show me what all this aerial combat crap is all about . . . blood me, if that's the correct word . . . after all, I should be safe in company with one of the RFC's top aces, shouldn't I?"

"It'll be dark in a short while, Major, don't you think we should wait until the morning?" asked Bob, angry.

"Now!" said Jessop.

Bob shrugged. "I'll see you down at the hangars, sir," he said, snapping to attention, saluting.

Sergeant Williams watched the young Captain approach, saw the compressed lips and hollow-eyed fury, barked at his team. "Get it out, for fuck's sake, and be quick about it . . . the Captain is in a mood."

"Get my machine out, Sergeant, will you please?" barked Bob. "And the spare one for Major Jessop."

Jessop came up a few moments afterwards, as Bob was going over his machine carefully.

He was wearing a brand new Sidcot, all stiff and smelling of new leather. He still wore his cavalry boots and jodhpurs with a spur clip on the heels.

The Major didn't bother to go over the Camel, just jumped in, waved impatiently for the mechanic to go through the starting routine.

The two Camels went down the field, tails lashing like aerial fish, took off and were soon climbing high into the clouds.

"I wouldn't like to be a Hun with that young fellow around this evening," observed Williams to his crew.

"He looked pissed off about something," said the Cockney fitter.

"The top brass have fucked up his plan," said Sergeant Williams. "I'd be pissed off if it happened to me."

"I hope the Major knows how to fly that crate," said the Cockney Corporal. "That leg of his don't look too kosher to me, and he's got Chesney's machine . . . didn't have chance to calibrate the new Vickers, after the Hun removed 'em . . . he'll probably shoot his prop off."

"Why didn't you tell me?" demanded Williams, angrily.

"Didn't think about it until too late, and that new Major don't look like a feller you could have a chat with," said the Corporal. "He's living on his nerves, and that batman he brought with him . . . Corporal Johnson, looks like a fucking garden gnome, asked for a bottle of Johnny Walker for his officer as soon as he got here . . ."

Williams shrugged. "Don't do it gain, Corporal," he said, resignedly.

Bob and Major Jessop crossed the German Lines at twelve thousand feet, to the usual accompaniment of the black blobs of Archie. The German gunners, after a few exploratory rounds, got the range and were soon blasting the two Camels unmercifully.

Bob noticed the Major's obvious nervousness, swerving whenever a blast came close. Banks of cloud covered the entire sky in cathedral-like columns, turning faintly blue in the dying light. The sun shone low on the horizon, ready to dip below the rim of the earth.

Over Boucheresnes, three ungainly German observation balloons floated, like a row of sausages in an aerial pan, the observers in their tiny baskets looking like Tom Thumb men.

Bob scanned the sky above them unceasingly for signs of ominous black dots that would herald enemy aircraft.

Archie was still tearing orange holes in the sky, the black blossoms floating away behind them like cotton wool in an Xmas window display.

Bob saw Jessop waggle his wings and point downwards at the three observation balloons. Bob shook his head, pointing upwards. There was something suspicious about those three sausage shapes. They were less than three miles away and still the ground crews had not attempted to pull them down.

Jessop waggled his wings again, jabbing his thumb downwards at the balloons, imperiously. Again Bob shook his head, pointing upwards, viciously, making mimes of aircraft approaching.

Jessop searched the sky above them, saw nothing and again motioned towards the balloons, this time pointing at Bob and then downwards, brandishing his fist. Without warning, just as Jessop turned his Camel over in a sweeping roll, the Archie ceased. Bob tried desperately to warn Jessop, but the Major's Camel was already diving steeply, almost vertically now, towards the three balloons.

Bob saw the four Albatrosses and three Fokker triplanes come out of the clouds as he was about to follow Jessop down.

"You stupid bastard, Jessop!" he howled into the slipstream, as he rolled and began climbing steeply to gain some advantage from height over the disparate numbers against him.

The four Albatrosses, all with the blue Lion inscribed on their fuselages, ignored Bob utterly, and went down after the Major in his lone Came, leaving the three triplanes to tackle him. Just as the first Fokker made its run at him, he saw the parachutes of the observers from the balloons open out, and the ground crews begin to haul down the massive envelopes at speed.

Spandaus rattled behind him, and the flack-flack of bullets hitting doped canvas along his port wing warned him of imminent danger. He flicked the Camel round in a vicious right-hand turn that caught the Fokker unawares.

He barely had time to fire a two second burst before another triplane was on his tail and bullets were hitting his rear section. The third one held off, waiting a suitable moment to apply the coup de grâce.

Searching desperately for the nearest cloud bank, fear drying his tongue into a thong of leather, he twisted and turned to avoid the hail of bullets that came in from every angle. The nearest cloud was a mile away, and the triplanes had placed themselves between he and the sheltering mass of vapour.

The Germans were skilful pilots and were plainly manoeuvring him for the kill. The third triplane with black chessboard markings on the top plane, hovered over the melée waiting its moment of truth.

Bob could feel the cold fingers of doom clutching his gut. This was it . . . he knew it. His Camel was being shot to pieces around him. His own plane was still being repaired from the morning's foray and this machine was Murchison's, strange to him, an unknown quantity.

A wire went, and a strut splintered, jagged holes appeared near the starboard aileron. The Camel began juddering and lurching, despite his attempts to control it. A triplane was on his tail, Spandaus flickering viciously. The dashboard went into a mass of wreckage, his windshield vanished in a million splinters. Bullets whanged off the engine cowling. He aimed a swift burst at the second triplane as it crossed his path and then both guns jammed. He could see the bulging cartridge in the breech.

"Fuck it, fuck it, fuck it!" he screamed, hammering away at the silent Vickers, sweat, cold and clammy, trickling down his spine, as he awaited the shattering impact of lead in his spine, and oblivion glazing his vision.

To his amazement, the three triplanes with their Maltese crosses, were alongside him, the pilots under their black leather helmets, smiling and waving at him, acknowledging his difficulties with a stiff salute of appreciation.

Then they were gone, all three making for the cloud cover with the amazing manoeuvrability for which the Fokker triplane was renowned.

His tongue had stuck to the roof of his mouth with fear, a thick band of ungovernable cloth, dry and acid.

In the same instant, four Camels dropped alongside him, the pilots all grinning and waving. He recognised Shalter and Murchison, Burgess and Clements.

Looking downwards, his legs shaking uncontrollably, he saw the wreck of a Camel burning furiously beside the ground positions of the three observation balloons.

He waved at the four Camels to signify the end of the mission, just as the sun dropped over the horizon's rim and purple shadows began covering the earth below.

****

Chapter 22

Captain Fossett's bandaged head looked larger than life in the light from the single hurricane lamp hanging by a piece of string over his desk. His blue eyes were frosty and hard as he stared at the five men before him.

"You all disobeyed orders," he screamed, wildly, his mouth writhing in his fury. "I'll have you court martialled for this last piece of disobedience, Captain!"

"What the hell are you talking about, Captain?" snarled Bob, his legs still weak from the fear engendered by those last few moments with the Fokkers over Boucheresnes.

"You took Major Jessop up with the deliberate intent to place his life in jeopardy," yelled Fossett. "You knew damned well he'd never been over the Lines for years and you needlessly exposed him to peril."

"Major Jessop ordered me up, Captain!" snapped Bob, trying to stop his hands shaking.

"That's enough, Captain Spiers, I won't hear any aspersions cast against a gallant officer . . ."

"Captain Fossett, do you honestly believe that I would wittingly fly over the German Lines at dusk and attack three observation balloons without written authorisation to carry phosphorous bullets, and without adequate cover for my ass? You are out of your mind if you believe that, and what's more, no responsible RFC officer would believe you either."

"You were hoping Major Jessop would be shot down so that you could put your little scheme into operation, didn't you, Captain?"

"You are talking out of the back of your head, Fossett, and you know it," roared Bob exasperatedly . . . the memory of those Spandaus a short time before had petrified him with a fear he hadn't known before . . . a feeling of utter despair had filled his mind. It lingered on now, even though the danger was past. It hung like a curtain of foreboding over his whole being.

"These men went up after you," said Fossett, feebly, realising the cul de sac into which he had driven himself.

"If they hadn't, Captain Fossett, there would have been another casualty on the Squadron's list this evening . . . myself," said Bob, trying to cool the situation. "Major Jessop wanted to go down after three observation balloons over Boucheresnes . . . I made my objections known to him, because it was plain that those balloons were a trap. He ignored my warnings and went down after them. I was attacked before I could go to his assistance, by three Fokker triplanes from the Lion Jasta. Four Albatross fighters ignored me completely and went down after Major Jessop. At the height at which he was then flying, around five thousand feet, he wouldn't stand a chance."

Fossett stood there, biting his lip, wondering what to do next, how to treat this situation.

"I'll make out my report, Captain," said Bob, quietly, now that the situation had almost resolved itself.

"Very well. Dismiss, gentlemen," said Fossett. His staff training had not included the management of front line fighting. His face was haggard and bitter, unable to cope with the problem.

****

In the mess that night, the men of 77 Squadron made merry round the piano, drinking and singing old RFC ballads, amongst which was the 'Young Aviator' sung to the tune of 'The Dying Lancer' and 'We Haven't Got a Hope in the Morning' sung to 'Old John Peel'. The air was thick with tobacco smoke, the smell of brandy, whisky and beer.

Captain Fossett had refused to join them on the grounds that he had reports to write.

Bob sang half-heartedly with the rest, his mind on Martin Jessop's last minutes and the conversation they'd had shortly before take-off about the Hun curing his leg problem before it became necessary for its amputation. The sight of that fiercely burning Camel on the edge of the balloon area haunted him. With Jessop's death, it felt as if the whole axis of life had shifted, the hinge had gone. Jessop's memory was vital and alive up to this evening . . . the man who had guided him through his first traumatic days as a pilot, and his eternal advice about height and not flying in a straight line for more than a few seconds at a time, had become a cornerstone of Bob's flying life. Now that umbilical cord had been severed and the past was now irrevocably dead. It felt as if there was no relationship between his past and the present. A void loomed that was not filled by family or friends, by Barbara or by Michelle . . . nothing made sense any more . . . he felt like the Flying Dutchman, doomed to spend his life watching others die and yet living on himself for the whole of eternity.

The Sergeant i/c Mess waved him over, miming the telephone.

"Spiers!" he yelled into it over the noise in the mess. He could hardly hear his correspondent. He waved at the singers to be silent a moment. Gradually the noise died away.

"Pierre? Pierre who? Ah, Lascalle? Yes, of course it is . . . why shouldn't it be? I don't give a fuck what they said to you . . . it is on in the morning, unless you want to call it off, of course? . . . I haven't heard anything from anyone . . . yes, it was one of ours . . . Major Jessop . . . our new commander . . . von D's mob . . . yes it was . . . very well, see you in the early hours!"

He stared back at the young pilots round him. "Lascalle," he said, unnecessarily.

"Then we're going over, Bob?" asked Shalter, his lean face eager.

"We put our plan into effect at dawn, gentlemen!" said Bob.

There were prolonged cheers at this. The two replacement pilots who had arrived to fill the places left by Langley and Chesney had flown in whilst Bob and Major Jessop had been out over the German Lines. They looked askance at this evidence of RFC madness, feel shut out of the evident esprit de corps that existed amongst the squadron members.

"There will be six only of us," said Bob, quietly. "You gentlemen will not be coming on the patrol tomorrow . . . no criticism of your abilities, but you haven't had the experience I require as yet, or the training."

"But, sir, that's unfair," protested the younger man, Blake, fair-haired, soft-mouthed, looking like a mere schoolboy. Even his uniform was fresh from Pope and Bradley without a stain or blemish. "We want to join you . . . how else will we know whether we can fight or not if we don't try?"

Mathers, the other man, older and more mature at twenty-three, who had been an observer in FEs for six months before qualifying as a pilot, also protested.

Bob bit his lip. With six only aircraft, the effect would be watered down considerably, reducing the effectiveness of the surprise considerably, also increasing the hazards to the more fully trained pilots if any of von Dolin-Berensky's men managed to make it back into the skies. On the other hand, he was debasing the currency of the value of the training he had inflicted upon the longer serving members of the squadron by approving their presence on the mission.

"Gentlemen, you'd last five minutes if one of von D's men got away from you and these Huns are not beginners . . . they are the toughest, second only to Richthofen's Jasta, in experience and determination."

It was Shalter, the Australian, who absolved him from his dilemma. "If you don't mind my saying so, Skipper, if these blokes don't come along, and if any of von D's fellows get off the deck, then we're in trouble . . . and I know all about your reservations about adequate training, but Chesney fucked it up this morning by going out without orders, and I know poor old Ches is in dock, but he well and truly fucked us up by taking it upon himself to fly this morning . . . he was a steaming bloody nit."

Bob wondered . . . was it really only a few hours since Chesney had landed his Camel after being the guest of von D at Cussigny? It felt like years . . . Lascalle's lunch with the squadron, the tossing of the coin . . . it seemed remote somehow and without any relationship to the present.

"Very well, then, gentlemen, but with this proviso . . . if you get into trouble, make for the Line . . . no arguments, is that understood? Nobody will accuse you of cowardice or chickening out . . . you won't be of any use to anyone, dead," warned Bob.

There were shouts of approval. Blake and Mathers were slapped on the back and made to feel easier about their projected roles.

"Nobody flies tomorrow morning without my express permission, is that clear, gentlemen?" rasped Fossett's voice from the doorway of the mess. "I absolutely forbid it!"

Bob raised his glass to him, mockingly. "Overruled, Fossett, old boy, you are merely Adjutant now . . . I have assumed operational control of the squadron's flying activities, so come and have a drink, there's a good chap, and forget it."

"Captain Spiers . . . I am OC of this squadron, not you," rasped Fossett, his face working with strain.

"Wrong, old boy, Major Jessop was OC until this evening, and there haven't been any orders since, countermanding my control!" snapped Bob.

Fossett bit his lip. The bandage round his head had slipped and he looked slightly like an Egyptian mummy who had recently cast its bandages. He looked at the hostile faces round him, grim looks, ferocious expressions and hesitated.

"Come on, Fossett, have a drink and forget it . . . by this time tomorrow night, you'll be the toast of General Snow's staff . . . the man who organised the destruction of von D's Jasta . . . and that'll really be something!" urged Bob.

"You're mad, Spiers, utterly mad!" said Fossett, hysterically.

"Of course I'm mad, Fossett . . . we're all bloody mad," said Bob, spilling wine into a glass, offering it to the staff captain. "Flying out at dawn to fight other young blokes over something we know nothing at all about and couldn't care less . . . who cares whether the Kaiser has a baby for breakfast every morning . . . do you? Do I? Do any of us? Do we believe that crap? Of course we fucking well don't . . . remember Meinwoller and Blosczik? Two stout fellows if ever there were any . . . human, just like us, and we're shooting at one another . . . bloody daft, I say . . . and all on the sayso of cretins like you, Fossett, old boy, who want to preserve the status quo of privilege . . ."

Fossett brushed the glass out of Bob's hand, angrily. "You are a traitor to your country Spiers, unpatriotic, undisciplined, and disobedient!" yelled Fossett.

The glass splintered on the brick floor of the mess, the amber liquid flowing over the brickwork.

Fossett glared at Bob for a few seconds before turning upon his heel and marching out of the mess.

Silence reigned for a few moments, everybody apprehensive at what would happen next. One of the mess waiters came with a dustpan and brush, began sweeping up the glass fragments.

"Hello, Bob!" said a voice quietly into the silence.

Every head turned.

Lieutenant-Colonel Martine stood in the doorway, immaculate, uniform pressed, boots gleaming, the red band round his cap a symbol of his authority.

"A-tten-shun!" snapped Bob. Boots smashed to the floor as everyone stood rigidly to attention.

"At ease, men," said Charles Martine, stepping into the stronger light nearer the bar.

Martine motioned the mess sergeant, who stood with his staff, stiff and still at attention. "Fill everyone's glasses, Sergeant," he ordered, quietly.

There was a stampede for the bar to have glasses filled. The atmosphere relaxed after the sudden shock of Martine's entry.

Martine gently laid his braid cap and swagger stick on a table, removed his greatcoat and hung it on a peg next to an assortment of flying helmets and Sidcots.

"A toast, gentlemen," he said, holding up his glass. "To 77 Squadron RFC!"

The young men cheered vociferously.

Martine held up his hand. "Gather round in a circle, if you wouldn't mind, chaps," he said, in the same easy, soft voice.

The pilots all gathered round him. Martine stood, one leg hooked over the back of a rickety chair, his polished cavalry boot negligently resting on the seat.

"The 77th is not renowned for its adherence to traditional ways of doing things, gentlemen," he said. "In fact, it has a reputation at HQ for being bloody minded and offensive and for downright disobedience on occasions when it feels it has right on its side. It also has made itself a lot of enemies within the hierarchy, who feel that their positions and ranks are being threatened by these actions."

Close up to Martine, Bob could see the strain on his hawk-like features.

"Not least of all, General Snow, himself, via the voice of Colonel Croxley-Blawford who feels that this squadron should be disbanded and dispersed amongst other RFC formations . . . he feels you are nothing but trouble-makers and a thorn in his side. We are shortly to begin the most decisive offensive of the war and the VII Corps will form the southernmost hinge of that offensive. 77 Squadron being one of the squadrons closest to our French Allies, God bless 'em . . . is an important unit in the scheme of things. Anything you do will present us with either opportunities or disasters . . . and I would like to think that it will be the former."

Martine paused, to hitch his elegant trousers from the top of his boot, gently and with a grace that Bob could not but envy.

"I have known Captain Spiers for nearly a year now . . . he and I were in the same Flying Training School at Denham together. He is an able man and a good leader, and like most able men, has strong ideas on what should be done about winning this beastly war. Unfortunately, those ideas very often conflict with the general plans of the Higher Command, not because they are antipathetic but because of their very revolutionary nature, they are hard to grasp by men who are immersed in the minutiae of day to day organisation of masses of men and equipment. They see him as an upstart, someone who is determined to rock the boat, when all the top brass want is an obedient and pliable executive leader . . . they dislike new ideas . . . they take time to absorb and the top bras feels they may be costly . . . God alone knows why . . . we've had some costly orthodox ideas over the past three years . . . however, I'm not here to criticise our higher command's methods . . . if we all did that, then chaos would result. Captain Spiers because of his exemplary record cannot be ignored, however, and it has now got to the stage that whenever General Snow hears the name he winces." Martine smiled.

There were some titters from the listening pilots.

"The General called me into his office this afternoon when it became known that Major Jessop had been shot down, told me in very polite, but firm tones, to get my ass over here, and sort this bloody lot out, once and for all . . . meaning, of course, the 77th."

Martine sipped his glass of whisky slowly, looking round at the ring of young faces.

"So, for the moment, I shall be your new commander . . . OC, leader, call it what you will, until I have sorted you all out." Martine's smile robbed it of any malice.

There was some stirring at this announcement. Martine held up his hand. "Unusual, gentlemen, yes, it is, but then again we're dealing with an unusual situation . . . a squadron formed from mavericks, I believe our American cousins call them, all of you here, because you are individualists and want to have a go at the Hun in your own special way. Alright, in a way, I'm a maverick. I enjoy this rank, because of two things . . . my old man is well up in the War Office and pulled some strings, and because the top brass feel that in a way I'm a thinking soldier . . . a book man, and wanted me upstairs out of the way before I became a nuisance."

There were some laughs at this.

"Now then, having disposed of my extraordinary rise to power in the hierarchy, I now want to hear about this plan for disposing of one of the RFC's biggest thorns . . . to whit, von Dolin-Berensky's Lion Jasta. Over to you, Captain Spiers."

Bob shook himself, scarcely able to credit his ears. A Colonel to command the 77th. The High Command must be worried, he concluded.

He explained his plan in detail, illustrating it with glasses on one of the tables.

Martine listened carefully, asking questions every now and then. "Makes eminent sense to me, gentlemen," he said. "So we meet Lascalle over Clery-sur-Somme at eighteen thousand feet?"

"You're coming, sir?" asked Bob, incredulously.

Martine smiled slightly. "I can fly a Camel, Captain, perhaps not as good as you, but you'll need all the men you can get to make this plan of yours a success, won't you?"

"Here's to Colonel Martine!" shouted out Shalter, raising his glass. "A very stout fellow indeed!"

The pilots all began singing 'For He's a Jolly Good Fellow!' lustily.

"Right, gentlemen, I suggest we all get a good night's rest . . . reveille at oh-five-thirty hours for a briefing . . . here in the mess."

The pilots all looked a little askance, but moved out of the mess when Bob inclined his head.

The mess Sergeant cleared away the dirty glasses and ashtrays around the Colonel and Captain. "Leave those, Sergeant," said Bob, quietly, seeing that Martine wanted to talk.

The mess was silent save for the muttering of the artillery at the Front that rattled the crockery and lit up the room faintly with flashes.

Martine straddled the chair, his long legs stuck out before him. He waggled his nose with forefinger and thumb. "Still damned sore on occasions, Robert," he grinned, wryly.

"How's Michelle?" asked Bob, feeling guilty at not having written to her for some time.

"I saw her the other day . . . in Amiens, my friend. She asked me to ask you about Sainte Saveit d'Erve . . . said you would know all about it," said Martine.

"But . . .?" began Bob, then stopped. How the devil had she found out about Barbara?

"I'll leave you with that one, Robert," he said, softly. "She also asked me to ask you about what you would like to do after the war, and I have succinct instructions to tell you that there will be a job for you . . .

guaranteed. Michelle seemed to think that this was important to you both."

Bob twisted his fingers in his hand. Somehow the future didn't appear to loom larger than twenty-four hours ahead these days, sometimes only twelve hours and then the gut-wrenching fear and smell of burning castor oil, smell of cordite. The sleeplessness lying guilt-wracked, tossing on his bunk through the small hours waiting for the sound of a Le Clerget to break the silence, save for the rumble of artillery at the front.

"I appreciate that, Charles," he said.

"I mean it, Robert . . . my family has influence and we will use it . . . for one of the family," said Martine, quietly.

"But we never . . ." began Bob.

"That wasn't what I received from my sister, Robert . . . she's under the impression that you and she wanted to get married, but more you than she." Martine tapped the back of the chair with his fingertips. He watched Bob for a few moments. "Look, Robert, I know the kind of pressures you operate under . . . more than any of the staff officers at HQ . . . Croxley-Blawford, Fossett, Moran, they're all members of the upper classes and have never been in the trenches, flown an aeroplane, or been over the Lines at ten thousand feet, they are remote from the men who do the dirty work . . . perhaps that's the reason for units like the 77th . . . for men, like yourself, who don't see the point of needless slaughter just for outmoded ideas. I've been pressing for every staff officer to spend at least six weeks every three months in the trenches, with the men they are supposed to advise. I haven't been very successful, and therein lies the reason for the Russian revolutionaries ganging up on the Tsar and his aristocracy . . . but my colleagues don't see it that way . . . they believe they should distance themselves from the men . . . keep a barrier permanently there. Croxley-Blawford is not a bad fellow, but he is frightened by events in Russia . . . they are all frightened men. They see this war as the end of an era already, and are becoming increasingly concerned about the left-wing Communists and others in the Army . . . the French, as you know, have had mutiny break out, and they believe that the ordinary British soldier may follow the poilu's example and rebel. So when you come up with ideas on taking von D's Jasta by unorthodox means they get alarmed, not at the idea itself, but what lies behind it."

"What's this got to do with Michelle and I?"

"My sister is again an unorthodox female . . . she follows this Pankhurst woman closely, votes for women and all that, and my parents are worried about her . . . she scorns getting married as the end product of all female desires, home, children and all the usual things women want . . . she's become liberated. You would have all your work cut out with someone like her as a wife, Robert . . . don't misunderstand me. If you are to be my brother-in-law I'd welcome the prospect, but I am thinking of you. Michelle is wayward, head-strong and you'd have your work cut out trying to cope."

"That's between me and Michelle, isn't it, Charles?" said Bob, curtly.

Martine held up his hand. "Alright . . . sorry . . . I won't interfere and say any more about it, but it is well worth thinking about . . . even when you're fifteen thousand feet up and a Fokker tripehound in the sun above you," he said, hastily.

"I have received the message, Charles," said Bob, stiffly, pacing the floor before the elegantly dressed officer in the chair. It was hard to believe that he was the brother of Michelle. They were so different, yet the family likeness was strong. "I promise to think about it, carefully."

"Good. Good," said Martine, standing up. "And think about Sainte Saveit d'Erve as well?" he reminded. "Where can I doss down for the night?"

Bob felt an irresistible urge to lash out at the composed face of Martine, for his ability to sound bored with even vital matters like his emotional future. Damn Martine and Croxley-Blawford, Moran, Fossett, de Vinguind and Launcey-Moore, and all their robber baron ancestry.

"Vyvyan was killed last month, Robert," said Martine, as if reading his thoughts. "Shot down by Werner Voss of Jasta 11 . . . Richthofen's crowd."

****

Chapter 23

Corporal Matthews brought his cup of tea at oh-five hundred hours. There was another figure with him, indistinct in the pre-dawn greyness.

"Who's that?" asked Bob, his eyes feeling like flesh in a bed of sand.

"Someone would like to make your acquaintance again, sir," said Matthews, in his horrible Glaswegian drawl. He lit the hurricane lamp beside Bob's cot.

As the light grew stronger, Bob recognised Corporal Johnson from his first day at Denham, the gnome-like figure, misshapen head and the slight hump on his back. His uniform was still the same slack carcass of blue, fit for a man much larger than himself. His poor teeth showed in a smile of welcome. "Nice to meet you again, sir," he said, softly, holding out his hand. "You remember me, don't you?"

"Ah, yes, Denham . . . Corporal Johnson, isn't it?" said Bob, shaking hands. "Sorry about Major Jessop, Corporal . . . fine officer." It sounded platitudinous, even to himself.

"He was going to have his leg done next week, sir," said Johnson. "Sad, isn't it?"

Bob nodded, unable to say anything for a second or two. He swallowed a mouthful of the hot tea. "Joined us permanently have you, Corporal?" he asked, to head off the phantoms that threatened to crowd in upon him.

"I'm going on leave, sir," said Matthews, stiffly. "And the Corp. has volunteered to take over until I get back from Blighty."

"Very good, Corporal. Have a good leave, when are you going?"

"The tender is taking me into Amiens this morning, sir, after breakfast . . . collecting rations at the same time . . . boat leaves Calais this evening . . . should be in Glasgow in a couple of days."

The two stocky men stood before him, embarrassed, diffident, wondering what to do next.

"Thanks for the tea, gentlemen," said Bob, sitting up. "I'll see you both later."

The ear-splitting roar of a Le Clerget drowned the sound of artillery from the Front. It was closely followed by another, until all nine were chuckling away to themselves, in rattling coughs and splutters, like metallic hens in a steel farmyard.

He pulled his Sidcot on over his pyjamas, slipped his bare feet into the sheepskin boots, shivering at the coldness of the material against his skin.

Finishing the tea slowly, savouring the acrid brew, he didn't even bother combing his hair.

He caught sight of himself in the mirror and for a moment was startled. The image in the mirror did not reflect how he saw himself. The face peering back at him was hollow-eyed, grey round the jaw-line under the stubble, the twitch at his eyebrow was almost permanent. There were deep crevasses round his mouth and down each side of his nose. His cheeks were hollowed, sunken into deep cavities.

He was mildly shocked. What transfiguration had taken place? His image looked like some horrible, Jekyll and Hyde, mutation. Was that truly his own self?

He felt depressed and irritable. The feeling of prescient doom was strong. A feeling of abject terror overtook him.

He began to tremble violently, his whole body shuddering. The grip of an ague he couldn't control. He saw faces flashing before his eyes, Riley, Jessop, Chesney, Langley, de Vinguind, and many others whose names he had forgotten long since, but whom he knew, instinctively, were those of men who had been shot down . . . he saw the face of Emile Meinwoller peering up at him from the rear cockpit of the Rumpler as he had the man's face in his Aldis sight, Charlesworth, Mason, his observer in the old FE, Foster and Phillips, his first Flight Commander.

His knees felt as if they were about to collapse. Cold sweat burst out on his forehead. The mirror seemed like a window into another world of death and oblivion. Try as he might, he could not prevent his hands trembling, or his legs shaking.

He tried to concentrate on Michelle's features, but could not remember what she looked like. Barbara next, and her face was all indistinct and vague. His mother and father, Melvin, anything to find some point of repose.

He fell back on the bed, his whole body seemed unresponsive to calls from his will. "This is bloody daft," an ice-cold part of his mind told him. "Pull yourself together for Chrissake!"

Gradually, the trembling in his legs ceased, and then his hands, until it left him weak and faint, his whole body bathed in a clammy perspiration. Nausea rose into his throat, the sickening taste of bile and food he had consumed the previous night. He put his head between his legs and nearly fell from the bed.

"You alright, sir?" asked a voice behind him.

Corporal Johnson stood there, his gnome-like body outlined in the doorway.

He sucked his breath in sharply in a shuddering intake of oxygen, filling his lungs.

"Yes, I'm alright, Corporal . . . is there any brandy?" he muttered.

The phantoms were receding now, fading into the darkness beyond the mirror, smiling, their lips writhing in meaningless signs.

"I'll get some for you, sir," said Johnson, turning to clatter down the spiral stairs of Number 4.

Bob stood up, shakily, his legs felt like rubber and wouldn't obey his will. He staggered to the door, holding onto the furniture for support.

The stairs seemed to go down for ever, as his weak legs propelled him downwards, each step an effort of will. It was agonising, as if in some slow-motion movie, and his feet were attached to legs twenty feet long.

He fell down the last three steps into a heap.

Hours later, black rain pouring down before his eyes, a strong hand helped him to rise.

"You should be in dock, sir," came Johnson's voice, as if from the wrong end of a tunnel.

His own voice boomed in his ears, hollowly lugubrious.

"Brandy," he muttered, weakly.

Corporal Johnson held the flask to his lips. The fiery liquid almost burned his stomach, but the adrenalin of alcohol brought new life to his sagging muscles. A minute later and he felt as if the previous minutes were all part of some bad dream, something that had happened to somebody else, not him.

"I'm OK now, Corporal," he said, removing Johnson's hand from his arm.

"You should report sick, sir," said Johnson, anxiously.

"I'm alright, I tell you!" he shouted, irritably, shrugging away from the little man. The brandy was still burning his stomach in wreaths of fire, as he staggered down into the bitter cold pre-dawn gloom towards the mess. Corporal Johnson hung back as if afraid he was going to receive another tongue lashing.

He walked into the mess, just as his legs almost gave way again. He clutched at the door, steadied himself, then walked in, smiling brightly at the ring of faces watching him. His skin felt like rawhide, and there were funny flaps round his ears as if the skin had not returned to its normal smoothness.

"Good morning, Captain Spiers," said Colonel Martine, standing in the middle of the group of pilots.

"You alright, sir?" asked Shalter in his Australian drawl. "Gotta wog or something?"

"No, I'm fine," he said, his smile brittle and fragile.

Martine was staring at him, in a funny way.

Bob walked in exaggerated steps over to the mess table, poured himself a cup of coffee from the charcoal urn. The mess table seemed to be at an angle. The scalding coffee eased some of the weakness in his legs, that seemed to want to splay outwards when he least expected it.

"Very well, gentlemen? We all understand our roles?" came Martine's voice from a long way away. His face seemed remote, like peering down the reverse end of binoculars. A blackboard had been set up in the middle of the mess, and a crude map drawn upon it in chalk.

"We come in from Le Catelet and wait until the Hun is almost down before we attack," said Martine. "No heroics from anyone, gentlemen, and if you get into trouble, head for home . . . is that understood?" He glared round at the young faces before him. "And you and Blake, Mathers . . . if any of von D's fellows get away, make for the Lines as fast as you can go. Got that?"

Martine used his swagger stick to point out some features around Cussigny and the German aerodrome. "There is a line of poplars to the east of the 'drome, and a church spire . . . so watch your height . . . don't get carried away and forget about that spire or those trees. This barn is an obstacle if you come down low for a strafe." He pointed to an old Norman building with tall arches and a tiled roof. "And keep your eyes peeled behind you . . . just because the Hun seems to be on the ground, there's no reason to suppose there won't be others above you and you'll be sitting ducks." He looked round, his voice faint as a Le Clerget roared briefly, then died away into its clattering and chuckling again. "Any questions?"

There weren't any. All were anxious to get started to kill the butterflies in the stomach and be doing something, rather than listening, standing still.

Bob held onto a table top, his stomach threatening to empty itself at any moment, and a tight feeling around his forehead was beginning to make his vision recede and return.

"Sure you're alright, Robert?" asked Martine as he passed him. In the brand new Sidcot he looked bereft of any identity, no different from any other pilot.

"Perfectly alright, sir," said Bob, moving carefully out of the mess. His legs were becoming all pliable again and wandering of their own volition.

Corporal Johnson was waiting for him outside the door, a large flask in his crooked hands. "Help you on your way, sir," he said, smiling in the gloom.

"Sorry I bit your head off, Corporal," said Bob, straightening with an effort and making his legs go in the right direction.

It seemed as if his feet were artificial, and too big for his spindly legs. They moved outwards at every step and he had to consciously correct this ill-disciplined movement.

Sergeant Williams and his crew were arrayed around his Camel, all watching him approach, concern in their eyes. They watched his agonised efforts to pull himself up into the cockpit, until Williams gave him a heave, his hand under his buttocks, that nearly pitched him forward into the narrow aperture. The smell of petrol, castor oil and cold air from the slipstream all intermingled gave his stomach more food for thought. He retched once or twice, but swallowed hard and quelled the feeling. He fastened the safety belt with clumsy fingers, flipped the ailerons up and down, elevator from side to side, from force of habit. The new dashboard looked strange and the windshield was free from oil stains. A new centre-section strut had been fixed and there were patches all over the wings. A new pair of Vickers graced the mountings . . .

He watched Martine signal for take-off as the first grey light of dawn brightened the cloudy morning.

He revved the Le Clerget to almost maximum before waving away the chocks and speeding off, fish-tailing down the field. He noticed the windsock was taut on its pylon.

As soon as they had cleared the field they began to climb steeply.

The numbness was leaving his limbs and strength seemed to be returning on assuming his familiar routine position. Corporal Johnson's huge flask had been strapped to the side of the cockpit.

There was a great deal of cloud scattered all over the sky. Huge banks of vapour hung like curtains and mountains all over the blue vault. The valleys and crevasses of the monster peaks were ideal hiding places for friends and foe alike.

They were still over the British Lines at fifteen thousand feet, and didn't cross to the German side until eighteen thousand feet showed on the altimeter.

It was bitterly cold at this altitude, and even in the sheepskin-lined boots his feet began to numb. His fingers felt frozen solid and the exposed part of his face was rigid. The Le Clerget roared away happily, even at this height.

The nine Camels were strung out in V-formation, Martine at the head, with Bob bringing up the rear of the huge arrowhead.

They kept well to the south of Le Catelet so that any observers, picking out the tiny specks above their heads, would assume that a British patrol of nine aeroplanes were heading for a possible target at Bellenglise. At eighteen thousand feet it would be difficult, but not impossible, to determine the type of British aircraft that were crossing the Lines.

At Roisel they turned slightly east of south and head in a long curve for Hargicourt. Over Hargicourt they turned due south towards St Quentin, following a tributary of the Somme river, to further confuse observers.

They were now deep into enemy territory and if any enemy fighters from a neighbouring Jasta to that of the Lions happened to be hunting, they were in deep trouble. Strangely, Archie was silent, either from lack of identification of the aircraft over their territory, or the gunners believed that no British aircraft would be mad enough to penetrate so deeply into the enemy airspace.

He scanned the sky above them, trying to penetrate the mountainous clouds that sailed eastwards over the countryside, for signs that their presence had alerted a German Jasta. There was nothing. The heavens appeared empty, save for the nine Camels flying south towards St Quentin.

He began to feel better by the minute since take-off. In place of the depression, a fierce feeling of elation gripped him. This was the culmination of all his planning, the nadir, the apex. If this worked, then a precedent would have been set, and one that could help put the RFC in a commanding position.

The stomach cramps left him, the tight feeling, the nausea, all departed leaving him experiencing a sense of well-being and power.

With one hand he unstrapped the flask, gripping the stick between his knees, he poured a generous portion of the scaling liquid into the bakelite cup and sipped it, scanning the air above and below him continuously.

Supplanting the elation was a feeling that something, somehow was not as it appeared. If Lascalle had carried out his part of the plan, then right this moment a colossal dog-fight would be in progress over the line somewhere between Boucheresnes and Combles, between the Spads of the Escradille Lascalle and the Fokkers, Albatross and Pfalz of von Dolin-Berensky's Lion Jasta, and perhaps even now the Germans would be breaking off the combat to return to their aerodrome at Cussigny.

The sun broke over the horizon and long shafts of golden light spread over the earth. Towards St Quentin a shower of rain was falling, giving a rainbow over the town.

He nearly choked suddenly, throwing the bakelite cup overboard in his astonishment.

The next moment cloud banks covered the sky above him.

He waggled his wings to attract Martine's attention.

He could have sworn he had seen several black dots above them . . . well above them at around twenty-one thousand feet . . . three thousand feet higher than their own ceiling. Only the Fokker triplane could reach anything approaching that ceiling. The Pfalz, the Albatross, and the Halberstadts could barely make their own present ceiling. He was certain that what he had seen were neither Fokker, Pflaz, or Albatross scouts. Martine was looking across at him, waving him back to his position at the tail of the 'V'. Bob refused to move, waggling his wings and pointing upwards in exaggerated gestures. Martine, with a long suffering expression under his goggles, reluctantly peered upwards. There was nothing. Even though he searched the sky through the massive cloud banks he could find nothing menacing.

The lazed back to his original position, uneasy and beginning to feel insecure once more.

The coffee had slopped out of the now topless flask, over the cockpit floor, and was flowing from side to side with the movement of the Camel. Cursing, he seized the huge flask and threw it overboard.

On the outskirts of St Quentin, Martine began his turn northwards towards Fresnoy le Grand. The Camels all turned in ragged formation, and gradually resumed their slack 'V' once more. He could see Shalter and Burgess staring at him curiously as they attempted to keep formation in the bumpy air.

What the devil had he seen? Three thousand feet higher . . . there was no German machine he knew of that attained that height. Unless this was something new in the Hun armoury . . . an aircraft that could reach twenty-one thousand feet . . . and then he had it . . . the answer . . . they were Spads . . . the new Spad XIII . . . what had Lasalle said they could do . . . twenty-one thousand feet plus . . . they had to be Spads. But what the hell was Lascalle doing up there . . . the Escradille Lascalle was to be the bait for von Dolin-Berensky's Lions over Clery . . .

The bastard, cursed Bob, helplessly . . . the bloody Frog had persuaded some other French squadron to perform that duty so that the Escradille Lascalle could be in on the act . . . it just had to be the answer.

What was he to do? They were now over Fresnoy and turning westwards towards the German airfield at Cussigny. Massive clouds covered the upper air like floating mountings, deep canyons opened out, the nine Camels of 77 Squadron flying between them like mountaineers in some science fiction scenario.

A few moments later, although the earth was shrouded in cloud, Bob knew they must be over Cussigny. He searched the sky in vain for some sign of the Spads, but could see nothing.

He felt even more uneasy. The whole operation was wrong, he felt it instinctively, with all the instincts of the hunter. The signs weren't right. Martine had fired his Verey pistol to indicate his intention of going down. It was too late now. Martine's Camel went over on its back in a long downwards roll, closely followed by all the others.

Bob held off. There had to be something up there. No shadows on the clouds . . . just the ethereal blue and gold and the blazing orb of the sun, now well above the horizon through a veil of clouds.

He eased the Camel over into a shallow dive, making for a massive cloud bank some thousand yards away.

The vapour surrounded him, long tendrils torn away by the propeller swinging back over the top plane. His goggles misted up. He pushed them up, the icy slipstream blasting into his face, making his eyes water. His compass was going wild, swinging round and round, the needle flickering and jumping. The burnt oil gunge from the Le Clerget had blackened half his face below his goggles and minute specks thrust backwards by the ferocious slipstream were stinging his eyes.

He emerged from the cloud bank to find himself under the wheels of a Fokker triplane. At least twenty others were in a scattered formation all around him. He barely had time to glimpse another formation stacked above them before he jerked the Camel in a swift turn into the cloud bank once more . . .

****

Chapter 24

"Jesus Christ!" he screamed to himself, those poor bastards down there!

He pointed the Camel's nose straight down and emerged from the cloud in a vertical dive. The wind screamed in the wires and struts. The Le Clerget howled and a million hellcats wailed in his ears.

The pressure forced his head back against the rest, his lips compressed in a rictus of tension.

The earth was still obscured by yet another cloud bank at ten thousand feet. With great difficulty he pulled down his goggles, his hand seeming to weigh a ton in the howling storm of air travelling past him.

He was into the cloud and through it in five seconds. The airspeed indicator read one hundred and thirty miles per hour and was jammed against the pin. The earth was below him now, a patchwork of green and brown, stitched by hedgerows and buildings. He saw the Camels of 77 Squadron flying like minnows across the gashed aerodrome of Cussigny. Ground crews manning Spandaus from pits were firing at the diving British aircraft. Something was on fire in the corner of the aerodrome, an oily blossom of black smoke rising skywards.

He went cold when he saw not a single German aircraft on the ground. Farther westwards there were no stragglers coming in to land. There was a blankness about the cloudy sky that filled him with dread. Above him, he knew, were those twenty-odd Fokker tripehounds, waiting to pounce.

He pulled out of his dive, narrowly missing a climbing Camel. The whole aircraft shuddered violently as the pressure on the wings built to enormous degrees. The Le Clerget was bellowing madly, and a stream of exhaust fumes were trailing back behind the tail section.

He almost blacked out as the Camel levelled and began reluctantly to climb. He felt a warm trickle of blood at his nostrils, and then his vision cleared, and he was amongst the Camels of 77 Squadron as they dived and strafed the airfield.

He located Martine a little higher than his colleagues, the Squadron Leader's streamers marking him out. Martine had his head over the side of the cockpit looking downwards at the empty airfield.

He fired his Vickers to alert the Colonel.

Martine came round in a swift right-hand turn, the Camel standing on its wing-tips. Bob jabbed madly upwards at the lowering cloud banks, gesticulating wildly at the incomprehending Martine, who merely stared at his mad Captain with disdain.

Bob didn't have time to do more.

Like vultures from hell the Fokkers were out of the cloud and into them, Spandaus blazing.

Three Camels were hit in the first thirty seconds and went tumbling earthwards.

The second wave of ten Fokkers were then into them, and two more Camels went spinning. The sky seemed full of triplanes, all with Spandaus blazing.

Bob clawed his Camel skywards, giving every inch of throttle, in order to gain precious height.

Bullets ripped across the lower wing, sending canvas fluttering in long strips. He turned swiftly, fired briefly at a bright green triplane that swam momentarily into the Aldis, and then another triplane was on his tail, Spandaus chattering and bullets were tearing into spruce and canvas behind him. Executing an Immelmann turn, he levelled out in time to catch a burst from a black chequerboard Fokker with the Blue Lion on its fuselage. The main bracing wire fell apart with a vicious twanging and began lashing the lower wing, tearing more canvas out in ugly streamers.

A Camel passed him, a mass of roaring flames and black smoke, the pilot desperately endeavouring to shield his face from the enveloping fire. A Fokker was trailing downwards, a long plume of smoke pouring from the engine, its left wing-tip a shred of canvas and shattered wood.

Above him, he saw Martine's Camel, streamers flying, bravely fighting off the attentions of three Fokkers. The Squadron Leader was in deep trouble, and his aeroplane had received several hits. One wheel hung from its axis drunkenly and the main undercarriage strut was a limp piece of matchwood.

He climbed onto the tail of a triplane, a yellow machine with jazzed blue lines. He barely fired a dozen rounds before the left Vickers jammed. A bulging cartridge gleamed in the breech. He hammered at it ineffectually to try to free the offending casing. It stubbornly refused to come free.

The yellow machine flew free from his grip, and then another Fokker dived in behind him. He turned, saw the flashes from the Spandaus and then tracer was lashing the cockpit coaming at his neck. He ducked, instinctively, felt something burn across his shoulder, as the altimeter went into a thousand fragments. The dregs of the coffee were travelling by capillary action up the side of the cockpit, but most of the liquid had dispersed.

Suddenly the air was free of Fokkers. Two triplanes were spinning down out of control to strike the ground not far from their own aerodrome.

A Spad came into his vision, as he hammered away at the jammed Vickers, and then another and then soon twelve of the French machines were arrayed all around his own and Martine's machines, the goggled pilots waving at them.

He saw Lascalle's Spad, an array of tiny Maltese crosses, signifying his victories, just under the cockpit coaming, fly alongside his Camel and wave at him, his white teeth gleaming. Lascalle held up two fingers, indicating two more victories, and then the twelve Spads and three Camels were hurtling westwards.

The Le Clerget suddenly began coughing and spluttering. His heart nearly froze. They were well behind the Lines. The village of Bellicourt was not even in sight. Blipping and coughing, the Le Clerget suddenly gave up the ghost, the propeller coming to a rest, and then the roar of the other machines was dying away, as the Camel lost airway and began to sink down. All the Spad pilots and Martine were looking down at him, concern on their faces. He couldn't recognise the pilot of the third Camel survivor.

The aircraft was sinking lower and he began to search round for a suitable field in which to attempt a landing. A prisoner for the remainder of the war! Dismay choked him . . . an ignominious end.

The Spads were still around him. Martine and the third man were above the Spads waving at him, trying to tell him something. All heads were down looking at his frantic efforts to maintain height.

He felt a sudden shock of fear as he gazed upwards.

A second wave of Fokkers and Albatrosses were plummeting down out of the sun onto the rear of the Allied formation. He knew that these machines must be the second bank of enemy aircraft he had seen on emerging from the cloud. He knew from experience, without the shattered altimeter to confirm it, that they were at less than three thousand feet, and like Aunt Sallies for the German airmen.

He jabbed his hand frantically upwards to warn his companions of their mortal danger, a sick dismay tearing at his gut. The trap had been well and truly laid by the German Jastas. How had they know of their plan, was the thought that went through his mind, as the fought to keep his Camel on an even keel without stalling. A thrill of horror went through him as a lick of scarlet crept from behind the cowling and seared along the nacelle.

He was at less than two thousand feet now and Bellicourt had just shown up, the church spire gleaming in the early morning sunlight, the cross surmounting the apex a bright flash of gold.

Without warning, the mixed Fokkers and Albatrosses were in amongst the Spads and Camels. He heard the insane chatter of Spandaus above the soughing of the wind in the wires of the Camel, the whine of straining engines, the scream of diving machines, and then he had to keep his attention riveted on a possible landing place. Every few seconds another tongue of flame would shoot from the engine to sear the side of the aircraft, and then die away.

Fear froze his tongue to the roof of his mouth . . . a flamer . . . the dread of every airman, and he was heading for such a death. He side-slipped desperately to keep the next tongue of flame away from the canvas of the fuselage, losing precious height in the process.

A line of poplars hove into view and a field of cows beyond. There wasn't going to be any time for a search. It was going to have to be this field. There was an Archie battery in one corner of the field, and the field grey soldiers were staring at the stricken Camel, mesmerised. Some horses were grazing in his line of approach. The poplars came closer, floating at him as if in some dream sequence. Another gout of flame shot from the engine cowling, as he jerked the stick back in desperation to avoid the trees. The topmost branches scraped the undercarriage, and then he was heading downwards, his port wing-tip at an angle.

The horses had seen his approach and were scattering. The soldiers from the battery were running towards him as if to stop him crashing. The undercarriage hit the turf at an acute angle, sending up a shower of earth and grass, and the he had straightened the machine. The tailskid struck, jarring his teeth. Another lance of fire shot from the cowling, singeing his face as the wheels struck again. The hedgerow before him was approaching at terrifying speed.

Every movement appeared in exaggerated motion, suspended in a time log-jam. The wing-tip caught the ground and the Camel lurched, throwing him against the coaming. The machine spun round in an arc of one hundred and eighty degrees, the opposite wing-tip crumpled and then the Camel was slithering along on its nose, the propeller shattering, sending splinters into the fuselage.

For a second he was dazed by the blow on his head, as the Camel came to rest, nose down, supported by the undercarriage. Flames were shooting out from the cowling now, the heat searing his face.

He released the safety belt, his left arm felt slightly numb and there was a sticky warm flow coming down inside his Sidcot sleeve over his fingers. He grabbed the top plane, trying to pull himself clear. Only his right arm had any strength, and his left hand refused to grip the trailing edge.

The flames were roaring now, the heat intense. With superhuman effort he managed to hook his toe over the windshield and jumped backward to the ground. He hit the trailing edge of the Camel's wing and a sharp stab of agony went across his left shoulder. Half blinded by smoke and flames, he crawled in desperation from the heat, using only his right arm.

Suddenly, several pairs of hands were dragging him from the wreckage, and voices were shouting in German around him.

Dimly he was aware of a vast explosion and an envelope of heat, and then blackness swooped down upon his consciousness . . .

****

Chapter 24

He was aware of days passing; the smell of ether, disinfectant, linen, and the indefinable odour of decay. Sunshine came through windows, dust motes danced in the afternoons, the linoleum on the floor was burnished to a bright copper colour. Faces came to peer at him, people clad in white, with face masks, men with stethoscopes round their necks.

One day, he was fully conscious, and aware of being hungry.

A blond nurse, middle aged, fleshy and plump, double chins, came up to him, smiled and said something in German. She thrust a thermometer into his mouth, held his wrist lightly, her forefinger on his pulse. She smelled faintly of perfume and soap.

"I'm hungry," he croaked.

A doctor came, a Captain, from the badges over his white overall. Tall, thin, hatchet-faced, smiling. "How are you feeling, Captain Spiers?" he asked in good English.

"Hungry," Bob repeated. "And thirsty."

The doctor said something to the nurse, who nodded, departed.

"What happened to me, Doctor?" asked Bob, trying to move.

"A machine-gun bullet in your shoulder, Captain, and some burns, but your main problem has been nervous . . . lack of will to live, and some quite extraordinary traumas. I am happy to tell you that you are recovering well, and if you are hungry, then that is a good sign."

"Am I a prisoner?" asked Bob, dismay suddenly striking him.

The Captain nodded. "You are in a German military hospital in Cologne, Captain, and have been here for the past week . . . ever since you were shot down by Freiherr Anton von Dolin-Berensky, over the Jasta's aerodrome at Cussigny." The doctor smiled. "Our artillery men from the anti-aircraft battery pulled you free of your burning aeroplane just before it blew up."

After the doctor had examined his shoulder, ordered new dressings, and left, Bob pondered his fate with a feeling of depression. A prisoner! . . . for the duration of the war, and that might be years!

As the days passed, he heard that the new British Offensive at Arras had all been in vain and had petered out after such names as Railway Triangle, Telegraph Hill, Wancourt-Fenchy, Monchy-le-Preux Hill. The British, at first, had been eminently successful, but the veteran German troops had launched counter-attack after count-attack to bring the assault to a close. The presence of British tanks had at first gained ground and the hope of a strategic breakthrough, but their misuse in penny-pieces had proved their downfall.

He was allowed up and out in the extensive grounds of the hospital beside the Rhine. He couldn't have escaped had he the desire to do so. His shoulder was still extremely painful and it was with only great difficulty that he could move it.

On the 10th April, the day that the British Third Army launched a final, despairing assault on Monchy-le-Preux, he had a visitor. A stocky man in the uniform of the German Air Service. The Pourle Merite, or Blue Max, at his throat, and Iron Cross accompanying the coveted decoration, Bob had no doubt that this was the bête noire of the RFC, the biggest scourge next to Richthofen, Anton von Dolin-Berensky, victor of sixty victories in the air.

"How are you, my dear fellow?" greeted the famous ace, extending his hand to Bob.

They shook hands to the accompaniment of the many military photographers, who travelled with the German ace wherever he went. "I was very sorry indeed to hear of your wound and trust that it is healing satisfactorily?" von Dolin-Berensky sat down on a deck chair on the lawn next to Bob, his high cheek bones faintly blue with evening shadow.

"I'm afraid you were one of the luckier ones amongst your comrades."

"What happened?" asked Bob, eager for news, as the photographers flashed away.

"We knew of your proposed plan days before, my dear fellow," said the German, smiling. "It was very bold and brilliantly thought out."

"How did it go wrong?" asked Bob, an acrid taste of despair in his voice.

"Your comrade in arms . . . Pierre Lascalle, my dear chap . . . vanity, I'm afraid. He could not resist the temptation to grab . . . how do you say it . . . limelight?" said von Dolin-Berensky.

"What did he do?" asked Bob, dully.

"He was shouting all around Amiens, the previous evening, of what he was going to do to my Lions the next day, and asked several of his fellow squadrons if they would agree to provide the bait for us, in his place." von Dolin-Berensky crossed his legs, the elegant black boots, shiny and beautifully modelled, glinting in the sunlight. "Unfortunately for Lascalle, and your comrades, one of them, eager to pander to the Frenchman's vanity agreed . . . well within the hearing of one of our better and experienced agents."

"But that didn't leave you much time to react, sir," said Bob, liking the stocky German, despite his despair over the outcome of his cherished plan.

"The man was due to come back over our Lines that night, and made his way to a telephone as soon as he landed . . . from a British aircraft, of course . . . you British are very quixotic about spies, and didn't know that the gentleman concerned worked for us as well as you British. He acquainted me with your plan, and we prepared a counter plan. As you know . . . it worked extremely well. I pulled in the services of our comrades in Jasta X . . . all twenty of them, and we waited for you to arrive . . . you almost gave the game away when you appeared amongst us, but it did not affect the final outcome." von Dolin-Berensky smiled, gently.

"How did it end?"

"You were the last of your comrades to fall to the guns of our Jasta, Captain Spiers. Colonel Martine fell shortly before you to the guns of Wener von Krebach, and was unfortunately killed when his Sopwith crashed near Cussigny. All nine Camels of 77 Squadron were shot down, and I'm sorry to have to tell you that your unit has been officially disbanded from the RFC, and a new squadron now occupies your village at Lourconter."

"What about Lascalle?"

"Captain Lascalle died in his flaming Spad over Cussigny also . . . a victim to the guns of Artur Feubald . . . altogether a good day for both our Jastas, Captain Spiers, not for the RFC or the French Air Force, I regret to say. Two of the top Allied aces removed from the active field of duty at one . . . how do you say it . . . fell swoop?" von Dolin-Berensky suddenly smiled, the lines about his nose deepening as he did so. "But, enough of this depressing talk. I did not come here to taunt you, Captain Spiers, believe me. You must be feeling very depressed about the whole business, justifiably so. I came to see if you were in need of anything . . . anything at all, and to extend to you an invitation to attend a dinner in your honour, to be held this evening in the Hotel Europa, Köln . . . Cologne to you . . . most of my Jasta will be present. You will be our guest of honour. How do you feel about that? We would consider it an honour if you would accept."

"Will there be photographers, like these?" asked Bob, looking at the faces of the newsmen around him.

"Naturally, everyone is curious about the great English ace . . . and so young, Captain," said the German, smiling.

"I will come on the understanding that these gentlemen are not present during the meal, sir," said Bob.

von Dolin-Berensky shrugged, still smiling. "If that is your wish, then so be it. I take it then, you will accept?"

"I'm curious to see my late adversaries, sir," said Bob.

von Dolin-Berensky laughed softly. "And they, you, my friend!" he said, patting Bob's shoulder gently.

"Do my late Squadron members know that I am a prisoner, sir?" asked Bob.

von Dolin-Berensky nodded. "von Krebach dropped a note on your field the day after the event, giving your officers a resume of what happened over Cussigny. I also had a letter addressed to your parent in . .

. er, Alton, is it not . . . I trust that your Adjutant is a man of honour and will post it for you?"

Bob couldn't imagine Fossett doing anything so chivalrous. The letter would probably end up on General Snow's desk, as evidence of his sympathy with the Germans. If they got to hear of his celebrations with the German aces in Cologne this evening, it would merely confirm their worst suspicions. It would not matter anyway now since he would be a prisoner for the remainder of the war, and by the time the whole bloody business was ended, everyone would have forgotten him, including Michelle and Barbara Welland.

von Dolin-Berensky seemed to divine his innermost thoughts. "If there are any letters you wish delivered over the Lines, then one of my fliers will be delighted to do this for you, Captain," he said.

They chatted on for several minutes about the relative merits of Camels versus Fokkers and Albatrosses, Spads and Nieuports, before von Dolin-Berensky took his leave, promising to send a car for him at seven that evening.

Bob watched the stocky German stride away in his tailored leather boots, followed by the horde of reporters and photographers, leaving him alone with his thoughts.

****

The black Mercedes arrived promptly at seven. Bob had been given a uniform during the late afternoon, and a little man had arrived soon afterwards who had carried out alterations on the spot to make it fit him. It was a genuine RFC uniform with puttees and boots, Captain's pips on the shoulders, and even the medals he had won for valour during his tour of duty.

There was a guard of honour of four Prussian guardsmen accompanying him in the huge car, stiff and straight, looking neither to the left nor right, during the short drive to the Hotel Europa. They held the door open for him, one assisting him to alight, amid a welter of flashlight photographs taken by a crowd of newsmen on the steps. There were cheers and hearty applause when von Dolin-Berensky appeared and put his arm around Bob's shoulders, whilst they posed for another photograph.

Inside the foyer, it seemed that the whole German Air Force had turned out to welcome him. They all crowded round him, smiling, thumping him on the back, shaking his hand, bowing, clicking their heels, to the inevitable flashlight photography, making him feel welcome.

Waiters moved amongst them, holding trays of Schnapps in glasses.

"A toast, gentlemen!" von Dolin-Berensky's voice rang out. "To a brave and worthy adversary . . . Captain Robert Spiers!"

All the aces raised their glasses to him, singing out "Prosit!"

Bob waited until the clamour had died away, then raised his own glass. "To the better man . . . Freiherr von Dolin-Berensky, and the fliers of Jasta Loewen!"

There were more photos and cheers, and then von Dolin-Berensky led the way into the massive dining room and, true to his word, the newsmen and photographers were kept out.

All was gilt, silver and crystal, starched linen and gleaming cutlery. Chandeliers blazed with the new gas mantles, shedding a fulsome light over the assembled fliers. At the entrance stood a tall figure clad in a splendid uniform, waiting to greet Bob.

"His Highness, Crown Prince Rupprecht of Bavaria," introduced von Dolin-Berensky, as the tall man stepped forward to shake Bob's hand, bowing and clicking his heels. "Commander of the 4th Army Group," added von Dolin-Berensky.

"I am very pleased to meet you, Captain Spiers," said the Crown Prince in halting English. "You have caused the German Air Force a great deal of trouble!" He smiled to take the sting out his admonition. "We are delighted to have you as our guest tonight."

Bob was placed on the top table, between the Crown Prince and von Dolin-Berensky, with the aces of the Jasta Loewen arranged down both sides of the stem of the 'T'. All during the soup course the Crown Prince plied Bob with questions about his family and background. He was surprised that the young Captain was not one of the aristocratic English families.

"It was a mistake," Bob admitted. "My name was similar to that of another gentleman who had aristocratic blood . . . by the time the mistake was noticed it would have caused too many red faces to reverse it!"

"My God!" muttered the Crown Prince, sooshing his soup through his teeth. "The English!"

After the soup came the entrée, and this time it was von Dolin-Berensky who rescued Bob from his royal inquisitor. He introduced my name each pilot of his Jasta long the table. The man in question would stand up, click his heels and bow to Bob, then resume his place.

During the meal the talk was nearly all of air war and individual combats, the cutlery and plates being used as pawns to illustrate technical detail of position and manoeuvre.

Despite his unease, Bob found himself enjoying the sensation of being a celebrity. His early misgivings all vanished under the influence of the wine and good company. His erstwhile enemies treated him with courtesy and respect, and listened whilst he described some of his own encounters with their Jasta, in silence and with avid interest.

There were more toasts and my the end of the evening, Bob found himself a little the worse for wear with the drinking. His arm, still bound tightly to his chest in a sling, had begun to ache again.

Von Dolin-Berensky noticed his fatigue. "We end it now, Robert," he said. "Your arm is hurting?"

Bob shook his head, but was unable to prevent himself biting his lip. Von Dolin-Berensky smiled, understandingly. "A brave man, Robert, but you have had enough," he said sagely, clapping his hands, calling his noisy pilots to order. But for the strange uniforms, Bob could easily imagine this gathering at a dinner in Amiens amongst his own pilots. The talk was the same, although most of it was in German, but it was all about flying and flying machines, combat and stories of miraculous escapes from death. The same horror of dying in a burning aircraft was expressed, that many of his own men had expressed. Not at any time were the English referred to as the enemy, but more often as 'our friends across the Line'. The nationalistic feeling was strong and 'Deutschland uber Alles' was sung with fervour and gusto at the end of the dinner. They even joined in when Bob sang in a very inebriated voice 'God Save the King!'. There were cheers and more praise as he was escorted out to the waiting black Mercedes and the four Prussian guards. Each pilot of the Jasta Loewen shook his hand, smiled and wished him well.

The Crown Prince even offered him an invitation to visit him at his home in Bavaria and do some hunting from his lodge in the Alps, when his arm was better.

He arrived back at the hospital more than a little drunk and bewildered.

****

He was transferred to a kriegsgefangenenlager at Stuttgart at the end of May, and was assigned a small hut to himself, away from the other prisoners, who were mainly infantry and cavalrymen from British units captured during the four long years of fighting on the Western Front.

He enjoyed privacy, better food and had all the English books he wanted to read and enjoy. He thought about escape after the initial pleasure had worn off and he became bored with the routine. He wrote letters to his parents and to Barbara and Michelle but it wasn't until November that he received a letter from Michelle via the Red Cross.

Her mood was depressed over the death of Charles the previous Spring and said her parents had taken his death badly. The very unexpectedness of the event, when their son appeared to be safe in a staff position, miles behind the Front was all the more traumatic.

Michelle's own emotion was one of deep sorrow, and concerns for his, Bob's, well-being as a prisoner. She was delighted to learn that his wounds had not been severe and that he had recovered although his arm was still stiff and lacked strength. She hoped he was getting enough food and attention in a medical sense. She repeated her offer of assistance when the war finally ended, to find employment of a character that would please and satisfy him so that they could get married if that was still his wish. Affairs in England were not good. People were depressed about the ever-increasing numbers of dead and wounded for so little result . . . another few yards of muddy marshland and then more death and destruction. There was hope that the Germans were collapsing under the pressure of the Allies and with the Americans now in the war it was only a matter of time before the Central Powers were defeated utterly and the wicked Kaiser banished. The collapse of Russia into defeat and revolution, the incarceration of the Romanoff royal family in the Urals were all news in England. Michelle was still working in the General Hospital in Amiens, and had nursed Bertie Launcey-Moore who had been critically wounded whilst in a dog-fight with Richthofen's Jasta. Launcey-Moore had been sent home to England where it was expected he would be invalided out of the RFC, or Royal Air Force, as it was now known.

There were no letters from Barbara Welland or his parents.

Christmas 1917 came and with it a personal invitation from von Dolin-Berensky to join his family at their country house in Munich. Such was the German ace's influence over the High Command, and his prestige with the German people, along with Richthofen, Voss and a few other selected aviators, that Bob was permitted to leave the prison camp at Stuttgart to travel with von Dolin-Berensky to Munich.

von Dolin-Berensky came to collect and sign for him two days before Christmas. Bob was obliged to sign a parole document giving an undertaking that he would not attempt to escape whilst enjoying the hospitality of the von Dolin-Berenskys in Munich.

Munich gave Bob the first signs of the grimness of the German situation as a result of four years of conflict. There were obvious indications that food was scarce and that disease was rife. Queues of women stood outside butchers' shops waiting for some scraps of meat for their families. The queues outside the bakeries were even longer. Children looked pinched and half starved.

The German ace was greeted as usual by the crowds of newsmen and photographers as he and Bob alighted from the train at the

Hauptbahnhof. They both had to pose for the inevitable photos and interviews. von Dolin-Berensky had celebrated his seventy-fifth victory and was now the front ranking German ace, ahead of the Red Baron, Manfred von Richthofen.

A large Mercedes was awaiting them outside the station. A chauffeur wrapped blankets round their knees and then they were off, heading for the outskirts of Munich.

People turned to cheer and wave at the German ace as they recognised his car passing amongst them.

The Dolin-Berensky estate was not large. The huge house was situated at the edge of a stretch of forest land, with a view over a lake, with a backcloth of a few meadows. A circular drive led up to the front door.

****

Chapter 25

The Dolin-Berenskys were five in number, Anton, Horst, Marianne, his father and mother.

Klaus von Dolin-Berensky, Anton's father, was stocky like his eldest son, huge shoulders and giant paws for hands. His mother was fair, blue-eyed, slight and looked fragile next to her bull of a husband. Horst was taller than either of them, fair, where Anton was dark, blue-eyed and slighter in build. Marianne was the middle child of the three at twenty, two years older than Bob.

They made him welcome and were soon all seated round a huge log fire, drinking German brandy.

They wanted to know all about Bob's background, his parents, brother and where he lived, how the English viewed this 'terrible war' that nobody in Germany wanted, least of all to fight the English . . . it was almost a civil war, when the Anglo-Saxons and the Teutonic peoples fought one another . . . the Franzozische . . . well, they were Latins, the Saxons and Nordic peoples should always stick together. It was awful that they were killing one another in Flanders.

His wife stopped him after he had launched into a dissertation upon Kultur and the great civilising mission of the Nordic peoples. His English was thick but lucid and his frequent lapses into German Bob could follow some of the time, for he had diligently set himself the task of learning the language in his camp at Stuttgart. The fast phrases and colloquialisms passed over his head, but he managed to grasp the gist of Herr von Dolin-Berensky's passionate flow.

They went tobogganning the next day, had a snow fight, and walked through the silent forest, the tingling cold and icy wind invigorating in its resin-tanged violence.

"What are you gong to do after this war is over, Robert?" asked Anton. "Are you going to fly still, or are you going to do something new with your life?"

"I don't know," admitted Bob, unwilling even now to show his true friendship for the young German. In this pine-forested wilderness, the snow crisp and soft underfoot, the wind soughing through the branches, the golden sunlight, the lack of any indication there was a war on anywhere within a thousand miles, no uniforms, and only the pleasant company of people his own age, it was difficult to think that less than a hundred miles from this forest mean were killing each other in hundreds, daily. And for what? The objectives of the conflict were even more remote away from the grind of confrontation. The Dolin-Berenskys were no different from him . . . this could be England, but for the remoteness and hugeness of the landscape.

"I understand how you feel, my friend . . . it is a madness . . . this war . . . and what will we all gain from it, no matter who wins it? There will only be death and destruction on a scale never before known and then the politicians will sit round tables, look very wise and stroke their white beards and tell us that now we must all be friends again."

von Dolin-Berensky seemed much older than he in some ways. At twenty-five, he was mature and remote on occasions, as if he were already an old man, wise in the ways of humanity, conscious of his mortality, subject to prolonged periods where he was withdrawn and silent. "Why don't you stay in Germany after the war, my friend? There will be plenty of opportunity, and for someone willing to learn our language a special place for an Englishman."

After the war . . . a point of repose, so distant that the farthest galaxies were closer. It was hard to think of a time when there hadn't been a war. Would it ever end? It was now in its fourth year, and he had been a mere boy when it started of fourteen. He was now eighteen and felt thirty-eight. The twitch had left his eyelid over the past few months and the nervous collapse that had been imminent a year before had now receded into the distant past, a mere dream. "I shall have to think about it, Anton," he said, slowly.

"I do hope you will. My father has many connections in the world of commerce and can always use his influence to help you," said von Dolin-Berensky.

Christmas came and went all too fast, and then he was saying goodbye to the family and embarking on the train back to Stuttgart, in company with the German ace of aces, to the usual accompaniment of newsmen and cameras.

Back in his solitary hut on the edge of the prison camp, he began brooding about the future. What would happen when he was finally released and allowed to return to England? How would he see things? He thought about Melvin, his brother, his father and mother . . . could he really go back to that tiny country town and become what? A clerk in a counting house? A farm hand, a bricklayer? It all appeared so inconsequential when put against a background of killing and death.

Spring came and with it the great German offensive against Amiens. On March 21st, 4,000 German guns opened a barrage on the British Lines, weakened as it was by casualties sustained at Passchendaele, and by the friction between Lloyd George and Haig. Within days a large and uncomfortable hole had been torn in the British defences and the hated Hun was within reach of the outskirts of Amiens. The British prisoners followed the news, what little of it there was, of the course of the struggle, until summer came and with it, what appeared to be, another horrible stalemate of trenches and artillery. By August it was apparent that the German Army was on the retreat at long last and the end of the war was in sight. Hope revived in the hearts and minds of the men in the camp. Home by Christmas . . . four and a half years after the war had commenced . . . the greatest, bloodiest war in history.

Bob had not heard from Anton von Dolin-Berensky for several months and concluded that their friendship had run its course, or that the German High Command had put a stop to the fraternisation in the interests of patriotism or the war effort.

In the early days of September he heard, via a German newspaper, of the death of the German ace the previous March, virtually coincidentally with the opening of the German offensive. The German

War Council had maintained a stony silence over the death of their favourite, believing that this news would shatter morale at home and depress people. The death of Baron von Richthofen the very next month at the hands of Australian Captain Roy Brown was a double blow. There was nobody to take the place of these two glamorous heroes and from that point onwards, the obvious superiority of the Allies in both men and machines began to take its inevitable toll.

The facts of von Dolin-Berensky's demise were kept secret. He had not been shot down in combat, otherwise the new would have electrified the Allies and would have been exploited to show the superiority of the Allies over their German counterparts. The ace's death was shrouded in mystery.

Bob wrote to Klaus von Dolin-Berensky as soon as he heard the news, expressing his heart-felt sorrow. The young German had been one of the few men he had ever formed a firm friendship with, apart from Charles Martine, and he felt the loss keenly.

Klaus von Dolin-Berensky replied after some weeks, thanking him for his letter and inviting him to visit them at Munich whenever the war was over and he was free to move around.

The Armistice arrived on November 11th 1918 at 11 a.m.

The Great War was over!

The news was not an unequivocal harbinger of glad tidings to everyone in the camp. Few men had illusions about the world they would have to face on their return to the UK. Four years of blood-spilling had not altered attitudes very much and privilege was still a factor to ordinary men that could influence their lives for good or ill. They had been stout fellows on the battlefield, on the home front they were problems.

Bob was repatriated on the 10th December 1918, and arrived in England at Dover on the 20th December.

The first person he saw was Michelle Martine, smiling and tearful simultaneously.

"Robert!" she cried, ecstatically, rushing up to kiss and hug him.

He had almost forgotten what it was like to hold a woman in his arms . . . the softness and pliability, the perfume and the femininity.

She demanded he tell her all about his adventures whilst in Germany all the way in the train to London. He stayed the night at the Martines, where her father and mother greeted him with some reserve and eyebrow raising. The war was over, heroes were ten a penny, and medals were being sold on the streets already.

Mr Martine promised to use his influence to find a position for Bob within one of the many companies on whose Boards he sat, and then, after a tearful parting from Michelle, he was on the train for Alton.

There was nobody to meet him, since he had told nobody of his arrival.

He dumped his kit in the Left Luggage office, walked home, seeing faces he vaguely recognised, but could not name. Men with the inevitable stamp of military discipline upon their features, yet like fish out of water, disoriented, afraid of the future.

Mrs Spiers nearly died when she saw him. "Bobby!" she cried. "We thought you were dead! No news for so long from you . . . how marvellous!" She hugged and kissed him with her moist kisses.

The house seemed small and cramped after even his hut in the prison camp at Stuttgart.

Melvin was in the Army Medical Corps and still in France. His father was still at work, although there was talk of reducing staff on the Southern Railway Company. His mother looked older, and his father, when he arrived home from work, looked a good deal older, washed out somehow, as if he had run a race and lost.

In the Station Hotel that night the talk was of reparations and making the Hun pay for the war and for the millions of dead. The beer was warm and unappetising.

His father talked of the bosses and exploitation as synonymous with capitalism and the Trades Unions who would provide for the future for all workers.

Most of it meant very little to Bob. It seemed as if he was some Rip van Winkle who had missed a generation somewhere and could not relate all this talk to war and death and killing. What had Trades Unions to do with the thousands of wounded and disabled, the men who had been taught to kill for four and a half years, for King and Country . . . the nation's heroes. Already, the heroes were superfluous and awkward problems.

He travelled to York in the early days of January 1919 to be demobilised, and then he went back to London to see Michelle. She said nothing about Sainte Saveit sur d'Erve or Barbara Welland. He had made no attempt to see Barbara whilst in Alton. And when he had almost plucked up courage to go and seek her out, he learned that she had married an American and had gone to live in the USA. Mrs Welland had gone with them.

He stayed with the Martines for a week, until the day arrived when Mr Martine made him an offer of a job with one of his companies. An assistant to the manager of an engineering firm in Enfield, where he would learn the job and eventually take over.

He stood it for a week, then quarrelled violently with the man who was his superior.

"I'm sorry, Michelle," he said to the tearful girl, the next day. "I can't stand it . . . I don't know why, but I can't."

"What are you going to do, Robert?" she wailed.

"I'm going to Germany," he said.

"What are you going to do there?" she cried, exasperatedly.

"I don't know, but I'm going . . . I can't stand this any longer!"

"But what about us . . . you and I, Robert?" she said.

"I'll send for you when I'm settled," he said, half heartedly.

She stared at him, tears welling from her eyes.

"Goodbye Robert," she whispered, reaching up and kissing him, tenderly.

"I'll send for you . . . promise," he said, knowing he was lying.

"Write to me on occasions, Robert," she whispered.

THE END